THE ANUK CHRONICLES

RISE OF
PROPHECY

VOL I

Abdur R. Mohammed

Images by: Stefan Keller

THE ANUK CHRONICLES

RISE OF PROPHECY

VOL I

Abdur R. Mohammed

Cover designed by Abdur R. Mohammed
Images courtesy Stefan Keller, Pixabay, & adobespark

This book is a work of fiction. Names, characters, places, and incidents
either are products of the author's imagination or are used fictitiously.
Any resemblance to actual persons, living or dead, events, or locales is
entirely coincidental.

Abdur R. Mohammed
Visit my website at www.theanukchronicles.com

Printed in the United States of America

First Printing: January 2019
Amazon

ISBN 13: 978-1-7324-7533-5

Dedication

"To the One True Master of the Universe"

Contents

Acknowledgments

To the following for their inspirational work:
Dr. Ken Atchity, Dr. Robert Sepehr, Erik Von Daniken, Andrew Collins, Brien Foerster, Dr. Robert Schoch, Graham Hancock, Robert Buval, Alicia Lindsey, and everyone who challenges the contemporary view of history.

To: Caroline Cardinale *for her support throughout this journey.*

CHAPTER 1: AFTER THE BEGINNING

F ar into antiquity when the world was young, it came. Out in the blackness of space an intruder approaches. The wondrous craft lumbers into high orbit, swimming along the sweet caress of gravity, skirting the edge of the warm planet. There is tremendous damage on the outer hull; scorching around other signs of a battle long past.

~SACRED TEXTS~
"After the beginning when the world was cooled, tribes of man roamed the planet."

The spacecraft stops like a giant whale about to sing; the behemoth drops its nose towards the southern continent. Seven smaller crafts detach from the aft section. They fly off towards the Northern continents. The mother-ship slowly descends to the green land at the bottom of the globe.

~SACRED TEXTS~
"The visitors fell from the sky in dragons, full of heat and thunder."

In a dense forest somewhere in the northern continent, the sun is in its retreat from the day. A primitive family gets ready for the evening routine when suddenly, a sonic "Boom" fills the sky. A small spec with trailing smoke becomes apparent, gradually increasing in size; it heads towards the forest.

One craft the size of a small field begins to settle on the forest floor. Afterburners blast trees off to the side, and animals scamper off in fear; only two primitive youths brave the unknown. One adolescent girl and boy sneak closer for a better look, silently observing the chaos.

Steam billows from the craft's underside. The thick smog dissipates to reveal a large ramp dropping to the ground. Several humans emerge from the ship. *They look like us, but taller*, the primitive boy thinks. They wear strange dark blue apparel, reflecting the fading sunlight. They survey the area with unfamiliar things that light in their hands. *Are they benevolent, or malevolent?*

The youths observe quietly. They spot two children running down the ramp, laughing as they chase a small animal.

The locals make their presence known by cautiously revealing themselves. The foreign children run up to them, smiling at the prospect of new friends.

~SACRED TEXTS~
"Our brothers from the stars welcomed us into their tribe, and we welcomed them."

-IN A SACRED VALLEY-

It is the beginning of autumn. Lush vegetation welcomes the brilliant hues of the season. A thick tree line peeks out at the village.

Children run around primitive huts, playing with wooden sticks as children do, swashbuckling, pirating. The smaller children giggle as they chase the taller ones, the visitors who are called human. They all end up at the center of a massive construction.

Small crude machines jump about on the muddy ground, hissing, grunting, spitting out plumes of smoke. Tubes weave around the area like the bodies of giant snakes, ending at a tan colored formation that's larger than all the huts in the village.

The structure is not like one ever built. The outer surface is made of a solid mixture of rock with sand melted to a liquid pulp, then poured over frames of metal. The humans say, "Anything can be fashioned from melted stone."

A full path leads up to a structure they carved into the rock wall itself. The locals talk about the night the humans started throwing light from their sticks; magic light, it cut through the mountain like a reed cutting through the water.

~SACRED TEXTS~
"We taught them the names of the beasts."

A human stands with a man in front of the local storehouse made of stone. They look up at the towering two-level structure. Here the village keeps a large number of meats, fruits, vegetables, and ale. Oh, how everyone loves the ale.

The human picks up a small box from a trailer behind them. Instantly, blue light envelopes a carcass on the bed. Like magic it slowly rises, gliding in the air straight into an open doorway.

~SACRED TEXTS~
"They taught us the names of the stars."

Night graces the village. The lake water is calm. A cold breeze blows, causing the human sitting with a woman on a rock to bundle up. He points to a corner of the star-filled sky, calling out strange names in a story. The woman weeps as the tale saddens her heart.

-LUSH VALLEY, A GENERATION LATER-

A massive waterfall roars in the background, throwing out water into a large pool. A temple is embedded in the mountain, shining with the morning light. A rainbow appears.

~SACRED TEXTS~

"We pledged our lives to the Royal house of ENlil. In return, they raised us out of darkness; they called us, Human."

~ MANY GENERATIONS LATER ~

It is the first year in the age of Virgo. Many lifetimes have passed since the strangers first arrived. Far in the Northern continent, they established the royal court of the Anuk. It was here that the seat of power existed, with all reverence directed to their land called Hyperboria.

Other houses belonging to ENlil created a great civilization towards the eastern part of the world; they called it Aryavan. Although loyal to ENlil, their culture became distinct over time. They indulged in many taboos such as breeding freely with man.

The lands of Illyria flowed from Hyperboria in the north across to Aryavan in the east. There the royal cousins set up principalities, engaging in trade with the other civilizations. They all lived in harmony until the brother house of ENlil, house ENki, was granted a burgeoning civilization to the south. Commonly referred to as the underworld, house ENki called it pTah, eventually changing the name to Egypt.

Persephone was the firstborn of the great Anuk King Shuru of ENlil. She married Osiris, the King of Egypt in secret, angering many royals in Hyperboria. Blood oaths were sworn against Osiris, resulting in the assassination of King Shuru. This unforgivable act sparked a global conflict.

Osiris was murdered soon after, leaving the new queen to fend off an offensive from the North. Sophisticated weapons from a Citadel in Hyperboria launched weapons at Persephone's allies in Aryavan. An attack was made on the rich southern continent. The ancient craft which first

6

brought the Anuk lay hidden there in the forbidden land of Lumeria.

In the vessel, weapons and technology exist beyond any currently in the world. The ship's exact location was known only by the original seven Anuk. They retreated there at the end of their cycle of several thousand years. Only one pure blood Anuk from amongst the houses knew of the forefathers' location, 'The keeper of forbidden knowledge.'

Today, the keeper rushes to find refuge with his beloved queen, to bring her hope. The plains of Giza appear welcoming, but he has seen the might of the approaching forces. He knows their true intentions; he knows what they want.

~ PERSEPHONE ~

An elegant temple sits in the shadow of the Great Pyramid. It is not as ancient but old enough to show years of weathering. Moss creeps through the stone tiles covering the walls with green. Just outside a magnificent monument in the shape of a lion stares out at the horizon. A massive river runs nearby.

Persephone sits in solitude in her private chamber, hunched over a small console. The escape from royal duties allows her to mourn her husband. Long flowing blonde hair, six-feet tall with a slim, elegant stature, piercing blue eyes; able to fight off a horde of Illyrian savages while still in a princess dress. She is still the envy of all the houses.

She looks at a bowl of exotic fruit. It just sits there waiting to be pushed off the ledge. *It's just so easy, do it,* she thinks. Her better sense prevents her from throwing a tantrum. She has been known to have quite a few; the Anuk were notorious for their tempers.

Her console begins to make rhythmic beeping sounds. She looks expectantly at the screen as information appears. Her face instantly becomes a mask of worry.

The high ceiling above her head brightens as a floating light-pod enters. The now worried but angry princess grabs the bowl, immediately launching it at the artificial creature. The dish connects with the device sending it crashing to the floor. The rash behavior does nothing to appease Persephone; she is still angry. Her chamber doors open revealing Thoth.

Tall and powerful in stature, Thoth is an Anuk to behold. His dark skin glistens from the long journey in the sun. His long wavy hair is pulled back into a tight ponytail. His sandals match gold on emerald-green clothing. He stands over six-feet-four-inches, with two hundred pounds of muscle.

Born to the house ENki, he is the last of this royal dynasty. He appears menacing to his enemies but is a kind, gentle human. Although adopting her husband's house as her own, Persephone is still of house ENlil; this does not devalue the love he has for his queen.

He walks briskly along the polished floors heading to his cousin. She is calm now, only watching the destruction brought on to the bowl. She decides to share her news before receiving Thoth's.

"The eastern settlements are destroyed," she explains angrily, "transformed to scorched sand. Those were innocent people."

"That's not all," Thoth informs her. "The Southern continent is frozen. Hyperboria's preemptive strike; Lumeria is under miles of ice."

There is a grave concern in Persephone's voice, "The forefathers, are they alive?"

"They are safe, still sleeping in the complex. They won't be for long if this onslaught continues."

"Surely, they won't dare kill the forefathers." A sudden chill overcomes the queen.

"Won't they? What better way to prevent judgment day?" Thoth sits next to Persephone, resting his large hand on her slender shoulder. Her stoic demeanor melts into one of sadness. She rests her head on him.

"Is this the end? Are we going to be the last of our house?" she asks full of sadness.

A glimmer of hope shines in Thoth's eyes. He looks at Persephone, trying to share through his expression that they will survive.

"We must go to Lumeria," he suggests, "from there we can end this conflict." His confident demeanor does not influence Persephone. If anything, her hopeless tone indicates this.

"Virgo ends in three thousand years. That's a long time before the awakening, before the forefathers can help."

Thoth decides that he will not let her mood sway his determination. "We can't trust or wait for the forefathers. We must do it ourselves."

"And what prevents them from finding us? Shall we trade a grave for a tomb?" she protests. Thoth smiles; there will be no convincing him they are on a foolish errand.

"I am still the keeper of forbidden knowledge. I have corrupted all routes through the network. They can try to find us, but not before we destroy them."

Persephone acts stern, although somewhere in the despair of her soul, she knows he speaks the truth. She tries one more attempt to plead with him. "Destroy them? They are our family, our blood."

"And when they kill us who remains from house ENki? Shall we leave the murderous line of ENlil to reign?"

There is no defeating Thoth's argument. Persephone resigns herself to accept it. She becomes curious as Thoth removes a small amulet around his neck.

About a third the size of a palm, it is made of gold and silver, cased in a grey colored ore, it falls apart in his hand. It is now three pieces; engraved symbols can be seen on the insides glowing brightly, and then quickly fading.

"I created this key at the Citadel," Thoth explains.

"To what?" she asks.

"The sanctuary complex," he explains while putting the two larger pieces together; he then holds up the third. It is similar to a cartouche, with sacred Anuk symbols still glowing brightly, adorning the surface.

"This is the heart. It powers the key. Together it gives us full control of the complex. Weapons of old and the ability to take the long sleep."

Persephone has to protest. The thought of joining the Forefathers scares her. *What happens when they wake and find us? What will they do?*

"That is forbidden. Only the forefathers can sleep," she reminds him.

"I am not suggesting that we must, only that we shall, if events prove to not be in our favor."

A brief silence passes. Persephone stands. A sudden ache in her stomach causes her hand to grasp the slight bulge. She heads over to a counter near a corner; an empty bag sits undisturbed with miscellaneous articles deemed necessary for any journey.

Amongst some clothing in a drawer lies a stuffed toy bunny; a childhood toy dressed in a white coat. Persephone holds it close as if she were a small child once more. She tosses it into the bag; it falls on top three leather-bound books.

On a wall, she touches a symbol. A drawer extends revealing several sacred metallic objects. Amongst them is a small red gem. She carefully picks it up, kisses it before placing it in the bag.

Suddenly, the doors burst open. A royal servant hastily enters. Sweat falls from his face. He is out of breath, trying to regain his composure.

"Your majesty," the short elder man starts, "Hyperborian forces have entered the perimeter. Two armed ships in the river, twenty more in the air."

Panic sets in with the queen, "Get everyone out. Flee to safety, hurry!" She looks at her devoted servant, regarding the man who took care of her since birth. "My heart is with you…go now, may God watch over and protect you."

The servant bows reverently. Before he retreats, he looks at his queen one last time. His expression is one of pure love. It breaks Persephone's heart.

The man runs off. With haste, Persephone begins filling her bag. "Our family is intent on destroying us and now, themselves. They forget, man cannot rule man."

"Your husband believed they could. That's why they killed him. Hurry, we must leave," Thoth insists.

At that moment when the bombardment started, when the temple walls shook, the queen made up her mind, *my enemies have to die. Maybe the time of the Anuk is over.*

Small pebbles begin to fall from the ceiling. The pair quickly makes their way out.

- THE TOMB OF OSIRIS -

The tomb is deep underground. Dark, damp, with artificial light emanating from pods secured into the rock. A robust grey platform is in the center. Four feet wide granite forms a catwalk-like perimeter around a moat. In the middle, another grey platform sits with a cavity filled with blue water. Four obelisks stand tall at each corner, with Anuk symbols carved into them. At the top, the capstones are polished to a smooth white finish.

Muffled explosions vibrate through the rock. They are coming from the surface. With no apparent way into the chamber, the enemy soldiers are attempting to blast their way through.

A nearby arch cut into the earth begins to glow blue. The light reveals a smooth depression cut into the surface. It goes some four feet into the wall, standing eight feet high. A flash of light brightens the space. In an instant, Persephone appears with Thoth.

They quickly jump on to the platform, trying not to fall into the six-foot-wide moat. The queen opens a compartment in one of the obelisks. She finds a box with a pair of pistols. *Never thought I would have to use these so soon,* she thinks to herself. It was not but two weeks ago that she hid the weapons there.

"How long before they find us, you think?" She asks Thoth.

Thoth holds out his hand. He appears calm, yet he is panicking inside. "Any moment now. The gem."

He takes the gem from Persephone. She passes him a pistol as well. He examines the items. Satisfied, he jumps high into the air, landing across the moat. Persephone does the same. "This will take a moment," he informs her.

Blue light begins to course through the symbols on the obelisks. A low hum starts, adding bass to the explosions above. Blue light emanates from the capstones, pulsating like lightning bolts. In a dazzling display of lights, they connect.

"Hurry!" Persephone screams. She drops to her knees, grabbing her stomach. She cries out with the momentary pain.

Thoth does his best to manipulate symbols which materialized in the air. A sarcophagus rises in the center cavity, pushing the blue water on to the granite floor.

"Remember, as soon as you arrive put the key in the main console," he reminds her. "The countermeasures are pre-programmed; it is all automated after that."

Explosions grow louder. Rubble falls from the ceiling. A far wall explodes revealing enemy intruders wearing the colors of house ENlil. They brandish their weapons as they climb through a small hole.

Persephone and Thoth fire their pistols. Concentrated light shoots out of their weapons, crisscrossing the incoming fire from the enemy.

Three soldiers fall, but more enter like ants scrambling to attack morsels on the floor. A well-aimed shot hits Persephone in the chest. The scorched garment mixes with burnt blood, smearing her golden-eagle crest. Another shot hits her, opening the wound as much as it burns the area around it. She falls.

Thoth blasts the shooters. He slams a symbol on the floor. Without delay the blue light above shoots through the air striking the men. It grows in intensity, forming a chain of death piercing flesh as it travels through the soldiers. They all fall screaming, dying.

Blood oozes out of Persephone's wound. Thoth panics. He picks her up with one sweep. He takes her to the waiting sarcophagus, carefully placing her inside. "Easy, try not to move," he advises.

A panel opens up on the side of the granite box. A small screen materializes. Thoth puts the gem into a slot. Worry covers his face; he gives it away with a frown.

"What, what is it?" she asks suspiciously. Thoth doesn't answer.

Fearing that she will be dead before long, Persephone struggles to remove the key to Lumeria. Thoth quickly reaches over to move her back down. As if to reveal his intentions, he picks up her bag.

"You will need the key," he says.

Realizing what the inevitable is, Persephone begins to sob. Her heart is breaking once more. "You're not coming, are you?"

"There's power for only one."

"Then you go. I can't do this," Persephone demands.

"No, you must. Now, be still," Thoth orders.

He selects some symbols. Light envelops Persephone. She screams in agony, cringing in pain, trying not to move. As the light diminishes, so does her screams.

"Is it done?" she asks.

Thoth looks at the screen. Relief fills the queen as he smiles. He moves closer to Persephone, looking at her with sad eyes. "I will go to Atlantis."

She struggles to get her words out, "There's nothing there but wild tribes of man." Thoth caresses her forehead, giving her some calm.

A tear rolls down Thoth's cheek, "It's a perfect place to start over. When the house ENlil falls I will find you in Lumeria, I promise. But first, you must automate the complex."

"By the ancestors and the Lord of heaven, we will meet again. Thoth, I..." He cuts her off with a kiss on her forehead. She smiles, lying flat in the box.

He taps a symbol on the lid; it rumbles loudly as it slides shut. He grabs the gem from the side before the blue waters flood the island. He jumps clear, quickly running to the arch. When the sarcophagus drops below the surface, he looks on solemnly.

"Goodbye Persephone, until we meet again." A blue light flashes. He disappears.

CHAPTER 02:
SQUATTERS

Eons have passed since the forefathers arrived; since they brought their wonders to humanity. Oh, what a golden age it was. Full of prosperity, honor, promise; the mighty Anuk had shaped destiny for all. No longer is such the promise, the hope, the guarantee. The Great War saw to that.

It has been nearly three thousand years since the fall of Persephone, since the demise of House ENki. In one day and night the world fractured, civilizations lost, life put on the brink.

Fire rained down from the sky in Hyperboria, bringing on destruction followed by the rapid freeze. The Southern continent was frozen too, Hyperboria's doing. Residual attacks brought devastation spreading from Illyria to Aryavan. The original civilizations were wiped away like the morning dew.

A thick band of desert formed across the planet a like a belt of destitution. From west to east scorching sands now occupy a once lush, fertile landscape. The broadest most pronounced areas are those beneath the Giza Plains, adjacent to the land mass to the east.

In this age of Virgo, humanity has re-emerged from the devastation brought on by houses ENlil and ENki. At the eastern end of the continent, the remnants of the Aryan houses consolidated their power, coming under their surviving Anuk sovereign. Stretching from the west of the continent to the eastern borders of Aryvan, powerful tribes of men grabbed large swaths of land to create their kingdoms; they called it Illyria, to honor the ancient name.

Just beyond the western edge of Illyria, five hundred miles across the ocean exists the island continent of Atlantis. Touching the northern freeze of Hyperboria, and then dropping to the southern seas, this land once had tribes of wild men roaming free, uncivilized. Three thousand years ago that all changed when the mighty Thoth arrived.

He raised the tribes out of darkness by teaching and building a society of tolerance. This ended when the survivors of house ENlil arrived.

Atlas was a minor house that escaped the destruction in Hyperboria; now they would claim Atlantis. They brought whatever knowledge they managed to save, managed to remember. Through this dynasty, the rebuilding began. Swiftly their influence grew, fueled by their lust for power.

From their new home, they reached out with converted armies, taking control of the land across the vast ocean, the wild Far West Continent. Closer to home, Egypt was in ashes, with only the great pyramid with the lion of Leo standing testament to the past. It was an easy conquest; the once great lands of Osiris were quickly scooped up by his enemies.

In the early days of Atlantis, the priests extended their greedy hands across all the realms. Not only were they influential within the Empire, but they also introduced their dogma to the other two civilizations. A culture of reverence to the forefathers flourished, making them gods amongst men. The new religion spread like wildfire, reaching all corners, quickly becoming popular with humanity.

One group resisted; they were called the nomads. They were born from the scattered refugees after the Great War. From Egypt, Illyria, and Aryavan, these peoples settled the wastelands. Their patriarch was that devoted servant to Persephone, who vowed to cherish the memory of his beloved queen. He is merely a myth now, only a shadow of the man who lived a long time ago.

These last years of Virgo are tumultuous times. Nomads terrorize the known civilizations; their motives remain unclear. Aryavan and the Illyrian Conglomerate of kingdoms enjoy a fragile peace. And Atlantis, oh Atlantis, it is still the mightiest amongst all; home to the only true pureblood Anuk dynasty, direct descendants of the first house of ENlil.

Two hundred years have passed since one Illyrian kingdom secured an arrangement with the Atlantean congress; protect them from the incursions of rapidly spreading nomads, in exchange for the rights to build a military outpost: sovereign Atlantean property, a garrison of might in Illyria. Once a fortress by which to launch attacks, now it functions as a training base.

Nestled in a valley, the base itself houses one hundred officers with support staff, playing parents to three-thousand recruits, all bound for the Atlantean Foreign Legion. It is a shameful sight for the facility once garrisoned ten thousand battle troops, an air-wing with one hundred assault aircraft, and a harbor at the inlet to the sea. It is an impossible task to maintain the facilities, as such, they are rapidly falling into ruin.

The locals continue to host the Atlantean soldiers, however. They welcome the money but despise the foreigners. The town itself is a pleasant one with all the conveniences of a mountain retreat, local cuisine, clean streets, and not so rowdy brothels.

Sandwiched between two small hills just off the main road, the 'Wild Pony Canyon playhouse' draws the military and locals alike. With red lights flashing in the black of night, it attracts the curious vehicles driving by like moths to a flame. Who could resist wanting to stop to use the bathroom facilities, have some ale, or entertain the prospect of a small-town prostitute?

~ ALEXIUS ~

At six-foot-two-inches with two-hundred-pounds of pure intoxicated indecency, Captain Alexius of house Badur enjoys the company of local prostitutes and pitchers of ale, while indulging in a lucrative card game.

His family was a prominent one, holding significant influence with the royal family at one point. He was brought up in a proper noble household, shielded from the vices of ordinary folk. So he was never much of a card player; cheating, now in this he excels. At age thirty-three, he has become good at it.

Alexius sits quietly with a garbage set of cards. He looks at the local sitting across from him. The scruffy man admires his hand, waiting to reveal the claim to a modest purse of money. Two other players are impatient. A chunky barmaid, Reisha, appears behind Alexius.

She makes the slightest of smirks while looking at his hand, ensuring the other players see her. She replaces an empty pitcher with a fresh one, leaning in close for her cleavage to catch lusting glances. As she picks up the empty pitcher, she sits on Alexius' lap.

"It appears that I may have to drop my hand and attend to a more, serious game," Alexius proclaims.

Smiling at the girl's ample backside, he grabs it, making her swoon. While the others are distracted by Reisha's voluptuous assets, he discreetly reaches down her undergarments to exchange his cards for a better set.

"Anytime M 'Lord," Reisha says. "You know where to find me." She hurries off to the bar, leaving Alexius smiling.

The impatient local drops his hand. The others do the same. "The whore brings me luck. Maybe I'll have her," the man declares. He reaches over for the pot. The other players frown.

Alexius drops his hand then quickly grabs the other man's wrist. "It appears the lady brought me luck. Now, the next round of drinks is on me."

"You're a cheater Atlantean," the angry local announces, "There is no way you would beat me otherwise." Standing quickly, he reaches for a weapon. Suddenly realizing that he had none, he considers his odds in a fist fight.

Alexius stands, towering over the man. His muscles bulge through his shirt, more so when he cracks his knuckles. The smaller man resigns himself for the drink.

"Barkeep," Alexius calls, "bring whatever my friends are drinking. Now if you'll excuse me, I have an appointment to keep." He scoops up the winnings then makes haste to a door behind the bar.

There are several rooms down a long hallway, private entertaining rooms. Alexius spots the one he wants. He knocks playfully then waits for an invitation. The door opens revealing Reisha.

"Now you promised you'd take me to your place." Reisha pouts.

"I promised you half the pot. You have any idea what will happen if we're caught?"

"I'll throw in my sister for next time." She watches Alexius struggle with indecision. His brain says no, but his shortcomings say yes.

"Hard to say no to that," he concedes.

"I bet it's hard. I'll get my things."

"Have to piss that overpriced ale first." Alexius leaves her, making his way around a corner.

Before he can open the exit door, a ten-year-old boy in rags attempts to rush past him. Alexius grabs the boy. Bruises on the child's arm catch his attention. A deep gash has dried up blood; looks like an old wound from an apparent beating.

Alexius kneels to meet the boy's terrified gaze, giving him a stern look. "Don't be frightened boy. You live here?"

The lad nods with a sad face. There is an air of misery about him, familiarity; not in the person, but the situation. Alexius reflects inwardly to when he was the boy's age.

~ALEXIUS (Age 10). FAMILY ESTATE, PARTHON, ATLANTIS~

Parthon is in the lower-middle section of Atlantis, situated on the eastern side of the continent. Primarily a farming region, it produces vast amounts of food and wine for the country. A substantial section of the province is owned solely by Alexius' family. They reside on a large estate close to the sea.

High up on a cliff, a large tree sits in solitude. Entirely out of place, it overlooks a precipice which leads to a deadly drop into the ocean. The rough waters smash onto the rock cliff, spraying mist in the air. The tree sits close to the edge far away from the tree line, almost 300 yards away.

A rope secured around the tree trunk descends over the cliff. A child's hand grabs the line from below, pulling himself up from the treacherous drop. Panting, Alexius rolls on to the ground. He has become skilled at this feat through years of practice. He looks at the tree, his only friend in this adventure.

The relief of reaching the top, despite how many times he's done it, never fails to overwhelm him. You see, the rope descends almost twenty feet on the rock face. It ends just at the mouth of a cave, Alexius' secret cave. There he escapes from life, to be left in solitude. His only companions are the treasures he has hidden there over the years; he started his pirate cove at age six.

The afternoon sun shines overhead. The rays are blasting bright through his closed eyes. The bright suddenly goes dark. He quickly opens his eyes expecting the worst; his mother stands over him, seething with anger.

With as much strength as she can muster, she swings a solid metal-like object at him, striking his arm. Blood pours from a fresh wound, but this does not stop her from attacking. Again and again, she hits the child, hoping for an unforgivable end.

Suddenly, Alexius pushes her off, sending her flying in the air. He sees her land at the edge of the tree line. His blood burns with anger; the pain is non-existent, his wounds are barely bleeding. His scars are internal, however, and he is desperately trying to hide them.

~BACK TO THE BROTHEL~

Alexius' momentary trip to the past quickly dissipates. He retrieves a small blade from his boot. The hilt is well crafted, with thin threads of gold winding across the ivory handle. He un-sheaths it; the polished metal shines in the poor lighting. The boy begins to panic, never making a sound, only struggling.

"Calm yourself boy, I will not harm you," Alexius says. "You see this?" The child's fear turns to curiosity. "The next time someone tries to hurt you, wave this around, then run."

He leaves the blade with the child. As he stands, he dips into a coin purse. He offers the child three gold pieces. Gratefully, the boy takes it then runs off. Alexius makes haste out the door.

-ATLANTEAN BASE IN THE VALLEY, THE NEXT MORNING-

The sun has barely risen. It is too early for anyone to be awake except for the furry woodland creatures, and soldiers. Along the perimeter of the base, a dirt road winds along a tree line. Behind the trees, a tall fence stands to keep the wilderness out.

There is a booming sound of cadence in the area, matching the thunder of running boots.

Fifty soldiers jog while they sing a tribute to the Foreign Legion; something about being gallant, fearless, able to destroy enemies. The lead voice goes up in pitch, and then the group booms repetition. On they go with their early morning jog.

Two runners at the tail end suddenly dart away, heading inside the tree line. No one notices the medium height, skinny cadet Bain, duck through the bushes then scramble for cover. His companion, a round heavy-set boy, affectionately known as Fat-boy, clumsily follows. He is out of breath, ready to die.

"You alright?" Bain inquires while he opens up his canteen, gulping away at the refreshing water.

Fat-boy looks at him, cringing from abdominal pain, his clothes soaked in sweat. "Do I fucking look alright?"

Bain produces a thickly rolled joint, "This will cheer you up."

Fat-boy responds by reaching down his pants. Instantly, he pulls out a small bag with white powder. "Be careful with this. It's from the Archon's stash. He gets it from the Far West Continent."

Bain grabs the bag. He sprinkles the powder on the joint. "Of course he gets it from FaW-C. That's where white powder comes from, idiot." Realization fills Fat-boy's face. Bain lights the joint.

The boys smoke to their heart's content. It doesn't take long for intoxication to overcome them. Their enjoyment of the contraband is so much that they are oblivious to the rustling in the bushes. The intruder carefully closes in. The figure stands behind them remaining silent.

Bain gets a chill. He quickly looks around only to be filled with horror. "Captain Alexius, Sir," Bain stutters, "we were just…" Fat-boy tries to hold the smoke in, turning blue in the process.

Alexius tries to stifle his amusement, appearing stern as his station demands, "Oh this will be good."

Fat-boy begins to explain, "You see, we were exhausted, so we stopped for a while…"

"Get your asses back to formation!" Alexius screams. "Give me that!"

The boys scramble to their feet, more annoyed at losing the contraband than being caught. The fleeing delinquents disappear down the road.

Free from observation, Alexius draws hard on the joint. He chokes while coughing up smoke. A sound in the bushes alerts him. "Hey, um…Reisha, you can come out now," he calls out.

The barmaid appears. She smiles lustfully, "So this is what soldiers do in the morning. Shall we go again M 'Lord?" She exposes her breasts.

"Sorry Luv, I'm out of coin. I'll see you later, promise. You have to go now. Are you sure your sister is out there?"

The barmaid nods then grab Alexius' privates. She lets go then runs off through the bushes. With another satisfying night of debauchery concluded, it is time to pretend the morning routine is underway. He runs the dirt road, heading to the main fields.

-TRAINING FIELDS-

One mile from the running tracks, a large training field spreads out in the open. Well cared for lawn grass blankets the area, with small dirt tracks interwoven from the perimeter. They lead to various points at a sectioned off area, able to host squads of twenty. This morning Captain Deidra with her small squad is formed up after their exercises.

Deidra is a thirty-two-year-old battle-worn soldier. Nearly six feet standing, she is a specimen of lean muscle, olive kissed skin, and raven hair. On her arms is a display of old scars serving as a mark of experience. She is a proud warrior devoted to the Foreign Legion of Atlantis. She stands on a raised platform in front of her squad.

"This part of your journey is almost at an end," Deidra announces. "You have endured just a fraction of what the Foreign Legion does." She steps off the platform to walk between the ranks. "Hunger, sleep deprivation, fatigue…"

As she turns her head to the left wall of cadets, she spots Alexius running towards them. There is a slight change in her tone. It goes from a stern, authoritative one, to an ever so slightly accusative one. She carries on while looking at Alexius with a suspicious stare.

"…confusion, faltering discipline, temptation," she continues. "You have faced your enemies. Soon you will face the flesh and blood ones. Squad commander!" she screams to the front of the formation.

A disciplined cadet shouts out, "Squad commander Andros awaiting instructions!" He steps away from his row.

"Take charge," Deidra orders. "Hit the showers. After, report to your classes. On your way out try your best to run through Captain Alexius," she demands with a devilish smirk.

All twenty cadets shout acknowledgment. The squad methodically turns to begin their exit. They run in unison toward the approaching Alexius. In waves of two, the cadets try to run him over, still keeping their steely gaze ahead of them.

The onslaught manages to throw the unsuspecting Captain off balance several times. He is irate, up until he sees Deidra in the distance chuckling.

Alexius makes it up to Deidra with a miserable look on his face, "Your idea?"

Deidra can't contain her laughter, "Cadet Andros has bigger balls than I thought."

"I don't like that little prick. He's just like his namesake…my brother-in-law. Rigid, never smiles, conniving."

"Maybe it's his shifty eyes or that snorting laugh," she points out still chuckling. They begin walking towards the main buildings in the distance. "Aren't you tired of all this?" she asks, "We are not teachers. It is…"

"I know. It's not us, not what we are trained for. Everything here is all so, predictable. No adventure or excitement. Just Illyria."

"You mean, not enough gambling, wenching, and stealing?" Deidra accuses. "You're more predictable than this shit-hole."

"Don't be a cynic," he complains. He quickly steps ahead to spin around while walking backward, smiling at her. "Hey, come with me into town later."

"What for?" she asks suspiciously.

"An adventure," he offers with a smile. Deidra scowls, signaling her distrust of his intentions.

"The Archon wants to see you," she says.

"Maybe he will go with me." He spins around to start his jog. Deidra reluctantly follows.

-THE OFFICE OF THE ARCHON INIAS-

The military forces of Atlantis pride itself on its unique structure. There are the lower ranks, the middle ones, the leadership, then the commanders. Depending on the force type, the commander can be either a battle-hardened officer or a High Priest at the rank of Archon. To get to this rank, one must belong to a particular branch of the priesthood; one devoted to military affairs, along with spreading the religion.

Inducted at age 15, now at 55, Inias has seen his share of conflict. At first glance, one would not place him as the Archon but rather a High Priest with a pudgy stomach. His neatly combed grey hair, well-manicured hands, combined with his round face and penchant to articulate words, is the opposite of a soldier's demeanor. With his shrewd nature, sharp tongue and wit, he has risen to the highest rank a priest can reach in the military. Now, he commands this garrison outpost, wishing for the day he will return to Atlantis.

His office is laid out with a precision severely lacking in the rest of the spaces. It is large and foreboding, causing one to incur a sense of dread at first glance. The feeling quickly fades when the décor is noticed. Standing in separate corners are two marble statues, one of a High Priest, the other a patron god. They are decorated with silks thrown over shoulders, hanging over colorful potted plants. Large glass windows welcome the sunlight shining on comfortable furniture. Further in is a large oak desk with a monitor amidst scattered papers. Behind the desk, there is an intricate bookshelf, with strange artifacts showing off the Archon's exquisite taste.

At present, Inias is supervising local workmen who are attempting to spread a newly procured rug. The monstrosity is causing some confusion with where to place it. The workmen are frustrated as Inias is challenging to please. They ramble on in their dialect, confusing the Archon as he tries to listen in. He finally becomes frustrated himself.

"No, no, no!" Inias shouts with pouty lips. "Not there. I want visitors to behold it, not glance at a thing in the corner."

The broad gesturing of his arms causes some snickering amongst the locals. Their behavior infuriates Inias, causing him to storm off to his desk.

Fuming, he opens a small purse of coin. He carefully picks out the gold pieces, leaving nothing but lower valued ones. Once satisfied he is compensated for the lack of respect, he closes the purse then looks at the workers.

Suddenly, the doors swing open causing a "thud." Inias peeks out around a wall to see Alexius walking in with an aide.

Inias claps several times at the workers, "That's enough. Out. Return in one hour." The workers begin their exit. He tosses the coin purse to one man, smiling. The room quickly clears. He decides to answer Alexius' questioning glare, "It is lunch money."

Alexius notices the hideous rug with an erratic pattern of reds and blues embolden with golden images of priests. He cannot contain himself. "New dust-mat your holiness?"

Inias turns red, infuriated at the insinuation, "It's not a mat! It's a work of art. Woven by Aryan monks, blind they say..."

"That I can see, blind for sure," Alexius interrupts. "Tavern wenches in Parthon would have done it for less."

"Yes, and bless it with decadence, whereas this is made with the holy...why am I explaining myself? Sit Down."

Inias sits behind his large desk; Alexius finds a comfortable chair. Inias' fat finger taps on a switch, activating a monitor on the wall behind him. "I called you here for an assignment."

Alexius' face lights up. The prospect of something to do other than dealing with cadets thrills him, "Finally, something that isn't teaching."

"No, it's less demanding," Inias explains. "I am tasked with consolidating certain, assets. A shipment is due to arrive at our local temple tonight. I want you to oversee the securing of it."

"What is the shipment?"

An image of a small chest fills the screen. It is intricately crafted, the body silver and bronze colors, with a golden-eagle crest adorning the face. The picture zooms out, displaying the box amongst other treasures; diamonds, rubies, with other items of value. Alexius is intrigued.

"Are you expecting trouble Archon?" Alexius inquires.

"No. All you're doing is receiving it, then bring it back here. I am tasking you with this..."

"Because I am your best soldier," Alexius states quite arrogantly.

There is a hint of amusement in Inias' response, "No, because the other squads are occupied."

"I'll take Captain Deidra then."

"I thought so. Anything happens to that chest, and you will pay severely, despite your family pedigree. Now, leave."

As he stands, Alexius congratulates Inias, "Marvelous your holiness, the perfect spot for a rug."

"Out!" Inias screams.

CHAPTER 03:
OH, THAT YAK

The kingdoms of Illyria have long since formed their conglomerate consisting of five vast realms, all ruled by man; quite an accomplishment since the destruction of the Anuk. Warring tribes united, all with the common purpose of commerce. Yes, economics is their strength, and they excel at it. No longer barbarians, the Illyrians conducted wars with currency.

Like with any flourishing civilization, the priesthood managed to weave their way into the fabric of Illyrian society; like cancer they spread, demanding absolute adherence to their religion. Humanity always knew they had to submit to a higher power, and the forefathers of ancient past were the power they owed reverence to.

The kings of Illyria opened their borders to each other when they formed the conglomerate. It is a guild of sorts, with the Chairman possessing more power than a king. A High priest presided at the Chairman's side, usually more corrupt than holy. Together, they controlled vast wealth, protecting the interests of the priesthood. No one challenged them, except, Nebpkara.

Nebpkara, also known as The Master, is a mysterious figure fighting a war against the Illyrian conglomerate for over 100 years; this villain remains elusive. Reason dictates that the Master is more of a figurehead than a person. Whosoever wears the mantle, they have proven to be detrimental to the priesthood and the trading guilds. A new word found itself into the vernacular of all the civilizations; thus all followers of the Master were labeled with it…terrorists.

~LIVIANA~

The early morning has already passed; the sun is out in this sleepy smoky mountain town. Everything starts late here. The leaves have already turned color, showing off their bright reds and yellows for autumn. People are scarce; only a handful of shopkeepers along the main street are out, sweeping the sidewalk, putting out their signs. The occasional car drives by, respectful of the speed limit. Only the sound of engines from Atlantean patrol crafts high in the sky interrupts the serenity.

Everything in the town is quaint, including the local hotel. Standing between a sandwich shop and an antique store, the structure's age is masked with fresh paint. The brilliant white walls occasionally get blasted with leaves thrown over by a gust of wind.

The rooms are warm, available in single, double, and family sizes. There are always occupants here; tourists are never failing to visit this friendly little town. One guest has taken up with the local custom of sleeping in late. Despite the invading light through the small window, she refuses to wake up.

Liviana stretches her naked body under the sheets. At six-feet-tall, her toes extend beyond the bed's edge. She appears to be in her mid-twenties, with her long blonde hair displaced and wild. She runs her hand along the vacant spot next to her. The emptiness forces her eyes to open, wondering where her bedfellow ran off to. The light streaming through a space in the curtains is beginning to aggravate her, so she decides to duck beneath the sheets. The door opens.

Mica enters rather loudly, not caring whether Liviana is asleep or not. He is a ruff, twenty-nine-year-old looking fellow, moderately built at five-feet-nine-inches, with a scruffy face and long neat dark hair. He has a cup of steaming tea in his hand, slurping the liquid rather loudly. The sound is aggravating Liviana; she makes it known by her angry tone.

"Mica," Liviana grumbles, "have you no decency?" She reveals herself from under the sheets. She is a mess to look at, once you get past the slender arms on the goddess-like frame, displaying shameless nudity.

"As decent as pie," Mica answers. "Your girl ran off…must've been something you did." He decides to aggravate her some more by opening the curtains.

Liviana cringes with the light, "What time is it?"

"Late. Barely time to find breakfast." He offers her the tea. She takes it gratefully.

She stands with the bedsheet around her, towering over Mica. He walks out, leaving her to get ready for the day.

-COFFEE SHOP-

The coffee shop is small with just a handful of patrons this morning. Only over-priced coffee with light pastries is served, making up a "second-breakfast" for some.

Liviana sits with Mica at a table near a large window, disgruntled that they missed breakfast at the hotel. They sip on their hot beverage, indulging in quiet contemplation.

A barista turns up the volume on a television. A reporter is talking about a horrendous attack on a guild-owned bank in a town not far off. Everyone looks at the monitor expressing surprise and horror.

Liviana gives Mica an annoyed look, "Why can't I tell him it's for Nebpkara? That would save some annoying foreplay. I don't understand the need for a charade."

"Don't you see what's happening? One mention of the Master and he will call the authorities or worse, soldiers. It will be alright, show him the coin and he will sing."

Liviana chuckles, "Just like that? Is it so easy to get information from these, shady types?"

"I know Stonebreaker, he's a weasel, but he is loyal to his code. Once he verifies the coin, he will give you the information."

"I could have stolen the coin…"

"You did…"

"There's my point," Liviana proclaims. "How can we be sure he's giving us accurate information?"

"Flirt with him, give him an incentive. He's not that smart," Mica suggests.

"Fine," she concedes. She sips on her coffee, falling into thoughts about the simpler days.

A teenage girl approaches with her mother, almost swooning as if they are meeting royalty. They stop at the table and are beside themselves.

Mica puts his hand on a concealed dagger, ready to dispatch the pair; Liviana ever so subtly gives him a look he understands to stand down.

"You're…" the girl begins.

Liviana quickly cuts her off, "No, I'm not. But thank you. It is very flattering."

The mother smiles then pulls the girl away. As the pair leaves, Liviana slips back into her memory.

~*LIVIANA (Age 06). WILDERNESS PARK, ATLANTIS*~

The Wilderness Park in Northern Atlantis is a treasure. It spans five hundred miles in diameter, consisting of mountains, lush valleys, lakes, and abundant wildlife; it is a paradise for those seeking an escape from city life. The clouds are fluffy, the breeze is cold, the streams are clean.

Liviana and her father Barish, are on a father/daughter retreat, spending their time in the family's mountain cabin. It is a midsummer's afternoon with ideal weather for fishing and swimming.

Little Liviana finds herself pouting at a window, growing impatient for her father to take her outside. The sound of approaching footsteps makes her smile. She quickly turns to see her father across the room.

Six-feet-four-inches tall, and two-hundred-twenty-pounds of muscle, few are not intimidated by Barish. He stands still, smiling enthusiastically. Liviana darts towards him then jump into his open arms. They begin their exit towards the nearby lake.

Small pebbles outside the cabin crunch with Barish's heavy stride. He kisses his daughter wildly, and she eats up every bit of his loving.

"Little Nephele...we could go fish after swimming if you like," Barish offers.

"Papa, you know I can't fish," Liviana reminds him. "Why don't you go fishing and I'll go swimming?"

Barish smiles at his daughter, "Then who will protect me?"

Liviana suddenly has a sad look, "I couldn't protect mama."

They reach the nearby lake; a literal stone's throw from their door. Barish drops to the bank, still holding on to his precious Nephele.

"You will have to protect us all one day my love when you are big and strong. This world is descending into the chaos that will see its end." He kisses the child, and then quickly throws her into the water. She screams with delight.

~BACK IN THE COFFEE SHOP~

A military vehicle drives by slowly. Liviana pulls her cloak over her head; Mica turns his back to the window. They look at each other, acknowledging together that it was time to leave.

-MAIN STREET-

More people are walking about now, ducking into alleyways to listen to local music from street shows. Everyone is bundled up as the cold mountain air blows. The streets host more cars now, which share the space with cyclists. A tall figure strides along the sidewalk, dressed in black city clothes. With her cloak drawn, Liviana approaches one of the conveniently placed souvenir shops.

The space inside is cluttered with all forms of merchandise: lamps, small statues, paintings, and cheap electronics. At a far wall the shopkeeper, Stonebreaker, takes a mid-morning nap. A short chubby little man, he has the appearance of any working-class anti-hero who is out to make money any way he can. These days it's working for the black-market cartels.

The door opens, ringing a miserable bell at the entrance. Stonebreaker jumps up from his nap, quickly wiping the drool off his face. He smiles from ear to ear looking at Liviana in her fancy outfit. The prospect of a rich out of town customer encourages him to neaten up his hair.

Liviana cautiously navigates around the merchandise, moving like a graceful cat. She spots two surveillance cameras mounted bluntly on the walls. She makes an apparent effort to avoid the devices while heading to Stonebreaker. She stops at the counter, looks at him for a moment, and remembers Mica's advice.

"I am here about the starlight package," Liviana announces.

Stonebreaker's smile disappears. He speaks with authority, "And who do I have the pleasure of speaking with?"

"Oona. Marcus sent me," Liviana explains.

She offers him a silver coin. There is an engraved image of an Illyrian senator on the face, with an out of place black dot on an eye. Stonebreaker looks at it, not satisfied.

"And who vouches for you?"

The question throws Liviana off. She was expecting to be welcomed as Mica promised. She suddenly remembers the idiot knew the man.

"Mica," she blurts out.

Stonebreaker becomes irate, furious at the mention of the name. "You tell that lying son of a whore to drop dead! I can't help you. Get out!"

A slight "click" sounds as Liviana un-sheaths her dagger. She grabs stonebreaker by the collar and pulls him down towards her blade. Fear fills the shopkeeper's eyes. "Look little man. Do you want to kiss my blade? Speak, now!"

She eases her grip, allowing him to regain his composure. He is more compliant, looking at the dangerous dagger.

"All I know is that it's not coming here…I swear," he says.

Liviana is not satisfied. She quickly makes her way around the counter. Expecting the worst, Stonebreaker drops to the ground.

She presses the blade on his neck, ready to slice, "I am here for the Master. If you don't know anything, then I don't need you. I'm going to slit your throat and the arteries in your leg. Then I will burn your store to the ground. You will be alive long enough to burn with it."

"Wait!" Stonebreaker screams. "Anything for the Master, please, wait. I'll tell you…I'll prove what I'm saying is true." The blade drops from his neck as he wets himself.

He cautiously slides past Liviana to quickly open a door, revealing a descending set of stairs. He waves her in, looking at the windows to see if there are onlookers. Satisfied, they make their way down. The stairs are wooden, creaking as they go.

Lights automatically brighten the basement, not by much, but enough to indicate that space is just like the outside, cluttered. Boxes and crates are everywhere congesting the room. It is dusty and damp. The lack of windows guarantees the air is foul. They stop at a table in the center.

Stonebreaker does not hesitate to activate a screen laid into the table's surface. Several symbols light up in the corner; he types in a combination rather quickly, hoping Liviana did not observe them. Images appear, then information.

"See," he points to the screen, "the Starlight package is bound for Atlantis…it's not coming here. This stop was just a decoy, see it says so right here." His enthusiasm for giving up the information shows on his face, hopeful, yet pleading.

"Who's the courier?" Liviana demands.

"Mercenaries hired by the priesthood, from one of the northern Illyrian cartels."

The information infuriates Liviana. "If you breathe one word of this, you and your entire line will die before tomorrow's light…I swear it by the Master."

Her promise causes the frightened man to nod his acknowledgment, while he wets himself once more. Liviana storms out.

-MAIN STREET-

It doesn't take Liviana long to make it back on 'Main Street.' She is aggravated, angry. Her long strides have a purpose in them; just about the only thing that does at the moment. She slowly realizes that her efforts have been for nothing, that the job she is here for was now out of reach. Her grumbling stomach reminds her to find Mica.

She crosses the busy street heading towards a restaurant at the corner; she is oblivious to the oncoming traffic. Angry motorists yell at her, but she pays them no mind. As she gets on the sidewalk Mica catches her eye; he is laid out on a bench taking a nap. On any other occasion, she would have done some mischievous things to aggravate him…not today. She stops at the bench and then kicks a leg.

The impact wakes him almost in a panic, "What the…Oh. Well, what did he say?"

"He said you should drop dead, and I agree with him. He was fine up until I mentioned you," Liviana growls.

"Why did you do that?" Suddenly he realizes something. "Maybe you shouldn't have said your name was Oona. That's his wife. I may have, you know."

"Incredible" she expresses with disappointment. "I'm hungry…let's go." She pulls Mica off the bench. They both make their way inside the restaurant.

The place is crowded, packed with patrons. There is a clamor of conversation, knocking cutlery, children crying. This chaos was not going to stop Liviana from enjoying a meal today. She has always been a "breakfast all day" girl. She was willing to put up with a short wait at the concierge. Her aggravation quickly disappears as she spots Mica stowing away a handful of complimentary candy. She does her best not to let him see her smile. An overly cheerful girl takes them to a booth.

They sit across from each other, grabbing the menus. Mica observes a large fellow in the booth after them, sitting behind Liviana; he even more so sees the man's female companion. She notices him, so he smiles at her; she returns a smile.

-NEXT BOOTH-

Alexius sits with a menu in his hands, reading the drinks section; he drops it to see Deidra smiling.

"Did I miss something?" Alexius asks curiously. Deidra ignores him.

She swats the menu from Alexius' hands, "You drag me out here for lunch?" Alexius ignores her.

-LIVIANA & MICA-

Liviana waits patiently for their waitress to arrive. Her steely gaze is fixed on Mica; he is looking around the spaces, counting exits, the potential exists and gauging the crowd. She knows he is doing this and is thankful for it. She, of course, will not share that.

"We're leaving Illyria, going back to Atlantis. This venture was a waste of time; the package isn't coming here," Liviana explains.

"Once again, no treasure," Mica states disappointingly. "Liv, I'm tired of this quest, tired of being poor."

"I cannot stop now; we cannot. If we fail, then being poor will be the least of your concerns."

A pleasant waitress stops at the table. She waits with her pad and pencil. One of the waiters quickly approaches with a trolley. She immediately makes way for him to pass. As he does, the aroma from a large slab of smoldering meat fills the air. The thing looks delicious, with fruit laid on the sides, and vegetables as garnish. The wonderful dish stops at Alexius and Deidra's booth.

"Can we have what they're having?" Mica pleads.

Liviana gives him a menacing look before responding to the waitress. "No, just breakfast for both of us." The waitress smiles as she leaves.

Mica matches Liviana's stare, "Did you know that sometimes you can be such a cu…?" Liviana has a wicked smile on her face. Mica knows that smile, and he doesn't like it.

"Go ahead, please, say it," Liviana challenges.

"I don't want to," he admits, knowing fully well what will happen. He is too hungry to take on Liviana's wrath, and he has not gotten beaten up in several days. "There are children present."

"You're the stupid little brother no one wants, did you know that?" Liviana scolds.

The insult does nothing to Mica as he relaxes, "Ah, but I'm not your little brother," he says happily. "He's probably stabbing some poor servant's guts out."

"Drink your coffee, and shut up."

-ALEXIUS & DEIDRA-

The slab of meat in the center of the table is smoldering. The pair looks at it with curiosity, lavishing in the ecstasy that awaits.

"What is it?" Deidra asks as she pokes the meat. She glances up to see that Alexius has already begun slicing into it.

"An adventure," he explains, "…or something they call Yak, I think. Smell good." He drops a slice on Deidra's plate then whispers, "Inias gave me an assignment…you're coming too."

A moment passes as he shovels pieces of the Yak into his mouth. The toe-curling flavor is seen in his expression.

"Well, are you going to keep stuffing your face or tell me?"

"There's a shipment of assets bound for the temple tonight. We have to secure everything, from mercs. There's this chest, with a golden crest…"

In the other booth, Liviana quiets Mica's grumblings then discreetly turns her head in Alexius' direction. She holds her breath waiting for the careless soldier to give up more information.

Alexius continues, "…surrounded by lots of treasure. It…"

"Are you insane? I am not stealing from the priesthood. That's the limit of our friendship," Deidra protests.

"Don't be so dramatic. We both know you won't do any stealing. All you have to do is, watch my back."

"And then what? What are you going to do after, run away?"

"It's just me securing my future, and yours if you'll have it."

Another moment passes as Deidra fumes. She decides to resign herself to the inevitable. She has known Alexius long enough to realize there is no stopping him once his mind is made up. All she can do is try to keep him out of trouble.

"This is the last time," Deidra shakes her head then mumbles to herself "This is what happens when I go soft."

They are preoccupied with the feast and do not take notice of one of the locals observing them. The man is tall, with a large stomach. His unkempt beard and long hair together with his rugged attire, tells that he is one of the mountain folk. A friendly lot, the mountain folk are protective of the locals and do not care much for outsiders.

The man makes his way to Alexius and Deidra, "You are soldiers aren't you?" He points to their civilian clothing, "You can't-fool me."

"Look, friend," Alexius says calmly, "we don't want any trouble."

The man smiles, apparently itching for a confrontation, "Trouble, trouble you say? We never had to worry about terrorists or curfews until you arrived. Put up your big base, training your soldiers. Why you have to come here? You should have stayed on your island."

Deidra attempts to calm to man, "We're here at the invitation of your king, to keep the nomads from spreading through your lands."

"Ah…fucking propaganda. You Atlanteans with your fancy gadgets and money. Think you're better than us…"

Alexius cuts him off in an arrogant tone, "We are better than you," he states. This insult angers the man, his grinding teeth giving this away.

He slips a hand inside his jacket and then leans into Alexius. At the same time, Deidra begins to move towards the attacker. She is saved the trouble of starting a fight when Mica suddenly bumps into the man.

Like a massive beast being dropped on a hunt, the mountain man falls on Alexius, limp and unconscious. The weight crushes him, but Mica tries to pull the beast off. The man's hand drops off to the ground, and so does the rest of him.

Mica calls out to the staff, "Some help here!" Two staffers rush in to pull the local off. He uses this opportunity to attach a small device on to Alexius' boot discreetly.

"Thank you, friend. What did you do to him?" Alexius asks Mica.

"Aryan snake venom. It's harmless…he'll be good by morning. Hey, can I try some of that?" He points to the chunk of meat.

Alexius nods. Mica doesn't waste time slicing a moderate piece off. Grateful, he returns to his seat.

-LIVIANA & MICA-

With one hand Mica holds the chunk of meat showing it off to Liviana; she is unimpressed. He drops it off on one of the freshly arrived plates. Like an entitled brat, Liviana attempts to take a slice of the Yak; Mica protects his prize.

"Well?" she demands a report. Mica nods, expressing delight as he chews. Instinctively, he cuts half the Yak and gives it to her.

"Ponchus is a good man but, we'd better be clear of here by morning; he won't take kindly to being stuck with snake venom. And I'm telling him you did it."

"Do you know everyone in this dump of a town?"

-ALEXIUS' BOOT-

A small octagonal device glows in a dim green color, and then it matches the color of the boot…fading away like a chameleon. The tiny transmitter has a range of 100 feet, and if Mica's gamble pays off, Alexius won't change out of his boots. The thing about soldiers who are posted in the middle of nowhere is, they will change their clothes, but they will always wear the same pair of boots.

Another one of his gambles was that Ponchus would know precisely what he had to do, all from Mica's nod. The beating Ponchus would deliver for the snake venom, however, was not something he had planned for.

CHAPTER 04: I NEED AN OLD PRIEST

One of the charms of Southern Illyria is the slow-paced atmosphere; even the sun seems unwilling to make its descent into twilight. There is still an hour to go, and the brilliant yellow streaks turn into rich red ones, showering the mountain-side with light. The local monastery sits at the top, a testament to the holy watching over the town.

There is a large temple at the center of the monastery grounds, surrounded by a well-cared for landscape. From there anyone can observe the roads spiraling down; it is advantageous since this is the only approach to the monastery. Presently it is carefully watched by the garrison soldiers waiting for their shipment.

Alexius and Deidra sit just outside of the temple. Like two overly bored adolescents, they find simple things to occupy their time. From pulling on the fresh grass to tossing rocks over the short wall; they are going out of their minds. Occasionally, pairs of Cadets stroll by, wishing they were full-fledged soldiers, taking note of their lazy superiors. Bain and Fat-Boy at the very least, complain about the two Captains just lounging about drinking wine.

The resident priest, Father Mathias, slowly approaches the temple from the monastery spaces. He is a kind old man, now in his eighties; strong as ever though, able to outwit the best of the residents there. He has dedicated the better part of forty years to the monastery, fathering four children, and amassing a horde of grandchildren. Not much is known about him before his assignment to this corner of Illyria. All the same, holy and unholy alike come to visit, paying homage to the man that is Mathias.

He is carrying a silver platter with a pitcher of local wine; a concoction of fermented fruit, wine, and a potent ingredient produced by the mountain folk. *It is sure to knock the soldiers on their asses*, he muses. He stops close to Deidra and places the platter on a nearby table.

"More wine my child? This is one of our favorites, locally brewed."

"No thank you, Father. I am quite alright with the regular brew." Deidra smiles warmly at the priest. She knows all too well how she behaves after several cups of the local favorite; she turns into a whining and needy wench.

"I'll have some," the irritating Cadet Bain announces, with Fat-Boy right behind him.

Mathias hesitates and then looks at Deidra. She must be feeling generous today, as her nod to the priest indicates such. He pours the drink, embracing the sweet aroma as it flows. The burgundy color entices Bain; Fat-Boy licks his lips waiting for his share. As Mathias extends a cup to the anxious Cadet, Alexius snatches it from Bain's grasp.

"Thank you, Father, most kind."

Bain and Fat-Boy walk-off scowling.

Mathias smiles at the comedy, remembering the impatience of youth. As he returns the pitcher to the table a pin on his collar catches the fading sunlight; it dazzles Deidra's eyes. The gold and silver triangle is small and looks more like a hand-made trinket rather than a religious object.

"That's an interesting pin," Deidra points out.

Mathias gives her a proud grandfather smile, "Oh this? My grandson made it. It's one half of a set, and he wears the twin."

"It's lovely," she expresses with genuine admiration.

Mathias looks at both Deidra and Alexius with worry on his face. There is a bit of an anxious feeling within him as if he is expecting trouble.

"I am uncomfortable receiving these assets. Normally this would not worry me, but these are different times. There's always some villain lurking in the bushes," he explains.

"Quite right Father. Not to worry though," Alexius declares, "you have the might of Atlantis to protect you." His tone is a bit arrogant, stemming more from the wine than any ill intent.

The priest smiles warmly at him, knowing full well what the drink is doing, "I knew your father. He was a good man, loyal…"

"He died when I was but a child, in Northern Illyria of all places," Alexius says.

"Wasn't he once Governor of FaW-C?" Deidra asks.

"He was, long before I was born. That's about as much as I know. Don't suppose you know more Father?" Alexius looks at the priest smiling at him.

There is a slight glimmer in the old man's expression. "Old age dulls the memory I'm afraid," he offers, not revealing what he knew. "His time in Illyria however, those were some exciting days." He makes a retreat before any more questions come his way.

Alone once more, Deidra exhales sharply, which does an excellent job at expressing her feelings about the wasted evening. She looks at Alexius pouring more of the potent wine. He looks at her and then fills her cup; this time she doesn't refuse.

"This is so boring, how much longer?" she asks.

"Inias said sundown. Relax, take in the cool air, the view; a break from everything."

"Some assignment this is." Deidra gets off the chair, then begins pacing, sipping on her wine.

"Do you always want to find a fight?" Alexius asks. "I requested you come so you can, relax. You are so uptight all the time."

"You want me here so you can fill your pockets," she reminds him.

"Whatever is in that chest must be worth a whole lot. Armed escorts?" Alexius asks rhetorically.

"So we are the villains, only not in the bushes."

"The priesthood is rich," Alexius reminds her. He decides to plead his case, hoping to ease her concerns. "They are possibly richer than Atlantis, surely all of Illyria, and definitely Aryavan. Think of it; they are revered by all except the nomads. You know, I've been thinking…"

"Here we go," Deidra declares sarcastically.

"Nomads live on the fringes, the borderlands, the wastelands. They live free. They don't pay tribute to the priesthood, nor carry banners to any lord or king…"

Deidra cuts into his rant, "And they worship their goddess, Persephone. Blasphemy." There is a conviction in her voice, almost a disdain at her mention of the once great Anuk princess, and Egyptian queen.

"There is the problem; they don't conform. So we fight the nomads. Ever asked why?" At this point, Deidra is noticeably uncomfortable with the conversation. She isn't buying his defense of the nomads.

"We fight them because they terrorize the civilizations with killings, destruction, and anarchy," she reminds Alexius. "We snuff them out; take their land and their lives."

"A handful amongst the many, seasoned by generations of hate and oppression."

Deidra looks at Alexius with concern on her face, almost worried, "Careful Captain, or you may be labeled a sympathizer."

"All I'm saying is that it has to end one day. Since it's not today, I'll try to get my piece of good living." He sips his wine with determination, trying to get past the bitter sting of flavor.

Deidra looks at him mockingly, "You're already rich, what are you complaining about?"

"My family is rich, not me. My mother saw to that," he explains.

Deidra continues her mocking tone, "Excuse me, your highness…Lord Alexius of House Badur, so says Deidra of Bastille Alley."

Alexius dips his fingers into his cup then sprinkles her.

-FAR SIDE OF TEMPLE-

Humans and goats alike avoid the steep mountain-slope leading up to the temple's backside. There are some trees rooted deep into the light brown soil. Green bushes sporadically spread out along the area. Pebbles and larger rocks come hurtling down from the monastery's border wall; not from anything less than the two figures sneaking up the side.

Making their way effortlessly, Liviana and Mica reach the stone wall perimeter. They rest for a moment under a large bush, observing the patrolling cadets above. There are only three on this side, armed with pistols and enthusiasm. Novice infiltrators may have been intimidated, but not these two; they regard the cadets as a let-down rather than a challenge. The ones they are more interested in are the two Captains.

"Where are they?" Liviana asks while retracting a climbing line.

Mica activates his armband. It's a rather innovative, sleek piece of technology. Wrapped on to his left inside forearm, one would think it is a regular black leather sleeve, and part of his attire. With a gesture a screen lights up, curving around the limb. A fully functioning monitor with three-dimensional capabilities is now active. A simple touch on the surface activates a series of buttons.

A small dot representing Alexius appears; sonar-like waves emanate from the dot, quickly creating a more detailed map. Some more information appears next to the image, giving a distance, bearing, and other representational data. As if urged on by the invisible waves, dogs howl in the distance.

Situated a sharp five meters up, a metal gate swings open. It smashes on to the side of the wall, reverberating with the impact. A patch of silver hair appears. Mathias carefully peeks down the incline. He spots the two lurking in the bushes, and then quickly waves them up. A climbing line shoots up, hooking on to a section by the gate. The pair now ascends to the inside perimeter.

The first to meet Mathias is Mica. He grabs the old man's hand, pulling firmly, trying not to topple him. Liviana is next. She appears to need less help than Mica but grabs Mathias' hand. As she enters the gate, her towering stature looks imposing. Mathias drops to the ground.

Liviana quickly, but gently pulls him up, "It has been too long."

It could be the exertion, but Mathias is flustered, and tears are forming. "I am sorry; this whole affair came about suddenly," he explains.

"No apologies necessary. Get yourself and yours somewhere safe. We will talk soon."

"There are three young men on patrol," Mathias warns. "Shouldn't be too hard to evade. Now, come." They duck behind a wall being careful not to alert the Cadets above.

-DOWN AT THE MONASTERY'S MAIN COURTYARD-

The slow setting sun has finally dropped below the horizon. Bright floodlights shine throughout the courtyard making the entire area appears as if it's daytime once more. The lights on the main entrance's wall come to life, staying dim but illuminating the beautiful flowers and plants nearby.

Tall walls enclose the front gate. There is a paved road from the gate leading up to the central courtyard. Precious orchids and other majestic plants adorn the spaces. Suddenly, a teenage boy and girl run to the entrance. They open the gates allowing two rugged trucks to enter; the mercenaries from Northern Illyria.

The vehicles make haste to the receiving area, coming to a sudden stop by kicking up dust and gravel. Everyone wants to see the occupants; they are expecting a rowdy bunch to step on the holy ground. Alexius and Deidra calmly stand with Mathias, several Cadets, and some youths.

The truck doors open, a husky man dressed in black, armed with pistols and daggers climbs out. He doesn't speak; he waits for his companions from the other truck to join him. Together they march up to Mathias; there are six in total, four men, two women, all dressed and armed alike. Each one has to be over six feet. Their menacing demeanor does not stop the youths from offloading the contents in the trucks.

"Your holiness. We request refreshments and your prayers," the lead mercenary says while bowing to Mathias.

"Of course, my child," the priest responds. "You are welcomed to the facilities. Please, join me in the prayer hall in let's say one hour?"

The man nods then kneels. He kisses Mathias' hand then touches his forehead. Pleased, he stands and barks orders at his companions.

"Quite the holy bunch aren't they?" Alexius whispers to Deidra; she doesn't respond.

Four mercenaries enter the monastery with Mathias; two remain with the trucks. The youths complete their task with the last of five crates being loaded onto a flat trolley. They begin to roll the cargo toward the back. Alexius starts walking towards them.

Deidra is irritated, "Don't," she advises with concern. "Wait until they are gone."

"Just a look," Alexius informs her with a cocky smile. She knows that smile; it never ends well for them.

"Those are mercenaries; no code, or honor. Doesn't take much to set them off."

Alexius ignore the advice. Small gravel crunches under his boot as he briskly walks towards to youths. One of the mercenaries steps in his path. The man is bigger than he is. The merc glares at him, snarling really. All he could do is smile at the man.

"I'll wait here," Alexius concedes. Deidra relaxes her grasp on her pistol. She breaths easy.

-IN THE TEMPLE PRIVATE PRAYER HALL-

The lights are dim in this large prayer hall. Although a private one, there is enough standing room for fifty devotees. At the end of a path, an altar stands raised three feet off the ground. The walls are well decorated with tapestries, the five banners of Illyria, and plants, all making the décor quite inviting. Standing just beneath the Northern Illyrian banner are the four mercenaries.

They patiently wait for Mathias to call them to prayer. The priest is on the altar burning incense and chanting prayers. The crates are sitting beside the altar, being blessed. They see Mathias wave them over. As they begin to head off, a beeping sound emanates from one of the men's armband. He sends the other three to be blessed.

Mathias smiles at his guests as they arrive, gesturing them to kneel. He looks over to the fourth man, wondering what was happening. There is a bit of nervousness in his voice, as he chants the ancient prayers. He decides that the wheel of fate cannot be stopped tonight, and if it is his time to travel beyond this realm, then he is more than prepared to do so. The fourth man quickly joins them, offering an uncharacteristic smile.

The sound of the prayers echoes, traveling to each corner. One of those corners, thirty feet away, conceals a hidden door in the flooring. It leads to a secret room in the ground, about fifteen feet square in size and eleven feet high. It is an old hideout, and an occasional smuggling depository; this monastery was once used by Illyrian outlaws and the Master himself. Now, Mica and Liviana patiently wait in it.

Mica observes the activities outside as best as he can. The view is not advantageous, but he can see enough movement to know they are still in prayer. He huffs and drops back down to the floor. Liviana sits in quiet contemplation.

"They've been at it for thirty minutes," Mica grumbles. "How long does it take for a blessing?" he asks rhetorically. Liviana turns to him, her steely gaze informing him to be quiet.

Ten minutes pass, then, a noise from the only exit alerts them. The door opens revealing Mathias; he smells of incense. The odor annoys Mica but does nothing to Liviana. She grabs Mathias' outstretched hands and brings him down to her eye level.

Mathias' face is a mask of concern, "It's just as you feared, they are staying the night."

"When is the handoff?" Liviana asks.

"Dawn. Not to the soldiers. A transport bound for Atlantis."

"Weren't the soldiers supposed to receive it?" Mica inquires.

51

"Yes, according to Archon Inias," Mathias responds. "The mercenaries just now received new orders from Prince Timon himself." He looks at Liviana, who is quite annoyed.

She intended to steal the chest from the ill-equipped and ill-manned soldiers. It would have been an easy task, with little collateral damage. Mathias would be exonerated, as it would be reported as a robbery by agents of the Master, and the soldiers would serve as witnesses. Now, there will have to be bloodshed, inviting the scrutiny of Prince Timon of Atlantis.

"That little prick always wants to be one step ahead of me," Liviana declares, her annoyance showing on her face.

"If all goes well my son will be at Demon Rock, you know the place. He has men you can trust," Mathias informs them.

"My tracker died," Mica says. "Where are the soldiers?" he asks Mathias.

"Two in the main hall, the rest are patrolling." He looks at Liviana, almost pleading "They are just children, surely you won't…"

"The grown ones aren't," Liviana cuts him off. "There are no innocents here." She looks at Mathias. She gently places her hand on his face; he closes his eyes, melting with emotion. "Flee this place Mathias; I cannot have your death on my hands."

"I have severed these long years. I welcome death for it is the only true friend I have yet to embrace. I love you and your father. It will be an honor to die in service."

Liviana kisses him on his forehead. She then pulls out her daggers to check the blades. Mica checks his pistols. Not wanting to be left out, Mathias checks his prayer beads.

-TEMPLE MAIN HALL-

Adjacent to the private prayer hall is the main hall, which is separated by a solid wall; the echo accentuates the grandeur of the space. Only Alexius and Deidra lurk quietly in the area. They sit comfortably on the wooden benches, regarding the scattered sculptures and tapestries. There is an air of defeat between them, more so Alexius. With his grand plan to liberate some riches already soured, he has resorted to just doing his duty; merely waiting for the Atlantean transport to arrive.

Deidra tries to hide her intoxication, "Accept it, it's over."

"You're right," Alexius admits with defeat in his eyes, "But we did have some good wine." Deidra smiles for the first time tonight.

He moves closer to her, noticing a bit of wine stain on the side of her lips. He licks his hands and then wipes the side of her mouth. Tenderly he rubs, and she doesn't resist. Maybe it's the foul drink, but the needy wench seems to be coming out; her skin is becoming flush, and her senses are heightened. She leans in closer, ready to plant a passionate kiss. As she moves in, Alexius' hand moves to her lips, stopping her.

He is listening to an echo; there is a faint sound coming from the private hall. A louder crash alerts him to trouble. Now aggravated that someone else is stealing his treasure, he decides to make one last effort to get what he can; the thought of doing his duty may have entered his mind, briefly. He takes off running with Deidra following closely behind.

It doesn't take them long to enter the area. They arrive on the scene to find one mercenary dead, two are fighting with a cloaked figure, and the last one is engaging a thief who is almost at the crates.

Liviana expertly blocks the large men's blows. She grips her daggers tightly, waiting for an opening; the moment one man's elbow drops, she swings her blade high slicing his jugular. The second attacker is now behind her reaching with his arm over her shoulder, attempting to grab her neck.

Not missing a beat, she breaks the man's arm. She flips him over her, and with a sharp plunge, brings a dagger hard down through his throat. She pulls it free, and then launches it at Mica's attacker, hitting him squarely at the brain stem. The mercenary instantly falls twitching to his death.

The soldiers rush both thieves; Mica is at the crates, and Liviana is twenty feet away, making her charge towards them. They spit up, with Alexius heading for Mica and Deidra contending with Liviana.

Deidra throws her punches hard, but with no effect; Liviana is moving as if she is the air itself. Their arms connect with Liviana blocking the oncoming swing with her left arm. She quickly pushes Deidra with her right hand, getting a short distance between them. It is enough for her to land a powerful kick to the soldier's chest, sending her flying several feet off the ground, and then smashing into a wall; the impact knocks Deidra unconscious.

Meanwhile, Alexius reaches Mica who at this point has smashed open the largest crate. He grabs the smaller man before he could remove the contents. They begin trading blows, but Mica is no match for the larger soldier; he is getting beaten.

In a split second Liviana moves clear across the room to Mica's aid. She separates the two men and engages Alexius. This gives Mica a chance to grab the partially exposed chest, and then flee.

Unable to effectively do much else, Alexius tries to land a powerful punch on Liviana. They seem matched in strength, and this causes a slight panic in the soldier. Her grace coupled with strong blows and counter-attacks, makes her moves seem rehearsed. Somehow, Alexius manages to barely stop Liviana from landing a deadly blow.

His attention is on her hands, but as her hood drops revealing her face, he becomes distracted. This is enough for Liviana to rise in the air to deliver a powerful roundhouse kick to his face. This sends him reeling across the floor. His eyes are still open, and he glances at Liviana across the room. In a split second, she is gone; *it must be a trick of the mind,* he thinks.

A barrage of muffled gunfire can be heard quickly reducing in tempo, and then goes silent. Alexius shakes off his beating then rushes to Deidra. She is slowly waking; he helps her up.

"Hurry," he urges while pulling her up. They both run to an exit.

As they clear the structure, they see several Cadets on the ground unconscious. *Alive thankfully*, Alexius reassures himself. They continue running towards the monastery's main area. A fool would hope to think they can catch the intruders. They still try, but as they already know, it would be too late.

The receiving area where the trucks were parked is now littered with unconscious Cadets, two dead Mercenaries, and a busted vehicle. Smoke is coming from the remaining truck, and the tires are shot up. There is no hope of chasing. Deidra mumbles to herself, cursing the pilot who dropped them off, *Damn Inias and his no waiting rule*, she fumes.

Mathias appears from a door. He rushes out to the Cadets to help them up. He suspects what will happen next. The Archon Inias will send for him, and he will have to answer for what transpired.

CHAPTER 05:
IN HOT WATER

A new day always brings the promise of routine at the Atlantean base; studies, physical training, and assigned duties…not today. The garrison is graced by a distinguished Commander of the Forces of Atlantis, Andros. His armed transport sits ominously on the landing ramp with seasoned soldiers stationed nearby.

Curious cadets pass by admiring the handful of troops in blood red and black uniforms. These are the men and women they aspire to be one day, serving as infantry, pilots, and infiltrators…all proud members of the greatest fighting force in the world. Today these veterans serve as escort to Commander Andros; his assignment, to retrieve an important shipment, now stolen.

In a restricted section of the garrison, one building is surrounded by armed guards. Trees overshadow the structure with moss and wild vines running along the walls; indications that this part of the base has been all but abandoned. It now serves as an interrogation area for the priest Mathias.

The Archon Inias's car arrives, stopping rather slowly at the front entrance. It is the only one there, bringing some relief to the priest that Commander Andros has not yet commenced his interrogation. Andros was known to be brutal, and part of his psychological tactic was to make a prisoner ponder the horrors to come. Inias was not that kind of beast.

As he exits the vehicle, there is an air of sadness in him. Mathias, after all, is a member of the priesthood, a colleague and a friend. Circumstances have forced this eventual predicament, and as Inias knows in his heart, the outcome of the interrogation is inevitable death. The question that looms with him was if and when his demise would come. He is an Archon after all, and it would take an order of the Priesthood, ratified by the Senate of Atlantis to request his death warrant. *Rules never seem to apply to Prince Timon,* he reminds himself.

He enters the old building alone, walking with purpose trying to hide his anticipation of events from the few soldiers posted there. They are his charges, but with Andros' arrival, he has been relegated to nothing more than an agent of the priesthood, holding no more power than Mathias. He arrives at a cell, and the guard opens the iron door.

Inias enters the dusty and damp room looking at the old priest with affection. Mathias sits in a corner, looking at his friend as he enters. Sunlight streams from an oval window overhead, with the rays only shining on a small edge of the wall. The door closes as if predicting Inias' fate.

"Mathias you old fool. What have you gotten yourself into?"

"I don't suppose you have any wine?" Mathias asks with a smile. Inias shakes his head. "I thought not. Well, it shall be a thirsty death then."

"I'll get your wine. You do know I can't help you with this. I've always turned a blind eye to your, activities."

"Whom do you serve Inias? Atlantis or the priesthood?"

"How dare you ask me that?"

"We are agents of the past my friend. Not the collection of the self-righteous, self-serving, parade of idiots of the present. This age is at an end, and prophecy shall have its day."

"Nonsense. Stories told by the ancients."

"Maybe so. Would you rather take the chance that you are wrong?"

Inias sits on the ground with Mathias. He puts a hand on his friend's shoulder and tries to reason with him, "Please, tell Andros what you know, maybe he will show mercy."

"There is no mercy to be found this day. Will you say a prayer for me brother?"

Inias nods and then embraces the old man, "And you do the same for me, for I may be joining you in the afterlife." He stands and then pounds on the metal door.

Mathias looks at him with a smile on his face, his tone is hopeful, "With the forefather's return comes the wrath of Persephone; her vengeance. Save yourself brother, or be consumed by the wrath of a god."

The door opens. Inias quickly takes his leave.

He walks briskly towards the exit, slowing his pace at the sight of approaching figures. As he gets into better lighting, he sees all the temple youths from Mathias' monastery, a handful of the family, and armed soldiers behind them. One figure catches his gaze; it is Commander Andros.

He is a clean-cut, medium built, arrogant man, with the features of an aristocrat, and that red cape; oh, how he loves to wear that red cape. He smiles wickedly at Inias.

Andros waits until they pass the Archon by several paces then asks a question, "Where are you going Inias? Come, join us," he orders.

Inias turns around to face Andros; the commander has his hand out as if gesturing peace, smiling that smug and evil smile. There is no escaping this morning's events.

-OFFICE OF ARCHON INIAS-

The office is quiet, with Alexius and Deidra being the only occupants. They sit by a large window contemplating their fates. Two squads run past them on the outside, singing their cadence and providing a welcomed distraction for the two Captains. As the squads disappear, so too does their momentary escape into silence.

"Andros can't blame us for what happened," Deidra says. She looks at Alexius, he is angry. "Do you think he will…"

"He'll have you executed, me, he'll want it to hurt, a lot."

On any other day, Deidra would consider his words to be a mere exaggeration. She knew of Andros' reputation and the hatred for his brother-in-law.

"Who was that in the temple, that woman?" she asks.

"I don't know, Nomad I suppose. If they had just a hundred like her, they could take out this entire base."

The doors burst open startling the soldiers. Inias enters in a fury with a stern look on his face. The pair quickly stands in military fashion, silent and looking straight ahead. Inias looks at them; his face is red and his breathing steady and controlled, like a bull ready to attack.

"You two, come here!" Inias orders.

Without hesitation, the soldiers march to the Archon. They are still silent, waiting to be allowed to speak. They have been in this position before, but due to innocent mischief and misbehavior. Now the eyes of Atlantis were on them, and that spotlight burned hot.

Inias screams, "By the gods, you have managed to destroy me. You had one thing to do, one simple task." Alexius attempts to say something; Inias stops him "Did I say you can speak? And you,

I expected him to fuck this up, not you, not Deidra. Go on, speak."

"Your holiness," Alexius begins, "plans were in play contrary to your expectations, to your orders."

"I know," Inias declares, a lot calmer now.

"You knew?" Deidra asks, sounding slightly accusative.

Inias tosses a thin brass tube on the floor. It lands next to Alexius' boot, but he dares not look down at it.

"Encoded message to be delivered via courier, yesterday. Arrived just now," he explains.

He gets closer to the soldiers as if to whisper. He looks them in the eyes, knowing full well that despite him being shorter, he is successfully intimidating them. His words will carry much weight now.

"You have one chance at redemption, one chance. We have intelligence on the whereabouts of the thieves."

"What about father Mathias?" Alexius asks.

There is a hint of anger in Inias' response, "He's dead, and soon I will be if you don't bring me that chest! Just so we're clear, if I am to die, you will suffer a fate much worse."

"Where do we start Archon?" Deidra asks with her head lowered.

Inias calms down some. He pushes past them to grab the monitor on his desk. He swings it around and then touches the screen. A map appears with the topography of a mountainous forest area.

"Demon rock. They are somewhere in that region…" Inias points on the screen. "There were transmissions sent to these coordinates." He taps the monitor revealing a more descriptive screen.

"Are you certain it's Demon Rock? That's a massive area to cover," Deidra protests.

Inias gets in Deidra's face, "No, but you better be sure. Take an entire regiment, with air support." He looks at Alexius, "Burn the bloody forest down if you have to."

"What if they left by air?" Alexius asks.

"Unlikely...the airspace is monitored, and it's been quiet. Go now, get ready. Oh, one more thing, Andros' troops will be joining the hunt. Ensure they don't find the chest before we do. Now get out."

The soldiers bow to the Archon then make a hasty retreat. As the door closes behind them, Alexius spots Commander Andros heading his way.

The wretch will surely have something to say. I'm in hot water as it is...no need to drown in it, Alexius cautions himself. Deidra looks at him then pats his shoulder. Not wanting to witness a potential brawl, she quickly leaves.

Andros has an evil smirk on his lips as he walks smugly towards his brother-in-law. He stops three feet in front of Alexius and looks up into his eyes; he is ecstatic at the thought of being able to "stomp" on this creature once more.

"Brother," Andros greets Alexius.

"Commander," Alexius responds.

Alexius' formal tone throws Andros off his plan. An informal response would have opened the door to a less appetizing dialogue; by addressing his superior with an honorific that door closed, keeping conversation to the business at hand. He knew Andros was trying to force him to lose his temper.

"I will lead the air forces in this recovery. Get yourself ready, we leave in one hour," Andros says in a formal tone.

"By your command." Alexius remains in a respectful pose, watching Andros stare him up and down. A moment passes before the Commander steps towards Inias' door.

"Oh Captain," Andros says with a hint of pleasure in his voice, "one more thing, you will join the ground force at the perimeter."

Alexius could sense the amusement the commander is getting from this. Keeping him away from the leading group would ensure Andros claims all the glory. He waits for a moment, then leaves. His mind is racing as he traverses the long corridor ahead of him

-OFFICERS QUARTERS-

The private building is for the officers only; no Cadets allowed. The interior is uniquely designed for the Foreign Legion's tastes. Trophies, awards, expensive ornaments, and of course a well-stocked bar. Several of the garrison soldiers are hosting Commander Andros' troops, but only a handful are in the building patiently waiting for their orders.

Alexius sees the air wing Captain he is looking for, Parish. He is a well-groomed man in his late twenties, dressed in a flight uniform. He is from the prosperous city of Darnen, in the African region of the Empire. A proud individual, he is not easily swayed by questionable affairs. He is very competitive, and this was a weakness to be exploited at the moment.

"Parish!" Alexius calls out. "Didn't expect to find you here." He meets him at the bar.

"And where else would I be? We are still on schedule to clean up your mess."

Alexius smiles, clutching a leather-bound folder, making it obvious that he was protecting it. The corner of a page is sticking out, with the beginnings of a number sequence visible.

"What do you have there? Looks like coordinates," Parish says.

"This? Oh, it's just something Inias gave me. So, you're taking Andros up I hear."

"I am. His pilot deferred to me because I am that good. Maybe he will be impressed with my flying and transfer me to his legion."

"The only thing to impress that man is results. Too bad I will find the prize before you."

Parish looks at him then grunts, "In your dreams."

"Care to make a wager?" Alexius asks with a serious look.

"100 ducats say I beat you to the prize."

"You know I don't have 100 ducats; make it twenty." Alexius places the folder on the counter and then sticks his hand out.

"Confidence escapes you, my friend…an easy win," Parish points out.

Alexius smiles, "Did I say twenty? Alright then, I am so certain I shall win, I am willing to bet, 200 ducats."

Parish looks at Alexius, skeptical about what just transpired; *is he running a scam? Or does he have some information that will ensure success?* "Done," he announces and shakes Alexius' hand. "Since I'll be taking your money, order whatever you want, I'm buying."

With a smile on his face, Alexius walks further down the counter to meet the bartender. The folder sits undisturbed on the table.

CHAPTER 06:
TREASURE AT
DEMON ROCK

The afternoon sky is alive with brilliant colors; similar colors graced the skies less than twenty-four hours ago above the local monastery where a violent theft occurred. This act is not going unpunished, for the offense was against the mighty Empire of Atlantis. Now, high in the sky, five armored transports scour the forests for the villains.

Four of the crafts are local, each holding a maximum of twenty-three soldiers. The fifth craft is the largest and carries fifty heavily armed and dangerous Foreign Legionaries. The formation moves together like a synchronized swarm of bees, moving slow and cautious above the treetops.

Further ahead by about five miles is the scout-ship, also serving as the lead vessel. Aboard Commander Andros calmly observes his pilot work the controls. The cabin is not cramped, but neither is it spacious. The commander sits midway at the back, raised higher than the two pilots up front. Captain Parish expertly navigates through the mountainous area, trying to impress Andros.

The treetops give way to a dangerous cavern below, which then opens up into a valley. Parish plunges his craft into a steep dive and then levels off close to the surface. A deserted camp catches his attention. He looks back at Andros who gives him a nod. With determination on his face and the flick of a switch, the ship is reconfigured into combat mode. It pulls up then darts high into the air, speeding over the mountain.

There is a lake about five miles ahead. Nothing is visible on the banks from this high up, just a thick rolling fog. Instruments begin to chirp signaling activity below. The Co-Pilot Signals Parish, who then looks at Andros; there is a smile on the Commander's face, one of victory.

Three tents are spread over the bank with sure signs of occupation. Two vehicles are parked and armed with long-range guns. The ship pulls up sharply ascending into the clouds. It levels off inverted in the opposite heading, then rolls level. It is higher than the approaching ships now, looking at the attack formation as they slowly advance.

-GORGE NEAR DEMON ROCK-

The area is becoming damp from a drizzle of rain; the drops are tapping rhythmically on the thick tree cover. A canopy of branches blocks the retreating sunlight, which is slowly being covered with rain clouds. There is just enough sunlight for three approaching figures to see their way through the forest; onward they hustle sloshing through the mud. They carefully climb an incline towards a large mossy log sitting securely on a high hill.

The drizzle quickly turns into a rapid downpour. Large branches laden with leaves provide shade for the three soldiers, well, two Captains and one Cadet. Alexius, Deidra, and Bain, all soaked, crawl next to the mossy log. They drop their heavy rifle butts into the mud, clutching the weapons as if expecting trouble. Deidra retrieves a pair of binoculars from her satchel. She passes it to Bain. He looks at her with a complaint on his face.

"You're the lookout, Cadet," Deidra reminds him.

"Be quiet," Alexius cautions. "How many are down there?" he asks Deidra.

65

Deidra aggressively grabs the binoculars. She peeks out at a gorge in a small area; the depression is about one-tenth of a mile down, and a quarter mile away. Three tents are visible, with movement inside. Flood lamps begin to light the area, revealing mounted weaponry.

"Seven. Not much cover, they will see us coming. That is if we get past those perimeter guns mounted on the trees, see there."

Alexius turns his back in frustration. He sighs and tries to figure out a plan. The forest ahead of him is darkening, severely restricting their field of view. He frowns at a pair of eyes glowing in the branches above. Several yards going up an incline in front of him stands large redwood trees; he has an idea. He dips into his satchel and then begins uncoiling a thin, almost invisible line.

Deidra looks at him, "This is a bad idea. Where is the air support?" she asks. Alexius shrugs his shoulders.

"Shall I call it in?" Bain asks enthusiastically. Alexius quickly shakes his head and tosses the thin line to him.

"Secure it to both those," he orders, pointing to the redwood trees several yards away.

"I am a soldier, not a slave," Bain protests.

"Boy get over there now!" Alexius aggressively points to the trees. Bain makes his way clumsily through the thick flora, grumbling.

Alexius looks back at Deidra, "The answer to your questions is…Parish has his coordinates; we have ours." Deidra shakes her head noticeably irate.

"I hope you know what you're doing…I don't."

"We're flushing out roaches. So…did you hear Inias say, 'fuck'?"

Deidra couldn't help but break down with a chuckle at the memory, "It almost made all this shit worth it."

"So…still got my back?" Alexius asks.

The question frustrates Deidra more than angers her. Here they are, in a bad position as it were, but clear and innocent of any wrongdoing; and Alexius still wants to steal the treasure.

"Unbelievable," she fumes. "You expect the three of us to take on…her?" The memory of Liviana brings some fear to the fearless Captain. She touches the sore portion of her chest.

"She may not even be down there. Besides, that's why we brought these," Alexius clarifies while caressing the heavy rifle.

Bain crawls by them, headed for the other tree. He trips and falls, making a commotion beneath the thick leaves. He gains his footing then jumps up with a smile on his face. He quickly runs off to another tree.

"Why…the fuck…did you bring him?" Alexius asks with much annoyance in his tone.

"To tell the Archon how we died: stealing his treasure," Deidra responds sarcastically.

"It's not a heist. These nomads are killers. You do remember the bodies they dropped at the monastery?" he asks rhetorically. "Besides, a little compensation for our troubles is expected. We're not taking much, just a little. Inias will have his prize."

"Then let's get on with it," Deidra concedes, knowing fully well that her complaints will fall on deaf ears. Bain crawls back to the log and takes up his position.

"Yes, Captain Deidra. Bain, be careful; don't fall," Alexius says with sarcasm.

Bain watches Deidra playfully slap Alexius behind his head. The path down is treacherous, and it will be a while before they get to the camp below. He checks his communications device, getting ready for what comes.

-LAKE AREA-

The Foreign Legion's heavy transport sits in a clearing some distance away from the lake waters. Bright lights from the craft shine on the soldiers standing watch. Commander Andros' scout ship is closer to the banks, pointed towards the water.

Outside the tents are several people on their knees with their hands on their heads. Soldiers point their weapons at them, wishing for a reason to fire. Andros walks in front of the men, looking at them stare back at him menacingly. One of the rough mountain-folk gives him a dirty look; this gives him cause to stop at the man known as Ponchus. Parish walks up to Andros, looks at Ponchus then nods to his commander.

Andros stands over the kneeling man, "Where are the stolen items?" A soldier pulls Ponchus up to face Andros.

"Eat shit Atlantean," the mountain-man exclaims.

Andros nods to a soldier, who happily drops his knee on the subdued man's face. As he falls, Ponchus discreetly pulls a small device from his inside pocket. He smiles with blood dripping from his mouth. Parish notices the inconspicuous box in his hand.

Ponchus looks at the soldiers, "Live free, die free," he says smiling, then presses a switch.

Parish dives on Andros, knowing fully well what is about to happen. The mountain folks vehicles erupt in explosions, followed by the tents. The soldiers are on alert looking for attackers; there are none.

Without hesitation, Andros grabs Parish's sidearm as they both stand. He points the weapon at Ponchus then discharges a fatal shot.

"Search everything," the commander orders.

-LIVIANA'S CAMP-

The rain has stopped as suddenly as it started, leaving the ground muddy. Liviana steps out from a tent then looks around expecting trouble. She lights a cigarette, exhaling as if it was the only one left. A rugged truck approaching distracts her.

Mica stops next to her in the stolen vehicle, splashing mud all over her expensive boots. He smiles that cocky smile of his, waiting for a witty insult. Liviana looks at him while blowing smoke in his face.

Mica coughs, "Those things will kill you." Still nothing. "Liv, time to go."

"I have a funny feeling," she explains.

"We can make the temple by sunrise...but we have to go. Load the chest."

"No," Liviana says calmly. "We can't take it with us, too risky. I have what we need; it goes to my father. Sentry..." An armed man walks up from behind a tent. "Break camp. You know what to do." The man acknowledges. She jumps in the truck, and they speed off.

Twenty minutes go by. Two of the three tents are broken down and are being stowed on to a waiting truck. An explosion erupts on the high ridge. Two enormous tree trunks crash on the loose dirt then slide towards the camp; several other trees break ground and follow the slow descent.

The sentries panic, hurrying to grab their weapons. A young priest runs out from the standing tent, clutching the stolen chest. He rushes to a nearby log for cover, trying not to get in the middle of whatever is about to happen.

Shots ring out from Alexius and Deidra's rifles. Suddenly, the perimeter guns begin to fire at the intruders. The bullets hit the ground rapidly, displacing dirt and rainwater. The pair springs out of the way in opposite directions.

As they do, the tree trunks and debris rumble into the clearing forming a wall. Two of the three perimeter guns are disabled; Alexius fires at the third, destroying it. Deidra engages the two sentries while ducking from incoming fire.

A sound startles Alexius; a large sentry barrels down on him with a heavy log. He drops his rifle and then stops the oncoming blow with his two hands. He struggles while trying to prop up the pressure descending on him; the attacker is powerful and enraged. His legs begin to buckle, forcing him to adjust his stance. Luckily, shifting his weight causes the log to slam into the ground.

He begins to fight the sentry hand to hand. The man is strong but unskilled. With a few moves, Alexius manages to knock his attacker out. The massive beast drops to the ground, causing a small splash. The shooting has stopped.

Alexius looks at Deidra standing over her two dead sentries, "You said seven."

Deidra looks around with panic setting in. There were the two who drove off, the one Alexius dropped, her two, and the cowering priest. She realizes they are still in danger, "Bain," she exclaims as she runs off.

Alexius starts towards the priest. Suddenly, a boy no more than thirteen years old rushes out from the bushes with a log. With hate and violence in his eyes, he swings his little weapon at the soldier. "You killed my father!" he screams.

Without thinking, Alexius smashes his mighty fist on the boy's jaw, sending him reeling back and falling to the ground. His head hits a nearby rock, instantly killing him. Berries fall out of his pockets, and a small gold and silver triangle reveals itself on the collar; Mathias' grandson.

Regaining his composure, Alexius looks at the dead boy with horror, the remorse that is taking over quickly turns into rage. He picks up his rifle and runs to the priest. Seething with anger, he points the shaking weapon at the holy man's face.

"Please, I am unarmed," the priest declares.

"Move!" Alexius screams as he shoves the man aside. He attempts to open the chest, to no avail. "Open it!"

"I can't. I don't have the key," the frightened man explains.

As the priest begins to protest, Alexius fires his rifle at the box. The lid now swings free, ready to reveal the treasure inside. This did not matter right now, for the numbness has already taken over.

He slowly peers into the box, with confusion filling his face, "You raided the temple for books? Where's the gold?" Somewhere in the back of his conscience, Alexius couldn't believe he was asking for gold. It all seemed automatic at this point.

"No gold. These are sacred books for the master. You don't understand. Please, leave," the priest pleads.

Suddenly, the seventh sentry appears with Bain tightly in his grasp; a pistol is jammed into the Cadet's side. There is panic on Bain's face; he is almost at the point of crying.

"Let him go…do it!" Alexius orders the sentry, pointing the rifle at his head. Deidra appears with her weapon aimed at the man.

The sentry shows signs of compliance. His grip on Bain begins to ease, slowly and carefully dropping. Bain's expression changes from fear to determination. He trips his captor, which drops them both to the ground. They struggle until the pistol goes off.

The bodies remain motionless as the gunshot echo fades. Blood oozes into a puddle. The sentry pushes Bain's dying body off of him, being careful to show his surrender. This does not stop Alexius from rushing him. He pounds on the man's face, waling on him as if to redeem himself for Bain's death, and that of the young boy.

"Enough Captain! Enough" Deidra shouts while holding him back.

He stops his beating and then drops to his knees. Deidra goes over to the body, and holds Bain, trying to conceal her emotion. Fresh rain starts to fall.

CHAPTER 07: DEATH BECOMES US

The Illyrian forest roads at night are dangerous; dark, winding, mountainous. All manner of creature avoids the roadway for you can never tell what will come barreling down the dirt pathways. The many animals who brave a crossing, do so at their peril. Tonight, a stupid deer wanders on to the highway of death. Minding its own business, the walking feast stops to sample a tasty treat.

A pair of lights appears minuscule at first, too far away to pay attention to. The deer quietly enjoy a shrub at the path's edge. The lights grow larger, now accompanied by the hum of engines. Faster and faster it comes, brighter and brighter it glows. He looks up, staring into the curiosity.

An Atlantean vehicle smashes into the animal, sending it into a bloody tumble down the side. So ends the tale of one stupid deer when it faced the driving skills of Deidra. She barely slowed during the impact. With a frame designed to withstand rolling boulders, the truck only suffered the stains of blood and skin on the front grill.

Her focus is on the winding road as she speeds towards the garrison. Alexius is silent by her side, lost in his thoughts. The radio crackles with questions from the squad they left behind; their location and status being irrelevant now. They had the prize, the stolen chest of treasure. Alexius thinks to himself, *What a treasure it is, worth several lives, including one Cadet, a kindly old priest and his household, and one innocent boy…all for worthless books!*

"Don't respond," he cautions Deidra as she reaches for the radio. "Andros is surely monitoring. No one should know we have it."

He leans back in his seat and closes his eyes, losing himself to fatigue. *Maybe I can rest for 15 minutes*, he teases himself. Deidra's constant swerving doesn't bother him anymore; neither does the persistent calls on the radio. All that mattered now was sleep.

~ALEXIUS (Age 5) MEMORY OF CHILDHOOD~

It is a sunny spring afternoon in the province of Parthon. The hills are alive with fresh flowers and green grass flowing up and down through the landscape. Alexius and his family are visiting one of the local aristocrats. They live at the border to the next province. More importantly, Alexius' friend Daniu lives there.

The boys are playing in the fields, a game they've invented; something about hitting rocks on a stick, then running. A majestic tree grows at the edge of the area where they play. Sitting underneath it is Alexius' sister Cassandra. She is eleven, and quite the carefree babysitter. Daniu's elder brother is engaging her in conversation.

The boys start fencing with sticks, making their way to the tree. Daniu's brother suddenly slaps Cassandra; Alexius sees this. He stops swinging and is struck by Daniu's wooden sword. He yelps, but doesn't take his eyes off the couple.

The boy walks away from Cassandra, leaving her in tears. Suddenly, a massive log connects his back, dropping him to the ground. He quickly rolls to face his attacker. Little Alexius swings the giant trunk, striking him repeatedly. Blood starts to pour, and bones break. Cassandra screams at her brother and pulls him away.

~LATER THAT NIGHT~

Alexius peeks into his father's locked room through a metal grate. This hidden spot inside the wall is the only window into the private study of Arias' 'secret circle' of friends. A new man is there tonight, looks like a priest.

Another is a younger thin fellow with black hair. The last man seems a bit heavier, sturdy and robust with flaming red hair. They are sitting around, smoking, laughing, and drinking wine. Is this all that grown-ups do when the children go to bed?

A strange man with the complexion of oatmeal addresses Arias, "There is the rage in his eyes, his skin, his soul. One so young should not possess such strength or ferocity, for every bystander will suffer."

"He is my son…" Arias snaps at the man, "not a plague." They all become silent.

Suddenly, hands grab Alexius' tiny feet. His older brother Remus begins to pull him out of the crawlspace. Being the big brother meant he had to protect Alexius from everything, even from himself. Remus scolds him.

~BACK IN THE TRUCK~

The rough road is smoothening out; the dirt is turning into paved concrete is a welcomed relief to all the bumps and slides. The garrison gates can be seen up ahead, along with the bright spotlights. High in a tower, a lone armed sentry stands ever vigil. The truck screeches to a halt at the gate. Alexius wakes.

A gate guard emerges from a booth. He points his rifle at Deidra then at Alexius. Deidra rolls down the window ready to scream at the recruit.

Alexius beats her to it, "Boy, put that fucking thing away, and open the gate!"

The young guard is surprised, "Captain Alexius," he acknowledges. He peers into the vehicle. Once satisfied, he gives an apologetic look.

"Get on with it before I shove that rifle up your ass."

The cadet rushes to the back of the truck and lifts a covering: three men are restrained with three corpses beside them; one of the bodies he recognizes, Bain. He immediately calls in the request to open the gate.

With haste, they drive through, happy to be out of the cold forest. Alexius switches the radio off and looks at Deidra. She has been a true friend, and they have been through a lot. They have killed many together, and lost many too, but never once has Alexius murdered an innocent.

"I didn't mean to kill that boy," Alexius says solemnly.

"I know. It was an accident," Deidra assures him.

"You're right, things happen, we were being shot at, and he did attack me."

"Then get over it, quickly, because you have Andros to deal with."

The truck makes a sudden sharp turn to the left, taking them away from the main buildings. Alexius looks at Deidra with concern, *what is she up to?*

As if reading his thoughts, Dedira explains her actions, "We're going to Back End...I suggest we park the truck there, only until we know where Andros is."

"Good thinking...I don't think he will try to take the chest, nor condone it. His people though, now they may try."

"You are going to be alright?" she asks with concern. Without the deaths, she would take every opportunity to torment him about his inability to steal the imagined treasure; not this time.

76

They arrive at a corner of the base called Back End. A dismal vehicle depot, it smells of metal, oils, and decaying rags. It is a mechanics paradise, with parts strewn all over the place, and a multitude of ground vehicles to play with. No one is there at night.

"I'll get the patrols to take the bodies and prisoners…get us a ride back," Alexius says. He types on a lighted keypad then jumps out of the vehicle.

He retrieves the chest, looks at it then shakes his head in annoyance. A corner of junk catches his eyes, the perfect place for this box of horror. The golden wings on the side intrigue him even in this state. No matter now, the only ceremony it shall have is the covering with a dirty rag.

Deidra pulls up to the curb on a hover-bike. He hurries over and jumps on the back. She taps the throttle with her right foot, and they speed off.

-THE ARCHON INIAS' OFFICE-

Inias sits calmly behind his desk, quietly reading incoming messages. He begins to smile at one point, leaning back on his chair, then reaching for his wine goblet.

The office doors swing open, revealing Alexius and Deidra; Inias spills his wine on his clean white tunic. They stroll into the office tracking mud on to the freshly laid rug. Inias looks at them furiously, then at the devastation done.

"You filthy animals!" he bursts out.

"Apologies your holiness," Alexius offers with a serious look, "We wanted to report as soon as we returned. We have the chest."

"Yes, yes. And you bring a few bodies, one of our own, and worthless prisoners," the Archon chides, throwing his right arm in the air.

Alexius grunts with some annoyance, "We retrieved...books." He looks at Inias' expression, wanting to see the surprise. There isn't any.

"Yes, books. What, you thought they stole gold?"

"Don't know what to think at this point," Alexius states bravely. Deidra lowers her gaze.

"It is all irrelevant now. We have the recovered asset, that's all that matters." Inias steps in front of the two soldiers. "I just received word from Atlantis...our time in Illyria has ended." He smiles triumphantly, overjoyed with his news. "The holy Prince Timon has ordered our return to the capital."

Deidra can't hide her smile, "Archon?" Alexius remains cold, unmoved.

Inias has a smile on his face, "This alliance between Illyria and Atlantis has been a taxing affair. Let Illyria handle their terrorists."

"Whatever his holiness commands," Deidra agrees.

Inias walks around the soldiers. He cringes at the sight of his rug. *What a glorious day. I have outwitted that fiend Andros, more importantly, saved my skin, and the imminent return to Atlantis.* He suddenly remembers something.

"Oh, your application." He looks at Alexius, relishing in the pause he gives. "It's approved. You will be re-assigned to the Far Western Continent. Deidra, leave us."

The joy Deidra felt quickly disappears. She gives Alexius a disappointed look as she leaves. She makes a point of closing the doors rather roughly. Inias' expression turns to one of condolence.

"I have sad news. Your mother has passed on. I truly am sorry."

Alexius appears unmoved. He stares straight ahead, "That is unfortunate," he states expressionless. "I am certain her loving family will take care of matters."

"Be that as it may, you will leave for your hometown in Atlantis tomorrow." Inias pours Alexius wine. "Parthon is it? You will attend the funeral, along with your wretched brother-in-law, to convey the condolences of the priesthood; your father was, after all, a well-respected statesman."

"Archon I must protest, Andros can…"

"Protest all you want. This is not a request."

The inevitable trip to Parthon could not be escaped. Alexius decides to unburden his soul instead, for even though he was not religious, he did honor the tradition of confessing sins. Inias was a tolerable priest. Considering all the time they spent together, he had come to value the priest's company, respect him even.

"I killed an innocent boy. Was his life worth some mere books? This is troubling me Archon, weighing heavy on my soul."

"As well as it should," Inias responds in an authoritative tone. "You were trained to kill your enemies. That boy was a nomad terrorist, plain and simple. Despite this, you feel remorse…that's good. It means you are human. Learn from it, grow with its memory. But never forget his place in the events that transpired. Do you forget who you are?"

"No Archon." Alexius lets the words sink in, finding the wisdom in them. The weight begins to fall off his soul, the fog in his mind clears. "May I ask, what is special about those books? Why did the nomads steal them?"

"Those old books are from a time before the great war. Over three thousand years ago, when the rule of the Anuk was all-encompassing. More valuable than this shit-filled kingdom we're squatting in."

"One less bounty for the terrorists then."

Inias stares past Alexius, remembering his friend Mathias' beliefs. There is sadness in his voice, despite his effort to conceal his feelings.

"There are some who believe at the end of Virgo, the ancient progenitors of civilization will return to judge humanity. If peace exists, a golden age begins; if war, then annihilation."

"Virgo ends soon. I haven't heard of a return of the forefathers. Sounds like more religion to me," Alexius says with some annoyance in his voice.

"That may be so. There are expeditions underway right now, to find the resting place of the forefathers. Lumeria."

"Adventurers, treasure hunters, fools chasing a myth."

"One of those fools is a dear friend of mine, a High Priest no less."

"I wish them luck. This world needs some judgment." Alexius places the wine cup on a counter and looks at Inias respectfully. "It is late, by your leave?"

"Yes, yes. One more thing Captain, have the chest brought to me at once."

Alexius bows then take his leaves. As the door closes, Inias looks at the muddy footprints on the rug. He scowls with annoyance.

-GARAGE AT BACK END-

The deserted area of Back-End is a dark, dismal place at night. The vast open skies are covered with ominous clouds slowly moving in. The stars are being covered up, and the air smells of rain; a depressing place to be, at Back-End.

A patrol car drives up to one of the garages; suspicious lights shine inside the space, with the raised doors revealing all the movement inside. The vehicle stops next to a hover-bike parked on a ramp; the lights are still on. The patrol officers stay in the car, observing Alexius inside the structure. Several times, a stray cat rushes in, expecting a treat.

Alexius uncovers the recovered chest, placing it carefully on the ground. He puts a mini-flashlight in his mouth and drops to the floor. He carefully opens the lid, expecting the old books to contain some mystery.

The three leather-bound books appear ancient. They smell of temple incense mixed with rain. Alexius carefully lays them out on the floor. There is a fourth book also bound in leather, but much smaller. It appears to be a journal with a crest on the spine. He opens the larger ones first; the pages are littered with strange writing, the ancient tongue. He flips through all three, finding more of the same. Finally, he picks up the smaller one.

Success, he finds familiar writing on the pages. He begins to read quickly, then fans through the pages. He gets to a section with illustrations, particularly one with the Cappadocian part of the Anatolian plains. Beneath the intricate drawing, he notices a crest; his eyes widen as recognition hits him. He immediately returns to the beginning of the book, frantically searching for a name; he finds it.

"Arias…father?" he whispers.

The sounds of footsteps approaching cause him to close the book quickly. He conceals it in his clothing then throws the rest in the chest. As the patrol officer stands over him, he begins cleaning the golden-eagle crest with a dirty rag.

"I may have damaged it…I didn't want the Archon to show off a busted box," he explains.

The patrol-officer is satisfied, "Yes Sir. Will you be here long?"

"No…Take this to the Archon. Please let him know I did my best to fix it."

The patrol officer nods then accepts the box. They both make their way outside; the officer climbs into his waiting car, observing Alexius mount the hover-bike. They leave together down the road.

-OFFICER BARRACKS SHOWERS-

The constant rhythm of falling water from showerheads is a welcoming sound, especially after being out in the forest all day. The rising steam quickly forms clouds, making navigation of the bath area somewhat tricky. Alexius makes his way to the back of the showers.

He has developed an affinity to form relationships with things, mostly inanimate, to cope with the isolation a soldier feels. He has his preferred parking spot, favorite cup, his favorite shower stall; a bit compulsive but a necessary comfort for the chosen profession he practices.

The sounds of falling water intensified since he first entered, now closer to his comfort area, new sounds begin to echo. He is curious who is back there this late, laughing. He breaks the corner only to chide himself; *I should've known...Deidra.*

She is lathering up with her girlfriend Cleo, in his favorite stall. He gets into the spot next to Deidra, as he does both girls become silent. He turns the water on, quickly soaking in the stream.

"Don't stop on my account," he tells the girls.

Deidra looks at him, blatantly annoyed, "FaW-C huh? You son of a bitch...you could have told me."

Alexius calmly responds, "You wouldn't understand."

"Did you even consider I would? Fucking shit."

At this point, Cleo is expecting a brawl. She quickly turns off her shower.

"I am sorry, truly am. What's done is done. You should be happy you're leaving this place."

"I've had enough of it," Deidra declares. "Time to return to real fighting, with honor and glory." She pauses, waiting to drop the sliver of gossip she received. She decides to put aside her annoyance for a while to share her news; *there is a chance Alexius would change his mind about FaW-C.* "Did you hear? Your mentor Commander Stavos is starting a campaign."

Cleo's footsteps slosh away on the wet floor as she heads to a stack of towels. She looks at Deidra with that look in her eyes, the look Alexius knew all too well.

"Your victim for the tonight?" he asks.

Deidra's lingering anger disappears. She softens up as she blushes, "Possibly. We've been on and off."

"Look…I've always wanted to experience the mystery of the land beyond the ocean."

Deidra's anger quickly returns, "Go fuck yourself."

"I have to tell you something…it has to stay between us," he warns. A short silence passes. "I took one of the books. It belonged to my father."

Deidra is appalled. She begins to protest, but Alexius quickly covers her mouth. She starts to calm down, "If the Archon finds out, he will have our heads."

"He won't," he reassures her. "Why were the nomads stealing these books? And what does my father have to do with it?"

"No great Atlantean such as your father would be mixed up with nomads. Simple coincidence, that's all."

"It could be. Oh, I leave for Parthon in the morning."

Deidra steps out of the shower, angry. "You really can't wait to leave me can you?"

"My mother has passed on. Inias insists I go."

Feeling stupid, Deidra steps closer, this time she tries to offer consoling words. She knew of the turbulent history with his mother, but somewhere deep inside him there had to be some version of love.

"Let go of the past," she advises. "Do what is right by paying your respects. She was your mother after all."

"For the sake of honor, I will go. Then I'll meet you in the capital." He watches her walk away.

"You do that," she exclaims, grabbing a towel from the rack.

-ALEXIUS' QUARTERS-

Garrison officers are afforded some luxuries due to their rank and station. One amenity is the convenience of private quarters. The Cadets all share rooms with ten per space, cramped in a stuffy compartment; not the case in Captain's Alexius' room.

The décor shows off expensive taste, with ornaments, drapery, decorative pictures, all rivaling the Archon himself. Alexius even has a rug from Parthon, woven by raunchy barmaids. Everything is neat and appropriately placed. His bed is of average size and carefully arranged with expensive silks. The past two days have been long; all he wants to do is finish packing.

Procrastination is something he excels at, always putting off a task in favor of a lucrative distraction. Tonight's indulgence is the book he stole from the Archon's chest. *By right its mine,* he convinced himself. This does not diminish his caution, for if Inias realized it was missing, soldiers would be breaking down his door before morning. *Maybe he didn't know it was there.*

He lays on the bed ready to skim through the diary. Sleep is crawling up his back, slowly taking over like a shadow, squeezing his eyes shut. Always a stubborn lad, he pushes through the fatigue in favor of reading a few pages. In a whisper, he reads.

"The houses of ENlil and ENki brought the Great War, devastating Hyperboria. ENlil invaded the lands of Persephone and Osiris, purging the royal house."

He closes the book, looks at the door, then opens it up again. Skimming through, he stops midway back to a map of the Cappadocian region in Anatolia. The illustration is detailed, showing hidden entrances to parts deep underground. He turns several pages then continues to read a notation.

"The path to the key of power starts in Cappadocia. The eye of Persephone will guide you to Lumeria. Protect the people Alexius, my son."

He slams the book shut, overwhelmed at the thought of his father's book being involved in everything that transpired. Confused as to what part he has to play in the journey that will unfold, tired of running away from his family, he tosses the journal into his chest. Sleep overcomes him.

CHAPTER 08:
IS IT LUMERIA?
-FROZEN WASTELAND IN THE
UNKNOWN SOUTHERN CONTINENT-

An endless blanket of snow stretches across the landscape, reflecting the sunlight to the point of being unbearable. This land was once green, fertile, one where life flourished. It exists as a barren icy wasteland now, with a history lost to antiquity.

All scans have returned the same result; it is devoid of any life or habitation. Many expeditions have braved the treacherous conditions, however, searching for the mythical land of Lumeria. Lost through the annals of history, it became a myth. A story told by survivors of the Great-War, enticing adventurers to undertake foolish errands.

The continent is vast, existing at the southern pole of the planet. No one wants to be here; no one dares stay here. For the myth promises that any who ventures in search of Lumeria, shall ultimately meet their demise. This does not convince the latest group of explorers to leave. They stumbled upon a massive pyramid, one they are convinced is the entrance to Lumeria.

One year ago, a scientific company was hired by the Illyrian conglomerate to conduct a survey of land holdings in the province of Ulimaroa. This province once belonged to the kingdom of Aryavan, located in the southern seas of their domain. It is an island continent as big as Atlantis, but far more diverse.

During the Illyrian and Aryan wars, Ulimaroa served as a major battleground. Many died during this tumultuous period, with peace only coming after the Empire of Atlantis joined the conflict. The Aryan monarchy was, after all, cousins to the Anuk rulers of Atlantis; it was expected that they would come to the aid of the house of ENlil.

The Anuk king fought alongside his kin, eventually losing all his children in the war. Devastated by this, he sought to end the conflict by any means available. Treachery had stolen his sons and daughters. He was forced to employ the same to end the war, ultimately taking Ulimaroa from the Aryans.

The Aryan ruler at the time attempted to usurp the Atlantean king by killing off his offspring. He then tried to put an end to the Monarch, the legitimate heir to the Anuk bloodline, the heir to the empire. The attempt failed with the Aryan ruler meeting the same fate he was conspiring to dish out.

Atlantis was on the brink of economic failure. Absorbing another continent would have led to financial ruin. The land was sold off to the Illyrian conglomerate, angering the remaining Aryan house. Unknown to Atlantis at the time was that Ulimaroa was rich in natural wealth. The Illyrians were now exploring the land resources.

A deep drilling survey team had stumbled upon a massive ancient area; an old outpost dated to be over twelve thousand years old. Since no records survived the Great War, the Illyrians relied upon the only authority they could, the priesthood.

Quicker than a thunder clasp, the priesthood secured the finds, designating it 'Holy ground.' The Illyrian conglomerate lost all rights to the site. Atlantis once more controlled a swath of Ulimaroa. Artifacts were discovered which pointed to the frozen wasteland much further south.

Now, one month in the barren tundra, the survey team has made camp at the base of a snow-white pyramid. Their communications are disabled, all means of transport inoperable, their numbers are dwindling; they are cut off from the rest of the world.

At the base of the pyramid, an Atlantean High Priest, Remus, is examining some old writing carved deep into the snow-free section of rock. His slave, Atmis, was the one who discovered it. Remus is a proud man, well built, with a full head of grey hair. Atmis, who almost never leaves his side, is in his early twenties.

"The ancients smile upon us, Remus announces. We have succeeded where no one has before. My boy, this is Lumeria."

Atmis smiles, exposing chattering teeth, "Prince Timon will be most pleased, your eminence. But, how do we get in?"

There is a glint of excitement in the old priest's eyes, "Ah, it is a matter of deciphering the ancient language. And I believe these symbols here will do the job."

Remus presses a series of the symbols in the rock. Suddenly, a bright blue light envelopes him and Atmis; they instantly disappear.

-DEEP UNDERGROUND, SOMEWHERE-

A soft glow of light begins to warm a dark chamber. The walls are artificial, with a metallic texture indicating this. Consoles are spread out generously in the spacious area beyond. With the brightening light, screens come to life as if waking from a long slumber. Displays with the ancient writing materialize by the walls.

Near the chamber, inside a smaller room with an arch, bright blue light explodes into the dark. Remus appears with Atmis, bewildered as to what happened. Remus smiles, giddy with excitement.

Atmis is awestruck. They walk out cautiously, being careful not to touch anything.

"What could this be?" Amis asks.

"I don't know," Remus responds, "but this is old, from the time of the forefathers. Travel by light is only myth told in stories. This is technology beyond anything which has existed since their time."

He points to a passageway, motioning Atmis to follow. They traverse a narrow catwalk; below it are unknown levels of darkness. There is both apprehension and excitement in their movement. The catwalk ends at the entrance of a larger room. As they approach, the lights inside come alive, the door opens.

They step in, expecting some horror to manifest itself. A medical bed sits in the center with blood stains on it. A pile of bloody clothing is on the floor. Above the bed is a glass covering. It hangs ten feet in the air as if waiting to drop on an unsuspecting victim.

A buzzing sound emanates from a panel. A hologram of the beautiful Persephone appears next to the bed, momentarily phasing out, then reappearing. "I am Persephone...Daughter...east, west, and...house ENki...Survive my child." The image disappears.

A symbol appears on a console, flashing as if it's an invitation to hear more.

Remus is dumbfounded, his beliefs challenged. This was Persephone, the heretic Anuk who was struck out of the histories of the world. Her story remembered only in part by the priesthood, is kept locked away from the masses. No one could know the truth, no one dares remember her. The console keeps flashing; there has to be more.

Remus instinctively hurries to the console. With a bit of hesitation, he touches the flashing light. The beautiful image of the blonde, sad yet determined ruler does not reappear. Instead, the room begins to hum. Slow at first, then a quick deep resonating thunder.

Streaks of light shoot out from the ceiling, landing on Remus and Atmis, instantly vaporizing them. The sound does not dissipate, and for now, it is as if there is power coming from deep below, getting ready for some monstrous purpose.

-AT THE CAMP OUTSIDE THE PYRAMID-

The ground begins to rumble. Panic sets in the small number of people stranded there. They look up at the sky expecting an assault.

High up on the pyramid face snow begins to melt. The rock surface appears to be about fifty feet square. There is a glow on the rock now, competing with the glistening sunlight. The surface rock gives way to a metal covering, it opens. Bright blue light shoots out of a cavity, striking the encampment below.

The inhabitants are running wild, trying to clear themselves from the pyramid's precincts. The beam strikes those that flee, vaporizing them. The inoperable crafts nearby are also hit, erupting in flames, melting to the ground. The remainder of the camp is ablaze in seconds. The light intensifies, assaulting the area once more, then it disappears. Smoldering ash remains.

The wind continues to howl, kicking up loose snow on to the black ash. It will not be long before everything is covered in white, erasing the footsteps of those who had ventured there. This is a secret that will be protected, one not meant for the likes of man.

The day will come when Persephone's message will be heard by the one it was meant for. Soon, for the days of Virgo are numbered, the time of the Awakening is at hand. The age of prophecy begins.

CHAPTER 09: HOMECOMING

Waves crash on large jagged rocks on the side of a small coastal elevation, spitting up foam and mist. The outcrop of land rises fifty feet with a flat area at the top. A solitary tree stands in an open field leading to a light forest. This is but one tiny corner of the estate belonging to members of the House Badur.

This House is a noble one, which served the great king of Atlantis, but eventually, it faded away into a passive existence. Their old wealth has secured the family much prominence in the country; at one time they held sway through the Empire.

Lord Arias of Badur was a close adviser to the King; his friendship would eventually secure a governorship of the Far West Continent. Arias experienced some unfortunate events during the last five years there, which forced him to resign the post. He returned to the capital, married his childhood sweetheart, a widow at that time, then settled in the family's ancestral lands. Together with his new wife and her children, he was content to leave public life.

Arias fathered one child, Alexius. Now a grown man, he is considered a disappointment, an undesirable to some of the nobility. He is only adept at being a warrior, an undisciplined one at that. This does not matter to his siblings for they love their brother no matter what, as Arias loved them as his flesh and blood.

Cassandra is six years older than Alexius. She takes after her mother, medium height, slim, carefree. *It is too early to be riding,* she chides herself as she approaches the solitary tree on horseback. Her flowing raven hair shines in the morning light. Her angry composure can only mean one thing; she is looking for her brother. *Not today of all days*, she exclaims silently.

Today a funeral service will be held for the family's Matriarch, Alexa. In her youth, she was a woman to behold, the youngest daughter of a nobleman, married to a commander in the Atlantean army. They had two children, Remus and Cassandra. They lived contently until revolt erupted in Egypt.

Alexa lost her husband to war. All seemed hopeless until one day, a young nobleman came to visit. Her childhood love, Arias, had returned from FaW-C, pledging to give up his adventures in far-off lands in exchange for her hand. She couldn't refuse, not because of his station amongst the nobles, but because she loved him.

They were married in a lavish ceremony; in attendance was the King himself, and much of the poorer folks in the province. Life was excellent; the troubles of the world seemed too distant to disrupt their happiness. Then, Alexius was born.

Cassandra dismounts her horse by the tree, *Alexius' tree,* she muses. There is a small mound of dirt near one of the protruding roots. Buried within is a set of climbing gear her brother used to descend to his secret pirate cave. It is undisturbed, leaving her to wonder how he got down there. It doesn't matter; she will take the plunge.

The cave is an eighteen-foot drop from the top. From inside the vast ocean can be viewed in all its glory. At the cave's mouth near the edge, Remus' five-year-old son, Steven, peers down at the dark blue water. He looks at his sandals, wondering if he should let it take the thirty-two-foot fall. He is fearless just like his uncle.

Steven looks back inside the cave grinning. He pushes off the edge. As his little body drops a few feet, he is instantly hoisted back into the cave. Around his waist is a thin cord attached to a brilliant pulley system. The cord retracts just enough for him to dangle in mid-air. A device connected to a rail then transports him thirteen feet towards the interior.

Steven stops at Alexius, laughing enthusiastically. His three-year-old sister, Chloe, sits on her uncle's lap, clapping and giggling wildly. She grabs a handful of grapes to offer her brother. Suddenly, she freezes as if caught in unexpected mischief. Steven sees her expression then quickly turns to the mouth of the cave. Their aunt makes her way down a rope.

Cassandra drops on to the cave floor, furious at what she sees. Alexius smiles at her, expecting a tongue lashing. She strides over to the band of troublemakers ready to pass judgment.

"You are the worst babysitter!" she declares as she unhooks Steven.

"Calm down, they are alright," Alexius points out.

Cassandra is irate, "Look at where they are, can't you even…"

"You're the one who insisted I take them out of the house," Alexius interrupts.

Cassandra puts Steven on the ground, grasping his hand tightly. *There will be no reasoning with this donkey,* she decides. She gives Chloe a stern look; the toddler begins to pout, waiting for a warning, ready to cry in defiance.

"You are a bad influence on them. These Children love you so much they will follow you down to the ocean if they had to."

"They were never in any danger, promise," Alexius reassures her.

Cassandra sits on a small box to catch her breath. The ocean breeze cools the cave; for a moment she remembers just how tranquil it is.

She looks at her brother, "I know why you're down here. You can't avoid today."

"What's to avoid?" Alexius says sarcastically. "There will be all the town's folk, wretched family, present associations excluded, and oh yes, your worthless husband, Andros."

"There will be a lot of them surely; fighting, arguing, trying to claim a share of mother's fortune."

"It's yours and Remus'. Don't let them rob you of it."

"And yours…"

"No, not mine," says Alexius.

"Alexius don't do this. The rantings of a sick woman are like a receding wave; all it can do is make a splash then never return."

"You're right…you're right," he agrees.

The silence invites the beats of crashing water. The rhythmic sounds start to relax the cave dwellers.

"This is where it happened isn't it?" Alexius asks, looking at the cave's opening.

"What are you talking about?" Cassandra asks with a hint of discomfort.

"You know what. Where mother jumped off the cliff into the ocean."

Cassandra's eyes drift to the children, "How did you know about that?"

"Whispers through the years. Uncomfortable stares from the town folk, dreams."

"It's true, mother was unstable, hearing voices, imagining things. So she tried to kill herself. If it weren't for Carrel and his fishing boat, she would be dead, you along with her. You were born that night, two months early."

"And now here we are," Alexius quickly adds, attempting to put an end to the topic. There would be no point in revisiting the past. Cassandra felt the same.

"How did you get down here anyway?" she asks as she looks at the rope.

"It's a secret." Alexius lets a moment pass to torment his sister. "There's a secret passage, let's go." He kisses Chloe on her head, then carries her towards the back exit; Cassandra and Steven follow.

-THE CITY OF RIHZON, ILLYRIA-

The peaceful city of Rihzon has always existed near the calm lake of Shekodra. It started as a small settlement after the Great War. Tribes of man flocked to the clean water supply, fearful that it was the only one left. Slowly, tents became huts, later turning into wood cabins; ultimately, marvelous stone buildings were erected.

Now it is a trading metropolis, rich in commerce and banking. Most of the buildings are constructed of stone, laid out intricately amongst more modern architecture. Cobblestone walkways are everywhere, adorned with colorful plants hanging over awnings. The residents carry about their days happily.

Vehicular traffic is always light, unlike the more popular cities such as Corinth, or Dalmatia. Here the residents relish the free public transportation system. High train rails spread across local destinations while large buses traverse the streets. One would find that many of the cars come from other places, showing off their colorful placards.

Not many vehicles are found abandoned within city limits, especially one from a south-western kingdom. A black truck is parked in a quiet alley, with bullet holes draping the sides. The same truck Mica stole for his getaway from the temple in the southern kingdom. By nightfall, it will be gone, stripped by the more unscrupulous residents of this neighborhood.

Not too far off is the city promenade; a favorite place that is remarkably clean. Plots of grassy mini-parks are everywhere, put there to accentuate the beauty of the area. Exclusive stores stand proudly on a short boulevard, catering to the wealthier clientele. As with any city poverty always finds its way into the social strata; even in this patch of Rihzon.

Liviana strolls casually on a sidewalk. Her clothing is ripe with perspiration, and her expensive boots are muddy. She fits right in with the transients who make their way into the boulevard begging for handouts from the many pedestrians. She stops on the sidewalk joining a crowd waiting to cross the street.

Two well-dressed chubby nobles stand at the corner with heads held high, arms locked; Carpus the pudgy man and Altia, the well-rounded snob are known around town. They are part of the banking cartel's board posted in Rihzon, overseeing the day to day operations for the Illyrian conglomerate.

Altia turns around to Liviana, who is standing behind her. She looks at the tribal markings on the woman's face, her dirty attire then huffs in that snotty aristocratic way; one who announces that she is of proper breeding. She returns her gaze to her plump husband.

"That trash may be following us," Altia points out. "Be a dear, give her a coin."

Carpus knows who the boss in this relationship is. He complies with a, "Yes dear." He selects a single copper piece from his coin purse. He offers it to Liviana, wincing at the thought of a beggar touching him.

Altia looks at the coin as it falls into the woman's right hand, making sure it's of the correct value. Her eyes travel up her dirty wrist to stop on a pattern of dots on her forearm; they look like a constellation in the skies. *It is not ink,* she decides.

With the worst impression of an Illyrian accent, Liviana says, "Thank you, M'Lord, M'Lady." Like a hungry cat, she scurries off, ignoring the oncoming traffic.

"Filthy gutter trash, this city is overrun with them," Atia says with her nose in the air.

"Yes dear. I hope the master gets her," Carpus adds.

"Watch your mouth," Altia snaps. "No need to wish that brigand here."

"Yes dear."

The couple casually crosses the street as if they were royalty; arms still locked, noses up in the air. Altia scans the crowd ahead for Liviana, expecting the waif to appear around the corner begging for more coin.

Altia would be disappointed, or relieved, for Liviana has already made her way several blocks ahead of them. She scans the side street behind her, then the major road. *Where is Mica? How long does it take to find a car?* She fumes.

A horrible sound catches her attention. It's a low sputtering, dying even, engine sound, accompanied by whines with occasional bursts of what has to be exhaust. She rolls her eyes, shakes her head, aggravated. As the noise gets closer, she covers her face with a palm, knowing all too well who would be in the driver's seat.

Mica pulls up along the curb, munching on food in a paper wrapper. The thing he is sitting in was once a delivery truck. The rusty body is covered in grey paint.

He looks at Liviana peeking out from behind her hand. "Get in...hurry up," he yells. He opens the door letting it swing with creeks and cracking sounds.

Liviana carefully enters trying not to be overcome by the excessive odor. "Really? This is what you find? Why not a fish truck? Or even better, a garbage collector?"

"Oh stop your whining, it fits right in with your stink. Did you get what you needed?"

Liviana sniffs her clothing, "It's the right temple, no mistake." She makes an awkward face from her odor. "You get the supplies?"

Mica gestures to a thick canvas covering what had to be the back seat. Liviana lifts the fabric revealing a bag of rope, a fusion cutter, a bound and gagged old man, and crumpled up food wrappers; the old man mumbles with eyes wide open.

"You do realize that I am hungry too?" Liviana protests.

Annoying Liviana gives Mica insatiable pleasure. There would be more time for that, but now they were on a mission. Time is a luxury they did not have.

He licks his fingers with delight, "Are you sure about this one?"

"I am. We are so close. It won't be long now. This has to be the one."

"I've heard that song before. You know, I think I just ate a pigeon…that I am sure of."

"Do shut up and drive."

Not wanting to be the only one sick from the meal, Mica pulls out a sandwich from his pocket. He offers it to Liviana, who takes it willingly.

The truck's engine sputters to life, making its way loudly down a side street. It passes Altia and Carpus strolling down the sidewalk.

"This is where I found you…seem like yesterday," says Liviana as she looks at Mica, who remains silent. "Any regrets?"

"Never," he says with a smile. "You gave me purpose, a reason to live. Who could refuse the…"

"Shhhhhh" Liviana cuts in quickly. "We have company. Who is he anyway?"

"Him? That's Dorovich, an old friend. He was kind enough to sell me to that slobbering pig Clabber." Mica reaches over to punch the hump under the canvas. "You see, he's not a slave trader…that would require a license, be legit with the authorities and all. No, he snatches children from anywhere he can find them, then sells his product to the temples. His latest venture, snatching babies for the Corinth sex temples."

"I thought sacred prostitution in Illyria was voluntary," says Liviana.

"It is, but this scum offers seedlings free of commission. Why pay a temple prostitute when you have a slave? One hundred percent profit; that's what's wrong with Illyria, it's always about the profit."

"And Clabber, is he mixed up in this?" Liviana asks.

"He's up to his clerical neck in it."

"Good thing he's our stop after this." She reaches over and punches the hump; the old man grunts in pain.

-A BREEZY EVENING IN PARTHON-

A half mile roadway leads up to the main house of the Badur estate, with tall fern trees draping the roadside; from a distance, you can see the massive structure sitting at the top of the hill. It fits for a family of high nobility. Many other buildings are scattered nearby: stables, smaller dwellings, garages. Just the mere size of it all in olden times would be considered an entire village.

Several vehicles are parked in front of the house. Later this evening everyone will travel to the town of Garthos for the funeral services. The local temple will be hosting.

Everyone is in somewhat of a somber mood, the family, the servants, the visitors. All who knew Alexa loved and admired her. For despite her being mentally ill, she was a kind, gentle lady. She died peacefully in her sleep, with her loving family all present.

Her youth was robbed by the sickness which she suffered with for thirty-three years. At the early onset of her dementia, she would only experience violent episodes around Alexius. Then there were times she would be kind towards him.

As the years progressed, she was overcome with blind rage fueling hatred for her son. *Demon, unnatural, evil,* were some things she would call him. Names would be the best part of her abuse, for on many occasions she attempted to put an end to her son's life. Alexius' escape was his cave, second only to his father's study.

The room is a large sanctuary, with walls of shelves filled with all sorts of literature. Strange ornaments amongst relics are scattered about near a sitting area which looks like it was meant for a king. There is even a small iron grate by the fireplace, where a small child could hide to observe the happenings in the room; this was not only Arias' sanctuary, it was also Alexius'.

He stands quietly at the entrance observing the oversized oak desk near the window. The drapes are pulled open, exposing the view of the lush landscape towards the rear of the mansion. Chirping birds can be heard singing their evening song; their music is relaxing. The tranquility is interrupted by a man entering the room.

One of the guests from the capital stands just behind Alexius. He is dressed modestly, with a small pin on his collar signifying his status as a High Priest. About five-foot-seven-inches, slim build, proper clothing with a thin face, he appears minuscule next to the giant soldier.

Alexius looks over his right shoulder to see long dark hair. A memory of a similar, much younger man sitting with his father in this room, flashes in his mind. *Who is this?* He wonders.

"This is a private area," Alexius states, watching the man smile.

"Yes, I know," comes the reply. There is a hint of nostalgia in the man's voice. "It has been many years since I've sat here. I am Calis, a High Priest of Atlantis." He offers his hand to Alexius, who takes it. "My sincere condolences for your loss."

"Thank you. Did you know my parents?"

"Oh yes, for many, many years. I was first acquainted with your father when he served the King. I have been a friend to your family ever since, even after his death."

Andros walks by the room; he stops to observe the two men through the open door. He decides to interrupt them.

"Your eminence, we shall be leaving shortly for the service" Andros announces in an authoritative tone. "Captain, you shall join Cassandra and me…"

"Alexius! That's my name in this house," he cuts him off harshly. "I will ride with High Priest Calis, Andros." The exchange bewilders Andros; he turns and walks off.

"My apologies, if you will be so kind, I am in need of your assistance."

"Of course…it will be my honor; my car is yours," Calis states.

They leave the room then make their way to a grand staircase. They descend the three levels slowly, looking at the mass of people walking to the exit.

"If I may be so bold," Calis begins, "by right all this is really yours. You are, after all, Arias' sole heir."

"That is bold," says Alexius.

Calis instantly becomes uncomfortable, for he did not know Alexius personally, but have heard stories of his temper. As they reach the ground floor, he stops to offer Alexius his humblest apology.

"Please forgive me."

"It's quite alright. You only state what you know. My brother and sister will inherit everything. I am but a soldier. None of this is mine."

They leave through the front doors, descending more stairs headed to a waiting area. A limousine with markings of the priesthood pulls up. The driver quickly jumps out then runs around to open the rear doors. Alexius is noticeably uncomfortable as he is not used to all the fanfare. They get in the car, ready to start on the thirty-mile journey.

The car's interior is beautiful, clean, and comfortable. *Maybe I can sleep all of the way*, Alexius muses. He decides not to appear as the mindless brute he is rumored to be or is sometimes. He runs his hand along the seats, admiring the soft fabrics.

"Nice isn't it?" Calis points out. "One of the luxuries afforded me by the priesthood."

"Inias would be impressed."

Calis chuckles, "Ah yes…Inias, that old buzzard. I hear he is returning to Atlantis, taking up the position of Archenieus."

"He is an uptight, miserable Archon," Alexius explains. "He will make an even more intolerable Grand High Priest." Both men chuckle. "We spent quite a few years together, can't say I will miss him."

"I also hear that you were responsible for the return of some, stolen assets. Thank you for that." Calis notices Alexius is a bit uncomfortable.

"I was doing my duty," he explains. *I wonder if he knows a book is missing.*

"Do you know what the books contained?" Calis asks.

"Inias said they were ancient texts from before the Great War. Nothing interesting I gather."

"Did you see them?" Calis asks, subtly setting the bait.

"No," Alexius lies.

"They are very valuable; in some circles, sacred. It's a shame; few outside the priesthood rarely ever get a chance to see the ancient tongue of the Anuk. Far fewer can read it."

"Can you?" Alexius inquires.

"In a fashion," Calis admits with a smile. "That knowledge was passed down to the royal family, only they, the pure-bloods, can fully interpret the language." He decides it is time to change the subject to one he has meant to touch on. "Say, your sister Cassandra has terrible taste, by that I mean Andros."

The uncomfortable few minutes suddenly disappears. Alexius had noticed stolen glances between Calis and Cassandra. It left him wondering whether his sister was finally going to get rid of that bottom feeder Andros.

"Your Eminence, if I didn't know better, I'd be certain you had some interest in my sister."

Calis begins to blush, raising his hand, shaking his head.

"At this point, I'd prefer the butcher for a brother-in-law to that idiot," Alexius states.

The men chuckle, promising the foreseeable time to their destination to be a bearable one. All that was left now was to endure a few hours of torture.

CHAPTER 10:
OLD THINGS
UNDER NEW

A cultural revolution had once hit the Illyrian kingdom of Rihzon nearly one thousand years ago; the citizens abandoned all religion then devoted themselves solely to the worship of economics. No longer was the priesthood revered, nor was devotion to the royal family of Atlantis required.

Most of the holy sites, including the ancient temples long in ruins, were buried. Some were converted into government buildings, while others were turned into shopping malls, but none were demolished. It was as if there existed some deep-rooted desire to preserve a link to the past. This longing would eventually open the doors to reform.

The priesthood was invited to set up a temple in Rihzon. They relished the idea for this was a chance to get into the heretic kingdom, to transform them from within. War was a horror of the past. No civilization wanted to repeat or experience the devastation of the Great War. So, the foreigners were welcomed with open arms. The bureaucrats lived contently with the notion of integration rather than face possibilities of invasion.

A new temple was unknowingly built upon the ruins of a much older one. Forgotten was the predecessor's name, but as it turns out it was once a place of great congregation. Far into antiquity worshipers would come from throughout the Illyrian kingdoms to pay homage to the priest, and to give praise to the Creator of the universe.

Mimicking Hyperborian architecture, the old temple was grand in scale, with lots of stone floors, columns, artwork, acoustics. Fires burned all day in a grand hall which was always filled with activity. There were also secret meeting places within, known only to the Anuk princes along with their trusted cousins, like Thoth and Persephone. Today, one of those places has been revealed to Liviana; her pursuit of the ancient texts has paid off.

This new temple imitates some of the old traditions by keeping blazing Urns on the stairs, accompanying grand statues at the entrance. This is about all that resemble existing temples in other parts of Illyria. The premises are locked up with no one allowed after sunset. The area is quiet, dismal.

It is dark now, with only a lone street lamp lending its' brilliance to the bushes by the temple's side wall. This is not desired by the two figures lurking there, for any passerby could see what they are doing. For the moment they are just making their way along the wall, heading to the rear.

Mica steps on a twig, causing Liviana to scowl at him. He gives her an apologetic look. The walls are high, but they are not trying to climb it. Instead, they are searching for a metal grate. That should be easy to open; then they can begin their search of the insides. They come upon an unexpected thick metal cover on the wall; about six-feet in diameter, it appears thick.

"Now what?" Liviana inquires.

"Give me the cutter," Mica demands.

He takes a small device from her then points it at the iron. With the touch of a button a red beam blasts towards the metal, cutting it with ease. Liviana positions herself to prop the weight.

"Will you hurry up," she complains as the weight begins to descend on her.

"Shhhh," Mica grunts.

"Fine...I want to see you take this on your back."

A complete circle is cut, freeing the barrier from the stone. Liviana is squatting now with the weight on her, but she manages to push it off to the side. She gets no sympathy from Mica.

With nothing smart to say, he climbs through the hole while tapping a part of his armband. A bright light from the device illuminates the darkness within. The walls are of modern design, freshly painted. Liviana bumps into him from behind, quickly pushing her way to the front.

"We have to go below, to the foundations," she announces.

She leads the way with Mica behind her. They hurry down the wide passageway which leads to a lower floor. It doesn't take them long to reach the weakest part of the temple, where the stone walls are turning into dirt ones.

Liviana points to the dirt, "Look for a solid piece of wall...it looks like, dirty marble."

"What in a mammoth's ass looks like dirty marble? And there's nothing solid here, just dirt," Mica points out.

"It's a grey, white color," Liviana explains, "maybe some mold and shit colors mixed in...All Anuk structures contain dirty marble. Just look, it may be just a small piece jotting out."

They frantically search the area, fearing that they came all this way for nothing. A rope protrudes from the floor in a corner. Mica tugs on it, breaking the surrounding ground. A hole appears after he pulls what turns out to be an ancient utility hole cover. He smiles at Liviana, who motions him to jump in.

"I'm not going first; you go first," he protests.

"You've got the light," she informs him.

106

There can be no winning with her, Mica thinks to himself. With some hesitation, he jumps into the wide hole. The drop is eight feet down, *not severe,* he thinks. Liviana soon after jumps in.

A dirt passage is in front of them, not too narrow but low enough to make them crouch to the ground. Like a pair of hunchbacks, they make their way through, down it seems to go, *Where will it end?* They both wonder; they soon get their answer. A substantial stone wall stops their advance.

There is a multitude of symbols on the face — each block containing a mystery, an old forgotten language. They look upon it, trying to guess what they mean.

"Can you read it?" Mica asks.

"No," Liviana replies, "this is unfamiliar to me. It could be ancient Illyrian." The frustration is evident in her voice.

Mica drops to the ground with his back on the wall, exhausted from the day; Liviana joins him. They take a moment, closing their eyes in the dark. The light from the armband falls on a piece of rock embedded into the dirt. It has a different texture on the surface when the light hits it. Small golden threads begin to glow briefly, barely visible in the light but lit long enough in the dark to be noticed.

Mica opens his eyes slowly to see it. "Hey, what's that?" he announces, then reaches for the out of place rock. He presses it, causing the piece to glow.

"No don't!" Liviana shouts, but it is too late. The ground beneath them opens up.

They quickly fall down a narrow incline, heading deep underground. After thirty feet the dirt ground turns into stone, then into a metal frame. They fall another twenty feet, not knowing where the journey ends. Suddenly, a dark void in the floor appears. They begin to panic as they approach a gaping hole that is about to swallow them.

They land with a thud on to hard floors; the tiles are each ten-feet square, the room is dark. Only Mica's artificial light illuminates their surroundings. The room itself is not as big as suspected; there is no echo. Their light falls on hanging torches, which they quickly ignite.

The flames bring the room to life exposing the fifty-foot square space. The ten-foot walls have Anuk symbols carved in them. A black granite sarcophagus is in the center resting ominously, partially covered with a heavy lid.

Liviana looks at the box smiling, knowing what it could be. "This is a travel point, a portal."

"Nonsense, they don't exist," says Mica. "Stories told to wicked little children like you, and me."

Liviana hurries to a corner, passing her hands along the inscriptions; she reads them softly, admiring the script. Some of the protruding blocks gain her attention. She stops by them then pushes one half of the way back into the wall, then another all the way. Suddenly, the blocks with the writing glow with a dull gold light. The symbols in them glow a bright blue.

"What does it say?" Mica asks.

"It's a note, stating Thoth was here." She continues reading down the wall. "It mentions the eye of Persephone." She freezes, then begins to smile.

"More stories. Liv, you told me there's treasure down here."

"I lied."

"Just great. Why are we here then?"

"To find a key…well, the location anyway."

"And that's where the treasure is, right?"

Liviana grunts a false acknowledgment. She did not like deceiving Mica, but his lust for treasure was the only thing she could use to convince him to join her. She knows all too well that it was not so much of the treasure he was interested in, but rather the hunt for it.

A gust of wind blows through the room, pushing the flames on the torches as if a malevolent spirit had entered. Mica is startled, almost frightened; Liviana ignores his yelps and groans of fright.

She begins to read a part of the wall, "When the house of ENki fell, Thoth fled Egypt. He…"

"Wait, I thought Thoth died with Persephone?" Mica interrupts.

"That's what the history books say. Persephone escaped to Lumeria, but Thoth ventured to Atlantis. It was just an isolated continent then. Hyperboria was still a paradise."

"The Northern wasteland? Would not have thought it," Mica chuckles.

"Legend has it that Thoth dismantled most of the old travel points. After that, he hid the key to Lumeria. To ensure it did not fall into the hands of man, he broke it into three parts. The heart, the eye, and the body."

"So, all three must be found? I do not like this," Mica admits.

"There's only one left, and, the gem of Persephone." She pauses to looks at Mica, knowing this would bring a smile to his face.

"That's more like it," he says with a smile.

"Thoth put humanity on the path to forget the ancient histories. He corrupted all knowledge so they would forget."

"Wine and whores work just as well," Mica states.

"Yes, it does…If I am reading this right, this should do it."

She pushes a small block inward, then turns a metal dial; nothing happens. She thinks for a moment, trying to remember something her father had once told her.

"We need blood," she shouts.

"You're not getting any of mine. Why blood?" Mica asks.

She pulls her dagger from her waist and then slices her palm. She looks at the red liquid, uncertain that she was correct in her assumption. Carefully, she smears the blood on the symbols around the metal dial. A series of blue light streak across the walls.

"Blood contains the code of life, the genetic blueprint of the ancients," she explains.

A buzzing noise emanates from the sarcophagus, startling them both. They make their way to the granite box, waiting for something to happen. A hologram appears on the lid in brilliant blue color. Liviana hits Mica on his arm, signaling him to begin recording everything.

A landscape appears with the Great Pyramid in the center. The images raise several feet in the air, causing the bottom to fill with an intricate tunnel system. A flashing red dot pulses, showing a sizeable cavity. Symbols appear around the dot.

Liviana smiles from ear to ear. "This is a map of the Giza tunnels. Look, It's the location of Thoth's library, the hall of records."

"It's near the Lion of Leo," Mica adds.

A new sound joins the buzzing; like a pulsing alarm, soft then suddenly loud, ending abruptly, quickly repeating. The images begin to fade as the ground starts to shake. The walls rumble with debris falling from the ceiling.

Liviana looks at Mica; both are beginning to panic now. He nods at her, keeping his arm pointed at the hologram which has almost disappeared. She runs to a corner then along the walls looking for a way out. She looks at the hole they fell through.

"Done," Mica announces. "Now how do we get out?" he screams over the noise. He looks at the hole. "You could jump back up."

Liviana nods then line herself up to make the ten-foot jump. Suddenly, the area around the hole comes crashing down; she barely manages to leap to safety. She looks at the sarcophagus, and then runs towards Mica, grabbing his hand.

They stop at the box, staring inside. Mica does not like what she is planning.

"Get in!" Liviana orders.

"In there? Are you crazy?" Mica protests.

"I have a feeling."

"Woman, I am not about to die with you in that box!"

Liviana starts to push the heavy lid, hoping to create more space for them to climb in. Despite his whining Mica helps her, mumbling all the while. Satisfied with a broad enough area, Liviana jumps in. Mica follows, stumbling on top of her; his face lands squarely on her breasts.

"There are worst ways to go," Liviana jokes. "Now, wait."

Next to her right hand, a small panel drops open. Symbols appear with a blue glow. The hieroglyphs are familiar. Liviana smiles knowing what will happen next. She touches a sequence, causing golden lines to connect the shapes. Suddenly, the lid slams itself shut; Mica panics.

The noise outside the sarcophagus begins to intensify. It is not the sounds of crashing rock, but a high pitched one, growing louder. Inside the box starts to glow blue, with heat adding to the vibrations. Pulses of light radiate through the pair, then it wraps around their bodies like a cord. In a split second, they disappear.

-OFF THE COAST OF SPLIT, IN ILLYRIA, UNDERWATER-

Ancient ruins lay submerged in the waters off the coast of Split, undisturbed for millennia. What was once a temple now serves as a home for an abundance of creatures, swimming happily

111

through the cave of coral formed around a broken statue.

A bright blue light flashes inside a portion of the cave, frightening a school of fish. A granite lid slides off from a sarcophagus, then plunges towards the seabed. Water quickly floods the box, sending Liviana and Mica into a panic. They frantically begin their swim to the surface.

Mica illuminates the way with his armband's powerful light. A glimmer of moonlight is visible through the clear water, giving hope that they were not too far down.

They surface, breathing deeply, thankful that they made it out. A few seconds pass before they realize land is in front of them, about a quarter of a mile ahead.

Mica gives Liviana an annoyed look after spitting out water, "You had to say it…It could be worse. That was worse!"

"Oh shut up, we're alive, aren't we? Where are we anyway?"

Satisfied that he got his complaint out of the way, Mica checks his band. A map appears, he smiles.

"Dalmatia," he answers. "How did you know we would end up here?"

"I didn't," she explains. "There was a symbol I recognized from the journal, for the Persephone gem. Arias figured it out. Now, to the fat man."

They take a breath, then begin their long swim to the shore. They were headed to Dalmatia, to an ancient temple. They had traveled 2780 miles in seconds. Now, they were one step closer to their prize…again.

-THE GRAND TEMPLE IN GARTHOS, PROVINCE OF PARTHON, ATLANTIS-

The town of Garthos serves as the provincial capital in this farming region. Despite it being the food belt for Atlantis, many Illyrian trade interests exist here. As such, the investment into the area has proven to be beneficial, with large buildings catering for lots of shopping. Despite this, the old charm remains, for it was here that the great Anuk Thoth first arrived; so the myth goes anyway.

~THE ARRIVAL OF THOTH~

Thoth faced many hardships in the first years after the fall, testing the resolve of any Anuk. Sickness along with other difficulties descended upon him. Ultimately, the veil of death hovered over this mighty human. It was not until a young boy would rescue him from death's door, that hope would enter his resolve.

One of the devastating things unleashed from Lumeria was a bioweapon designed to kill off all Anuk. This was the cause for Thoth's illness, for his inoculation from the virus had proven formidable, but not absolute. A variety of tribal medicines, however, would outwit the genetic engineering of Anuk scientists.

An adolescent boy named Badur nursed Thoth back to health while protecting him from the wild lands of Parthon. When Thoth regained his strength, a friendship was fostered between the two, and they roamed the continent for a time. As fate would have it, they returned years later to where they first met.

The warring tribes in the area were subdued, with Badur assuming the mantle of a leader with Thoth's help. Together they planned to bring Atlantis out of darkness, to renew the golden age. This did not happen, for shortly after peace was established, the survivors of the house of ENlil arrived.

It had been a refreshing ten-year period of peace, without the interference of any other survivors from the Anuk Empire; for it was assumed not many were left, least of all any of the great houses.

This was far from true, as the youngest brother of the usurpers from Hyperboria named Atlas, entered the bay of Atlantis one summer afternoon.

With his household, this would-be king assumed the title, claiming dominion of all lands of the decimated empire. Atlas created his military, then conducted a bloody campaign to subdue the realms before him.

Thoth, fearing that his carefully laid plan for the future was in jeopardy, fled Atlantis. His one trusted friend, Badur, now had to finish what the keeper of forbidden knowledge had started.

Badur was given a choice when the forces of ENlil entered his lands; submit or perish.

Nobility was bestowed on the local Atlanteans. They all became servants of the house ENlil, and over time, forgot the promises their progenitor had made to his friend; clear the path at the time of the awakening, to bring forth the heir of Persephone.

-THE GRAND TEMPLE, PRESENT-

As expected, most of the town is gathered at the temple. Many did not know Alexa personally, but they knew of her. There is a rich devotion to tradition in this region which demands one pay homage to nobility. The seating area is almost full; one thousand seats.

More seating is provided in the grand courtyard, with large screens mounted on the temple walls. It is dark now. The video feed lights the area. It would be another thirty minutes before the service begins, so many are going into the casket area.

Inside, the massive chamber is filled with Parishioners. The priest, Etos, is preparing to give his sermon. He is a short chubby fellow, dressed in

114

his priestly garbs. Everyone loves him; he is a cornerstone of the religious community. Several of the temple youths buzz around him carrying chalices of incense. Some are preparing various relics near an altar.

A family of four sits at the front; Alexius' brother Remus, his wife Anna, with their two small children, Steven and Chloe. The children are restless; Anna is trying to calm them. She looks at Remus; a bit annoyed that he is more interested in the crowd rather than helping her.

Remus is eleven years older than his brother, rugged but yet dignified. Unlike his sister, he takes by his father, tall with a medium build. His slightly greying beard matches his head of neatly cut dark hair. He has carried on the mantle of Lord for the family and has done an excellent job with it. Everyone respects him, including the nobles. Anna is the perfect match for him, with her quick wit and fiery tongue, she tends to keep him in check.

"You looking for that slut friend of yours?" Anna says to Remus.

"What? Be quiet, it's not a day for your teasing," Remus advises.

"Just trying to distract you from whatever is eating you. What is it?"

"Waiting on my brother, that's all."

"It is shameful that he thinks it more appropriate to be wandering around the place," Anna says.

"I'll be back," Remus informs Anna. He heads towards an exit, ignoring his wife's objections.

The temple catacombs store two things, the tombs of saints and the wine cellar. Not many have ventured into the catacombs, but the wine cellar, now there is a place frequented by many a delinquent. On his way into the wine cellar, Alexius decided to pay a visit to the departed.

Brazen images of saints stand tall in the vast chamber. The place is damp, dusty, with hanging torches begging to be lit. Fire blazes in some crude lamps towards a forgotten area. It is an unmapped section housing dead saints from a time long ago. Alexius stands in front of one stone tomb belonging to his ancestor, Badur.

He holds his father's journal close, letting the light from an overhead torch fall on the pages. He reads silently, occasionally passing his hand on carvings on the stone, then comparing them to the pages. There are some matching symbols on the tomb from the journal. One week ago, they would have been unfamiliar, but now they bear a striking resemblance to Archon Inias' recovered books.

Approaching footsteps can be heard, prompting him to stuff the journal in his jacket quickly. He pulls out an empty flask. To his relief, Remus stands behind him.

"You startled me," he lies.

"Everyone is gathered; they are about to start. What are you doing here anyway? And don't tell me looking for the wine cellar; if anyone knows where that is, it's you."

"How did you find me?" He looks at Remus pointing to the lit torches. "Oh. I just got sidetracked, that's all."

"And is it just coincidence you end up at the tomb of your ancestor?" Remus points out.

"Our ancestor," says Alexius.

"Sometimes blood is everything little brother."

"Doesn't take blood to make a family."

"Even Andros?" Remus asks.

"Don't push it," Alexius replies with a scowl.

"But really, why here, why now?"

"How much do you know about father's friends? The ones who would come to the house all the time. The ones he went off to Illyria with?"

"Not much really. One of them is here..."

"Yes, I met him," Alexius says. "What about the others, what were they up to?"

Remus is getting uncomfortable; it shows on his face. He points to the exit. Alexius begins to suspect that his brother has some of the answers he seeks, but today is not the day to ask for them; maybe tomorrow.

"I'm sorry I've stayed away for so long," Alexius says solemnly. "There is no excuse, but..."

"Don't brother," Remus says, putting his arm around Alexius. "You need not explain. It's been quite a challenge this past year. I often wonder if I should have become a soldier like my father. It seems our fates have been crisscrossed."

"I would make a disastrous politician and you a horrible soldier. Face it; fate has put us right where she needs us to be."

"Have you ever thought of coming back? There is always a place for you here; you know that don't you?"

Alexius sighs, "It won't be right. With mother gone, it would feel as if I am returning because of it. I was never meant to have a family it seems, to settle down, to just...breathe."

"Surely there is someone out there to make an honest man of you?"

"Not even the Princess of Atlantis can make an honest man of me," Alexius jokes.

They go around a corner then climb a flight of long stairs. "You mentioned challenges this year, such as?" Alexius asks.

"There has been a lot of oversight from the capital in our local government. I've even been called to counsel in Atlas. You know how much I hate that place."

"Are you going? What about the senator, shouldn't he be addressing your concerns?"

"Otto is an old man, stubborn and unwilling to give up his seat. I will admit that it is my lack of courage to sack him that cements his resolve. I'd feel better if we had someone there we could trust to represent Parthon; to represent the family."

"Oh no, don't even try it," Alexius says with a smile. "Politics is not my game. Get Andros to play senator."

"A senator's post will be taken as an insult. We both know he desires a proper lordship, not the lesser nobility he has inherited."

"The man barely deserves the titles he currently has." Alexius touches the journal in his inside breast pocket. "I can't be your senator brother. I have some important things I must attend to."

They walk the long halls to the exit reminiscing about days past. As they come upon a split at the doorway, Alexius starts to head off in the opposite direction. Remus knows he's going to the wine cellar. He shakes his head.

The crowd has settled now. Etos is going on and on about the patron god Garthos; a marbled image of him stands tall at a left corner, towering over the lesser essential statues. Etos begins his story about the afterlife; his voice echoes with the help of loudspeakers.

Remus takes his seat next to Anna. She looks at him curiously, waiting for an explanation for her brother-in-law's absence. He smiles then plays with Chloe. Anna looks over to the side passageway; she sees Alexius being discreetly dragged by Cassandra.

They make their way to the others, sitting in their assigned seats. Alexius attempts to sit next to Cassandra, but she quickly pushes him off to the adjacent position.

118

"Have some respect, it will be over soon," Cassandra chides.

"Where's your pack mule?" asks Alexius.

"Looking for you," Cassandra replies. "He should have started in the wine cellar."

Andros appears from the opposite end of the hall. He calmly approaches while smiling at his admirers. His family is also in the noble class, with a reputation for being shrewd. They are well respected, but not on the scale that Cassandra's family is. He takes his seat next to his wife.

"Fell into the wine barrel again?" Andros asks Alexius.

"If only I were so lucky," Alexius jokes. He reaches into his jacket, retrieves his flask, and takes a drink. He offers it to Andros.

"Don't disgrace your family, or me," Andros warns with a smile. Cassandra hits him on the shoulder, obviously not pleased with the exchange.

"How is Daniu?" Alexius asks Andros.

"Still locked away in an Aryan monastery. By now Daniu has probably shaved his head, surely wearing those infernal robes they…" he stops as Alexius chuckles. "What?"

"This is the first civil conversation we've had, ever," Alexius explains. Andros doesn't finish. Instead, he looks at the activities on the stage.

A line of young boys and girls enter the altar area. Their ages range from twelve to fifteen. One girl appears late. She is clearly in her twenties; it's Lizzie, one of the temple youths. They all carry smoking chalices of incense, swinging it slowly in front of them. They circle Etos with the smoke as he chants some prayers.

Lizzie gives Alexius a warm smile. She bites the side of her bottom lip then bumps into the lad in front of her. Alexius notices, then quickly takes a drink from his flask. He smiles back at Lizzie.

CHAPTER 11:
A POT OF GOLD
STEW

The kingdoms of Illyria have indeed become the wonders of man; all built on the ashes of the Anuk predecessors. If Rihzon claims to be the economic powerhouse of the conglomerate, then Dalmatia can aptly hold the title of being its big sister. The 'pearl of the Adriatic' is the capital of this kingdom, what a capital it is to behold.

Situated in an inlet surrounded by rocky cliffs, one would feel as if they are entering an ancient version of Atlantis. High walls with towers encapsulate a city of red roofs amidst stone buildings. Giant statues jot out of the rock to reach the skies in calm, bright blue waters.

The wealthiest of Illyria's citizens live here. Their fortunes made from trade in everything that could be bought and sold. There was never an item that could not be bartered; even influence had a price. No one was exempt from the allure of Dalmatia, not even the ministries of the priesthood.

The local monastery sat as most do, on a high hill overlooking the city. In this holy place, there was an overabundance of slaves; temple youths who were free citizens of other realms did not exist here.

The affluent High Priest Clabber lives in opulence. It has long been suspected that he is involved in illegal activities; black market everything, from slaves to stolen Atlantean technology. Yet, no one dares confront him, for as long as he brings in tribute to the governing order of the priesthood, he will have their protection.

Clabber is one of those priestly aristocrats who believes he is untouchable. His walk, his speech, his overall demeanor are the stink of a pompous snob who lives in the reputation he has gained.

The sun has barely risen. This means the High Priest will have his morning soak in the 'sacred pools,' inside one of the private quarters. Clabber regally walks across his marble floor followed by a slave girl, Neela; she's no more than ten. She very carefully carries a platter of fruit several paces behind her master.

They descend a winding staircase headed to a steaming pool. Fires blaze in ceramic urns, giving a mystical ambiance to the room. Columns rise from the floor, propping the low ceiling. A marbled bench sits across from the water where Clabber has now stopped.

Neela places her platter near a column then looks over to Clabber. He lifts both arms parallel to the ground as if waiting for some divine inspiration. He clears his throat, signaling his slave that he was ready to be attended to. She quickly runs up to disrobe him.

At first glance, one would look on in awe at the fat, hairy 'man-beast.' That glance would quickly turn into amazement at the short chubby arms disappearing into the body. If one's breakfast were not instantly regurgitated, then the overlapping stomach rolls, coupled with the ripe sour stench, would quickly bring on this reaction.

Clabber ceremoniously enters the pool, wading over to the far wall. He closes his eyes, enjoying the burning incense hanging above the perfumed waters. Today is a good day, for he is completing a five day fast in honor of some festival or another. A good soak before a good meal; this brings a smile to his face. First, he will have some fruit.

Neela walks over to the platter with her bare feet sticking to the wet tile. She is hungry but cannot eat until her master does; none of the children can. Her sad face is a testament to a lifetime of abuse on top of hard work. She begins to pick up the tray but is startled by Mica standing over her.

She looks up with wide eyes fearing the worst; frozen for a moment, unable to scream. A hand covers her little mouth, another holds her. She does not struggle. The grip begins to relax, the palm drops from her mouth. She looks at Mica with eyes that plead for help.

Mica knows her pain. He was once like her, a slave to High Priest Clabber. Stolen from Rihzon as a small child, from parents he will never know. His heart breaks for the little girl; all he can think about is making the fat pig pay. Liviana has forbidden any harm to the priest so there will be no killing this morning.

"Don't be afraid little princess," Mica whispers. "Run along now, get something to eat. Hide in your room."

Neela scampers off, her tiny feet hitting the metal staircase hard. The noise alerts Clabber who opens his eyes to see Mica standing near the marble bench. The intruder crunches into a red apple, disrupting the tranquility of the bathing room.

"What is the meaning of this!" Clabber screams with contempt. Mica ignores him, continuing to crunch. "Do you know who I am? I will have you…"

"Lord Clabber," Mica interrupts, "what is that smell?" He tosses the half-eaten apple into the water then selects a nice green one. "Smells like…disappointment."

122

"Who are you, what do you want?" Clabber asks.

Mica sits on the bench, taking his time to regard the fruit in his hand. He reaches for a dagger on his waist, slowly pulling it out, displaying the well-crafted blade to the priest.

The weapon's hilt is ivory with intricate gold carvings on it. The symbols shine with the meager light. Clabber sees enough of the images to give him some pause; he knew the markings belonged to the infamous terrorist group that had descended upon Illyria.

Mica slices into the apple, cutting small strips slowly. He tosses a juicy piece into the pool within reach of Clabber. The part is so thin that it just floats there. *Is this a trick?* Clabber thinks.

"You look hungry," Mica says in a serious tone.

Clabber turns red as a turnip then wades off to a corner. "I am the High Priest of Dalmatia. You will recognize your master!"

His arrogance is astounding. Even in this position, he fails to see his dilemma. He watches Mica smile while continuing to throw strips of apple towards him. *He looks familiar*, Clabber notes to himself.

"You fucking twat," Mica says in an aggravated tone, "do I look like your slave? You know who I work for," he states.

The confirmation that this was indeed a terrorist was all Clabber needed. A mere bandit or assassin from the cartels he could handle. Not these people, for they could not be bought or bribed. Caution enters his soul; maybe he will be the first that can sway one.

"Apologies," Clabber says with humility. "What does your master want?"

"Don't know, don't care," Mica responds.

A cloaked, intimidating figure steps out of the shadows. Fear creeps into Clabber once more, for this could be the master no one has ever seen. Those unfortunate souls who have encountered him have never lived to see another sunrise. The figure steps into the light, twenty feet away.

"Get your fat ass out of there. Present yourself properly," Mica orders.

Clabber hurries out of the water, his heart pounding. He gets to the submerged stairs then begins to climb out. Quite expectantly, he slips backward, creating a big splash.

Mica pauses his peeling, then looks at the figure; he notices a nod towards the falling man. Grumbling under his breath, he enters the water to help Clabber out. Once they make it onto the tiles, he rolls the 'beast' on his stomach, exposing the hairy backside.

"You're disgusting," He says to Clabber. He grabs the nearby robe, tossing it over the abomination. "Cover yourself."

As the priest covers up; Liviana reveals herself by dropping her hood. Light from the flames show off the tribal images on her face. Once Clabber notices her, his anger quickly returns when he realizes that this is not 'The Master.'

"Who is this cunt? I will have you both killed!" he exclaims with ferocious anger.

Mica knew never to call Liviana that word. He has slipped up in the past and escaped her fury with a warning. Now, this idiot has angered her.

In a split second, Liviana moves across the room, stopping behind Clabber. She presses her blade on his jugular making her intentions known.

"Call me that one more time, you piece of filth," she warns.

"You…" Clabber begins slowly, carefully choosing his words; he has an idea who she is now, or what she is, he thinks this may save him, "…are the…"

Before he can utter another word, Liviana slams the butt of her dagger behind Clabber's head. His body drops to the floor causing Liviana to jump clear. She stands next to Mica, who calmly slices off a large piece of apple, then offers it to her.

-TURNEY'S BROTHEL AND BAR, PARTHON, ATLANTIS-

It is well into the morning on this side of Parthon; the skies are clear, the wind is brisk. The parking lot at 'Turney's Brothel and Bar' is almost empty. There weren't many patrons last night, as they were at the funeral services for Alexa Badur. A vehicle is parked at the entrance.

The car belongs to the local priesthood, on loan to High Priest Calis of Atlas. He sits quietly in the back seat contemplating his next move. This was a bit unusual for him, waiting outside a seedy brothel; it was by far *not the strangest thing I've done,* he recalls. He looks at a clock display near him. Time was not on his side today, so he exits the vehicle.

Inside the brothel is quiet, with only one barmaid wiping down the counters. Krista notices Calis. She immediately drops to her knees.

"Good morning M'Lord," Krista says in a sweet voice.

"Good morning," Calis answers, then quickly helps the young lady on her feet. "There is no need for formality my dear."

He looks around the relatively large space. It is clean, well-organized, quite deceptive as the outside seems almost dilapidated, but yet the insides can rival any nightclub in Garthos.

Krista quickly gets behind the bar, "May I offer your holiness some coffee or tea?"

"No thank you," Calis responds politely. "It will be kind of you to take some tea to my driver." He begins to reach for his money.

"Yes of course…you need not pay. It will be my honor."

"Bless you, my child. I am actually here to collect one of your patrons…"

"Alexius," Krista quickly states with a smile. "He's with my sister Lizzie."

"Before you go outside, can you inform him that I am here?" Krista nods then scamper up a flight of stairs.

The upper level is spacious with a long hallway winding about like a hotel's. Krista stops at a door, presses her ear against it listening for activity. Since there is none, she hurries inside.

She sees Alexius flat on his stomach, asleep. Lizzie comes out of the bathroom. Krista quickly picks up some of Lizzie's clothing on the floor to throw at her.

"Cover up you tart," she instructs Lizzie. "We have a distinguished guest downstairs."

"More distinguished than him?" Lizzie asks in her country accent.

"Yes…a High Priest from the capital."

Lizzie yelps with excitement, then quickly gets dressed. Alexius begins to wake. She runs over to kiss him on the cheek, then joins her sister.

"M 'Lord, there is a High Priest downstairs waiting for you," Krista says.

"What? Wait, where are you going?" Alexius asks a bit confused.

"Time to go…we have to close up for the day," Krista informs him.

Bewildered as to what's happening Alexius gets off the bed, not realizing that he lacked clothing. The girls gawk then leave. He proceeds into the bathroom. So begins the slow routine to get dressed. *But wait….today, oh no,* he screams in his head.

The girls rush down the stairs, stopping in front of Calis. Lizzie drops to her knees then grabs the priest's hand. She gently kisses it before bowing her head. The hand touches her forehead, ending gently on her head; she smiles. Her sister receives the same.

"Bless you my child, both of you," Calis says in his priestly voice. He looks around as the girls run into a kitchen area. "Might as well sit I suppose," he says to himself, examining his hand.

He takes a seat in a booth. The girls bring a platter of bread, cheese, steaming tea, with a bowl of olive oil.

"Please, we insist," Lizzie explains.

"Oh alright," Calis concedes. Alexius finally makes it down. The girls run over to him.

"Thank you for the hospitality ladies," Alexius says to the two girls. Krista drags Lizzie off to the back.

Alexius smiles at Calis, "How did you know where to find me?"

"My driver is not as discreet as he should be," Calis explains. "I was concerned when Cassandra asked about your whereabouts, so I came to the only logical place you would be."

"You may think me a disrespectful son," Alexius states while dipping bread in the oil.

"Not at all. It is not my place to judge anyone, nor is it to tell anyone how to live." Calis glances at Krista taking tea outside.

"I thought that's what the priesthood is for? That's what they do."

"An unfortunate difference in methods, them and me," Calis explains.

"You don't act or speak like other High Priests; they would never enter this place."

"Let's just say that we have our differences."

"Say, I've meant to ask, who were the others who met in my father's, secret circle?"

"Is that what you called it?" Calis asks smiling. Alexius does not respond; he smiles with bread in his mouth. "Very well; there was my sponsor Samiri, Darius, myself of course, and…the King."

Alexius chokes on his bread. He looks at Calis who calmly sips his tea. The King of Atlantis has been absent from all the realms for over twenty years. No one knows why he left, never to be seen or heard from again. Only whispers and legend grew around him. The fact that he was there, with Arias in that sanctuary, sends a chill up Alexius' spine.

"The King? Why?"

"He was a close friend to us all, brothers more like." Calis looks at the wall, feeling nostalgic. "The last great Anuk King, a direct descendant of the forefathers, pure in blood, and from when I knew him, pure of heart."

"Why did he leave?"

"When you see him, you can ask for yourself. But for now, we should be going."

Alexius wonders, *Could this be a man worth befriending?*

-AFTERNOON IN DALMATIA-

The once serene grounds of the grand temple are now alive with activity. People swarm all over the place, setting up tents as if there were to be a festival. Two small crafts are parked on the grass; troop transports, able to hold twenty passengers each. Outside the main gates, armed nomads stand with weapons, diligently waiting for any disruption of what is transpiring.

Removed from all the activity above is the High Priest Clabber, locked away in a dungeon, his own as a matter of fact. He sits behind iron bars in a stone room about eight feet square. A 'shit-bucket' sits in a corner, with remnants of the priest's nervous stomach. *Oh, what have I done to deserve this?* He laments to himself.

From his cell he hears footsteps; just the bare 'pitter-patter' of a child. He smiles hoping it's one of his slaves coming to set him free, to rescue him. His prayer is answered as a little eight-year-old boy slowly makes his way towards the tired old man. He stops at the iron bars, looking upon his master.

"Be a good boy, find the keys, help me open the doors, will you?" Clabber says to the child.

The lad nods then walk around the area. He is not sure what he is looking for but will do anything to please his master. He returns with a stick then leans on the bars. Clabber frowns as he reaches through to slap the boy across the face.

"I said keys, not a stick!" he screams. There is not a sound from the lad; he sits crumpled on the floor.

More footsteps echo, this time they are loud; they are the heavy stride of an adult with purpose. Fear takes over the angry priest. He quickly retreats to the farthest wall. Mica appears, slowly walking towards the boy on the floor.

He helps the child off the ground. The lad runs off, leaving the adults to regard one another. Mica looks at Clabber then opens the cell; so many things he wants to say to him, so much hurt he wants to inflict.

"Where is the band of Osiris?" Mica asks calmly.

"I don't know what that is…please, I beg you, let me go."

"Where is the band?" Mica asks once more, moving closer to Clabber.

"You keep asking me for something I know nothing about. I already answered everything you asked."

"Where is the….what is that smell!" Mica shouts. He rushes over to a water hose coiled up in a corner.

He knew it would be there, as it always had been. He knows the water rushing through the lines would be powerful enough to cause welts on the skin, bruising the flesh, disrupting the senses; for an adult, it would do these things, to a child, far worse. He lets the water blast through, with the nozzle pointing at Clabber.

The priest drops on the ground with the bucket of excrement falling over him, flowing with the water getting inside his mouth. The powerful stream goes down to his testicles. The torture feels like an eternity. After one minute, Mica turns off the water.

"Where is the fucking band of Osiris!" Mica screams like a madman. He unclips his dagger. With hate in his eyes he rushes towards Clabber.

A slight beeping goes off in his ear from a tiny earpiece concealed under his hair. He looks at his armband to identify the caller; he can't ignore this one. Whatever he hears gives him calm. He looks at Clabber with disgust.

"Lord Clabber, are you hungry? We have a fine stew brewing for you."

"If you wish it, my lord," Clabber says almost to the point of tears.

Approaching footsteps brings a mix of fear with curiosity to Clabber. He sees two nomads enter, their facial tattoos giving him much grief. His gaze drops to a smoldering pot they both carry. They leave it with a bowl on the floor.

"Go on…eat," Mica offers.

It has been five days since he's eaten anything of substance. Only liquids, including milk, a handful of berries, and an egg in the mornings, were all that Clabber allowed himself to have. Whatever this was would be a welcomed relief to the burning in his stomach. He lifts the cover carefully.

With surprise quickly turning into anger, Clabber looks at his gold coins carelessly submerged in hot water. To add insult to injury, potato peels float about with a clove of garlic.

Clabber looks up at Mica with hate in his eyes, "I am not hungry."

"Not good enough? We will have to do better then." Mica nods at the two nomads, who remove the pot from the room.

A little calmer now, Mica walks over to a short stool to sit. Clabber is afraid to move, so he sits on the ground, fuming.

"Yes, we found your hidden treasures...not very well hidden. You don't remember me, do you?"

"I am afraid I do not recall our acquaintance."

"This room, you once locked me in here for ten days. 'What is that smell?' You would shout as you entered. Locked in because a lovely city girl befriended me, and I brought her here, to our home."

Clabber looks up at Mica with remorseful eyes. "I am sorry," he claims, starting to sob.

"We entered the temple; all Lyra wanted to do was say a prayer for her father," Mica explains. "When you found us you were furious. You flogged the life out of her, a seven-year-old girl. After you tossed her out like a common street urchin." Mica's rage returns, "She was not one of us, not one of your dirty, forgotten children!"

He drops down to meet Clabber's gaze, then slaps the man several times on his rosy cheeks. Clabber begins to cry, but this does not stop Mica. He drags the priest up. He puts his palm on Clabber's face, violently pushes his head back on the iron bars.

"Where is the band of Osiris?" he screams. He repeats the action until blood drips down Clabber's head.

He stops, intrigued that this filth can keep a secret. They were sure the band was here; Liviana was confident about the location. *Could the journal*

131

have been wrong? I knew we should have brought it...and now it's back in the hands of this lot, Mica ponders.

"Mercy...I beg mercy, pardon," Clabber cries. "Please, I am faint."

"Then you are of no use to us." Mica retrieves his dagger, displaying it to the frightened man.

"Wait, wait," Clabber begs with his hands in the air. "There is something that was left here; I know not what it's called. It is ancient."

At last, a glimmer of hope. Mica touches his ear to call for his nomad comrades. It doesn't take long for two to enter the dungeon. They grab Clabber. Mica stays behind for a moment, looking at the room where he once endured the priest's torture. He smiles.

The bright afternoon sun shines on Clabber's face, blinding him momentarily as he makes his way outside. His captors drag him out of the temple then down the stairs. He breathes the crisp autumn air, confident that he may yet live through this day.

Liviana is close by; she sits with a feeble old man, a slave. She gently feeds him from a bowl, treating him like a wounded child. She entrusts the man's care to a nomad. She sees Clabber at the bottom of the stairs.

The grounds are filled with people running about, alive as if for the first time. Nearly one hundred souls have been freed from Clabber's household. They regard their liberators with much respect, not afraid of the nomad terrorists. Neela with several children run up to Liviana, smiling as they try to hug her. She pats them all then continues on.

She stops in front of Clabber, who immediately drops to his knees then prostrates. She looks at one of the men standing behind him; he drags the priest up. Mica stops at the group.

"He should be fed, for his compliance," Mica orders. The men drag Clabber off to a table. "It's here; he will show us."

"Good work," Liviana says to Mica as she takes his hand. "What do you think he will do when he realizes his wealth is being given away?" She points to several tables, loaded with Clabber's once hidden treasures.

Mica smiles, "Take his life if he knows what's good for him."

"Come," Liviana says, putting an arm around Mica.

They walk towards the treasure pile. It is undisturbed despite the multitude of people walking around it. Freedom is more important to the slaves than all the gold they can carry. With all his talk about finding treasure, Mica finds himself disgusted by the sight of it.

"There's your treasure, you can have anything you wish," Liviana offers.

"This belongs to them," Mica says as he looks at the people, "and to the poor, the sick, the weak. Anyone who has been cheated by this animal should take what they feel is owed."

"Consider it done. Now, we have some business to attend to." Liviana walks off towards Clabber, but stops midway, realizing Mica is not following; she looks back at him.

He stands in front of the tables, looking at everything, contemplating what he had just suggested. *It would be a shame to leave empty-handed,* Mica reminds himself. He picks up what looks like a broken piece of a small golden disc with a chain attached to it. Smiling, he displays it to Liviana; she smiles back at him.

CHAPTER 12: THE INHERITANCE OF HUMANS

The late hour of the evening is marked by the declining sun poised to make its final drop behind the mountains of Parthon. A small river flows through the Badur estate, turning into smaller streams as it flows out in various directions. One stream pass along a fenced off area near a private road.

The three-mile retreat into the less visited areas of the estate is a welcomed hideaway for Alexius. He sits on the rocky banks watching his horse take its drink. *Such a simple life,* he thinks. Reality sets in. He brings forth his father's journal, ready to read some more.

~Journal~

A high burden I carry for my family, one that dwells beyond the confines of time. Doomed are the trustees who live in the misery. Long have I relished my title, yet my soul knows it is an unearned affair. The balance of things comes at the fulfillment of the oath.

Oh, how I lament the tale of Persephone, for she suffered a fate no soul should endure. Her burden must be set free, now, in this age of the awakening. Oh, how I lament the tale of Persephone. Share in her tragedy I must.

~End Passage~

"Some clues would be helpful," Alexius says to his horse.

A snapping twig startles him; he turns quickly expecting something sinister to fall upon him. He breathes relief when Remus appears with a horse.

"Clues to what?" Remus asks.

"What are you doing here? Shouldn't you be out doing your Lordship duties?"

"Don't be ridiculous…I can't stand those vultures any more than you can. They are all there unwilling to leave, roaming about the place as if waiting for some treasure to be bestowed on them."

Remus lets his horse join the other by the stream. He sits next to his brother, whom he noticed is trying to conceal a book.

"So where did Calis find you? Gambling? Wenching at Turney's? Or wandering around town?" Remus asks with a smile.

"Turney's; don't complain, I made it didn't I?"

"Barely. Andros was beside himself, assuring us you will not attend the burial."

"What did you think?"

"I knew better." Remus pats his brother on the back. "Even if you did not come, we would understand."

"It was the right thing to do." Alexius smiles, remembering this is what Deidra had told him. He carefully reveals the journal to Remus. "It's father's."

"I haven't seen that since, a very long time." Remus takes the book, handling it like a delicate flower.

He smells the cover, igniting memories of childhood. He closes his eyes becoming lost in the past. Arias treated him as his own born son. Remus cherished his adopted father, whom he honors every day by carrying on the family's name and title.

Remus takes a deep breath, "You asked me about the men in father's circle. From what I remember, one of them, Darius, was charged with his murder."

Surprise overcomes Alexius, "I thought father was killed in a terrorist attack."

"He was in a way, for that is what Darius had become, or so the tale goes."

"What became of him?" Alexius asks, still staring at his brother.

"No one knows. He fled Atlantis never to be heard from again. This journal, when it was but empty, was a gift to father from Darius."

So many questions are swirling around Alexius' head. The journal mixed up with ancient texts, a task bestowed by an ancestor, Persephone, a murdered father; there was a connection he could feel.

He takes the book. "There is a part here…It reads, '*The path to the key of power starts in Cappadocia. The eye of Persephone will guide you to Lumeria. Protect the people Alexius, my son.*' What does it mean?"

"You must find a way to Cappadocia," Remus advises.

Suddenly, Alexius remembers that he has been reassigned to the Far West Continent. Frustration overcomes him.

"I have to be in FaW-C a week from now." Alexius stands and looks at the sunset.

"A trivial detail, one I am certain you will overcome. It's getting late, time to head back."

They both get on the horses. They planned on making the journey a slow one, for the gathering at the house was not one they were thrilled to rejoin.

-GRAND TEMPLE, DALMATIA-

For the first time in decades, the Grand Temple is alive with celebration. No longer was the High Priest Clabber its keeper, more importantly, no longer was he feared. The former slaves set up a feast for their liberators, thirty or so nomads, with their two distinguished leaders. Urns burn bright, music echoes, revelry is abundant, and everyone is cheerful. One is hopeful, Clabber.

He is not amongst the crowd for surely his safety will be in peril. He stands in a remote corner of the monastery, inside a large hall that has long been locked away from intruders. Liviana stands at the top of a short flight of stairs with Mica, patiently waiting for Clabber's revelation.

"I have your word. I will be free?" Clabber asks Liviana.

"You will be free," she responds.

"Hurry up swine," Mica says, pushing the priest's back.

Clabber looks at his former slave who is now the master. He hurries to the far end of the room some thirty feet away.

"For a fat fuck, he sure can run," Mica observes.

"Do shut up," Liviana warns.

A marble wall is at the end where Clabber has stopped. He doesn't look back; instead, he quickly pushes a sequence of tiles. There is a short rumble on the floor. A descending stairway appears to his side. He hastily makes his way down, disappearing into a darkened corridor.

"Really?" Liviana chuckles. They both take off after him.

The dark corridor brightens with light from flaming torches. Standing eighteen feet away in a circular antechamber, Clabber faces the entrance.

There is an annular protrusion jotting out three feet from the stone floor. It appears to be made of a strange metal, grey in color, with silver particles mixed in. The texture looks wet, but it is stable.

As they enter Liviana notices a stone block on the wall barely sticking out with Anuk writing on it; it has a dirty marbled color. She makes her way to

137

it smiling. She retrieves her dagger, instantly putting the fear of death in Clabber. She slices her hand much to his relief; drops of her blood fall to the floor.

"Stand back," she orders.

Liviana smears her blood on the block. The ground rumbles once more, the circular protrusion rises four feet, then the top begins to glow with golden symbols. Clabber looks on in awe, immediately dropping to his knees. Liviana calmly walks over to read the symbols in the ancient tongue.

The top layer dissolves creating a depression. Inside, a small metal object sits in a thin glass holder. It is dark bronze, no bigger than a finger, thin as paper. Lines of gold are noticeable, with sharp angles weaving their way around the face.

"At last," Liviana announces, pleased they have found their prize.

A drop of her blood falls into the depression as she picks up the transparent holder. The spot where it fell glows blue. Curiosity gets the better of her. She slowly puts a finger in to touch the area.

Mica gives her a worried look, "Liv don't," he warns. He looks around, ready for some trap to be engaged.

She ignores him. The metal column quickly dissolves, leaving a small blue box on the ground. There is more of the Anuk writing on it glowing brightly. At this point, Clabber is prostrating devoutly.

Liviana reads the inscriptions. A golden thread of light wraps around the midsection of the box, then it opens. She carefully lifts the lid; what she sees puts reverence on her face, something Mica has never seen. Inside sits a small red gem.

"The gem of Persephone," Liviana declares with love in her voice. She picks it up with trembling hands.

She shows it to Mica, who looks on in awe. He had taken all that Liviana had told him to be a mere myth or excuses for adventure. Now, in their presence, she held real history. A confirmation that there was a deeper purpose to all that had gone before; all that there is to come.

Clabber stands to look at the gemstone with renewed faith. Even though he is a High Priest, indoctrinated into the new version of the old Anuk religion, he is not a believer. All his years of corruption seemed trivial at this point. He suddenly remembers a warning passed on to him.

His lips tremble, "It has been passed down through the years that anything removed from this room will bring death. The old priests said the essence of the gods themselves was brought here."

Liviana becomes irritated, "There is only one true God. You people have perverted the ancient religion, twisting it for the sake of man's lusts."

In a hopeful tone, Clabber says, "You promised you would leave. I have given you what you came for."

"Your prophecy is wrong." Liviana nods at Mica.

Clabber's expression changes from plight to fear as Mica draws his dagger then swings it at his neck. The priest's jugular is severed, sending blood squirting everywhere. He grabs his throat as he drops to the floor. He looks at Liviana while breathing his last breath.

"I bring death," Liviana says to Clabber.

The body continues to twitch.

-LATE AT NIGHT, IN ALEXA'S ROOM, BACK IN PARTHON, ATLANTIS-

Sleep escapes some at this late hour; Anna sits with Cassandra on the floor of Alexa's bedroom going through her personal effects. Chests are arranged neatly in the large room; some are packed, others are empty. The finality of death it seems comes when the belongings of the deceased are put away.

The slow rhythmic footsteps of children alert their mother; Steven and Chloe enter the bedroom with sleepy faces. Steven runs up to Anna to crawl into her lap. Chloe remains at the doorway looking at the two adults. Suddenly, large hands lift her off the ground. Alexius puts her on his shoulder and remains stationed at the door.

Anna holds up an ugly shawl, "Is there anything your mother didn't horde?" she asks Cassandra rhetorically.

Remus appears behind Alexius. He puts a hand on his brother's free shoulder. There were some memories in this room, happy for many, bad for one.

When Alexius was fifteen, Alexa succumbed to a dark stage in her mental illness. One stormy night her torment was overbearing, brought on by the mere presence of her son. After a series of outbursts no mother should deliver to her child, Alexius left his home. He ran off to Atlas where he met Deidra, then joined the Atlantean forces.

Remus remembers that night; he accepts that his brother acts out in his way, but still yearns to belong.

He takes Chloe off Alexius then quietly enters the room. He puts her on the bed then joins the women. A section of a trunk catches his attention. He picks up a stuffed toy bunny.

Remus dangles the toy towards Alexius, "Remember this?"

The white bunny is shaped more like a human than a rabbit. Its fur shows signs of old age. It is dressed in a cream sweater and a white coat. Remus' display of the rabbit brings Alexius into the room; it also sparks curiosity in Chloe, who now sits up on the bed.

Alexius takes the toy, squeezing it almost reverently. He gives it to Chloe, who welcomes the bunny with a hug.

"Take good care of her," Alexius says to his niece.

There is more digging in trunks by his siblings. Remus heads over to a corner wall. A moment passes before he returns with a small blue box in his hand. There are strange writings on the top -the language of the ancients.

Anna looks at her husband curiously, "What's that?"

Remus heads over to his brother, "Mother kept it for Alexius."

"I've never seen that before, what is it?" Cassandra asks.

Remus offers it to Alexius. Inside is a small silver cartouche shaped pendant attached to a thick silver chain. There are more ancient golden symbols engraved into the silver body. Alexius picks it up, revealing a handwritten note beneath.

"It's in mother's hand," he says. He looks at Remus, hesitates, then reads the note.

~ALEXA'S NOTE~

Alexius, my baby boy, I leave this heirloom to you as it was entrusted to me for you by your father Arias; passed down to him through the generations. Keep it safe; protect it with your life, for the agents of darkness seek its mystery.

My heart breaks for you, for you are a child of suffering. Please forgive me past ills. I have always loved you, my son.

~END NOTE~

A tear rolls down his stoic face, not genuinely revealing the confusion he feels inside. Cassandra goes to him to provide a warm embrace.

"She wrote that but a month ago," Remus explains.

Chloe drops off the bed with her new bunny in her arms. She darts out of the room, startling the adults.

"Do you have to leave tomorrow?" Cassandra asks Alexius.

"I must. Carrell sails at first light. It's a two-day journey," he explains.

"Fly to the capital with Andros; you can leave tomorrow afternoon," she explains.

"I can't. As much as I want to, I can't."

Chloe returns to the room, rushing in with purpose. She offers Alexius what appears to be a tightly woven band.

"What's this?" Alexius asks with a smile.

"A magic bracelet," the toddler responds. He hugs her then heads out of the room.

His entire life up to this point did not make any sense. He would not have answers to the questions that burned his soul. All he could do was follow the path before him, a path still shrouded in mystery.

-TEMPLE GROUNDS, DALMATIA-

It is now past midnight; the festivities have died out. All the monastery residents have returned to their quarters, anxious to leave the place at first light. The tables that once had all of Clabber's treasure are now empty; successfully distributed amongst the former slaves. The nomads are not leaving empty handed though, for they claimed a share as well.

The transport crafts begin to ignite their engines. Blue flames blast out the rear exhaust, creating a brilliant light in the darkness. One ship lifts off the ground then angles its nose towards the sky. It ascends slowly towards the heavens, making its way to a destination known only to a few.

The second craft's ramp is open. Liviana runs up with Mica, quickly making their way to the back area. The ramp closes creating a seal, equalizing the air pressure inside. They pass by their sleeping comrades, quietly taking seats at the rear. They prepare themselves for departure by attaching restraints.

The ascent begins. The windows show the ground quickly disappearing. Liviana closes her eyes, ready to drift off into much-needed sleep. She wakes to sounds of rattling.

Her eyes remain closed, she smiles, "So, what did you get?"

Mica acts aloof, "Me? Nothing much. Just a ruby, some coin, and this beauty." He reveals the necklace he picked out of the treasure. Liviana looks at the broken shard around his neck.

"That's worthless," she points out, "it's gold plated if you haven't noticed."

Mica smiles proudly, "Well I like it. Reminds me that even broken things have a home."

"Nicely put. Now get some rest and stop your infernal jiggling," Liviana grumbles.

"By the time the authorities realize what has happened here, we will be halfway to Rekem."

"We're not going to Rekem. We're going to Harapa, to see Old Mother."

A moment of panic sets in with Mica, "Can you drop me off at Rekem? You know how much I hate that place."

Liviana remains silent, which forces Mica to settle in for the long ride. He fumes silently, touching the worthless trinket around his neck.

The craft shoots off into the sky joining up with its companion. After flying in formation for a minute, Liviana's craft breaks off, heading to the Aryan border.

~DEEP INSIDE LUMERIA, THREE THOUSAND YEARS AGO~

Dark chambers suddenly begin to brighten as scattered screens come to life. Symbols

143

materialize in the air at various points; instruments start to hum. Light gradually fills the space, dim at first, then creeping up to a comfortable level.

A raised platform is in center of the chamber with a sarcophagus, dark grey with some silver mixed in. Blue light forms under the metal box, then it shoots around the platform creating a barrier of light. A dull droning sound matches the spinning light, rapidly increasing in pitch. Plumes of smoke emanate from beneath the platform; as suddenly as it began, it ends.

The sarcophagus' lid slides off to the side, revealing Queen Persephone. She struggles to climb out, barely managing to make it on to the platform's edge. Her bloody hand smears red on the metal. Her cauterized wounds are opened up once more; made fresh again from the journey by light. She stumbles down the short metal stairs, grabbing tightly to sturdy railings.

There are several panels on a sizeable table-like console with warning symbols flashing. Persephone looks for any vacant part with a crevice to match Thoth's key; she is in pain, wondering if she will survive the next few hours. She sees an empty slot then pulls the key off her neck. The moment she slams it in, red lights flash, alarms blare.

Persephone bows her head, "I seek forgiveness with the Lord of heaven, the Creator and Cherisher of the worlds." She taps several switches then turns the key ten degrees clockwise, then to sixty degrees, and back to ten.

The key secures itself to the panel as it glows gold. The chamber rumbles violently. It is joined by muffled roars of rockets igniting. Wave after wave of departing missiles shakes everything in the room.

Two displays materialize over the console; one shows the globe with targets spread all through the realms, the other provides live data. Persephone looks at the information then panic overcomes her. The noise and clamor dissipate, leaving a symphony of electronics to join the sounds of the sobbing queen.

She limps away, holding her mouth with one hand while grabbing the side of the wall with the other; she wants to scream, to wale, to let all her emotions pour forth, but won't because this is a sacred place. She makes her way to a catwalk with an endless abyss below.

She stops midway on the metal corridor; it is evident now that it is suspended above a great height. She looks down at the darkness inviting her to descend. *No!* She screams in her head then continues her journey to the circular room at the end.

The doors slide open, lights brighten. A single medical bed is in the center with a glass covering suspended in the air. Persephone limps over to the bed, ready to lie there, to fade away into oblivion. She strips off her bloody clothing, letting it fall to the ground before she climbs on to the bed; it automatically inclines for her, causing her to cry out in pain.

She feels around the sides for a compartment, realizing that her wound has begun to bleed once more. Her fingers run over a switch. A chamber-door slides open on the bedframe, allowing her to snatch a medical kit. Hastily she retrieves a small packet. Tearing it open, she then smashes it on her exposed wound. A green gel forms. It quickly 'fizzles' into a white powder; she exhales with relief.

The glass covering descend on her, stopping three feet away. She selects a sequence of buttons on the bedframe. A screen materializes in the space in front of her. She clears her throat, wipes her tears. She was many things, and vain is one of them; she straightens out her hair while looking at her mirrored image on the screen. Satisfied, she selects another button.

She clears her throat, "It is now the age of Virgo. I am Persephone, Isis of Egypt. Daughter to the house ENlil. The true heir to all the lands of the east, the west, and Hyperboria."

The chamber lights begin to dim, causing her to pause to look around. This place is, after all, Lumeria, home to the sleeping forefathers. *What else lurks here?* She wonders. Time was not something she had.

She continues, "Wife to Osiris of house ENki. I commit myself to the long seep, though I fear I shall be dead before judgment day, at the time of the awakening. The world is in ruin. I am afraid that I played no small part in this."

She pauses, ready to confess her crime.

"I launched weapons that will devastate the planet. Outposts of ENlil shall be destroyed, including Hyperboria. Lands will be frozen, and others will be burnt; a combination of devastation engineered by my ancestors. But they did not unleash this on the world; it was I, Persephone that did.

In my ignorance, I also set forth a bioweapon, a plague for all Anuk, and those with our blood. I know not whether any of my kind or the watchers will survive; if shelter and care are sought in time, then maybe.

You exist only in essence now. With the help of my cousin Thoth, you shall be preserved through time, hidden away for your safety. When you are born, know that you are from me and your father, the great king Osiris."

Tears roll down her face.

"Treachery and betrayal have destroyed my house, your house. You are the heir to the world. I pray that you are born into one free from the failures of our kin. If not, then you must fulfill your destiny, bring order to chaos.

Judgment day is at the end of Virgo when the forefathers will rise. Destroy the house of ENlil before they bring on the destruction of humankind. Vengeance must rain down on them if they live.

I love you my child, more than I will ever be able to share. Rise above our nature, become a beacon of hope. Rise above the winds of time, let the light of Orion flow through you. Until we meet, in this life or the next, I love you."

She taps a switch, the screen dissolves. As she closes her eyes the glass cover descends on the bed, sealing her in. The lighting in the room goes out, with only the lights from the bed illuminating the darkness.

CHAPTER 13:
THE CITY THAT
NEVER SLEEPS

The capital of Atlantis, Atlas, is a sprawling metropolis on the northeastern side of the island continent. The 34 square miles of the city ends at the edge of a lush forest, which climbs up the side of a sacred mountain. At the top exists the majestic residence of the royal family. It is one hundred acres of highly protected land, with a magnificent palace looking down at the city; it was not always like this.

Almost 2900 years ago, the 'Bay of Atlas' welcomed survivors from the house of ENlil. It was here that the sole surviving brother of the usurpers in Hyperboria, Atlas, would establish his power base.

He arrived with his household, some ten thousand strong, made up of servants, family, and military. They once lived on the borders of Hyperboria and Illyria, somewhat removed from the surgical strikes unleashed from Lumeria. Their lands were overcome with the 'Black Death,' so they fled out into the world, eventually arriving in Atlantis.

The early settlers faced some hardships adapting to the new land, mainly due to resistance to integration with the local inhabitants; it was not long before the tribal population was subdued. A large city was built, which quickly turned into a sprawling metropolis.

Today, the wealth of the empire can be appreciated just at the sight of the capital. New temples exist amongst old, including small pyramids scattered in the cityscape. Tall buildings flow towards the interior of the city, turning into skyscrapers reaching up to the clouds; stunning walls of glass have replaced the limestone blocks of the past. Monorails stretch throughout the skyline, with flying crafts gracing the restricted airspace.

~TIMON~

Prince Timon sees this view from his private quarters as he stands on his balcony in his underwear. He is forty-four years old, and rather short for an Anuk, quite possibly standing at five feet seven inches. His lean muscular build is a departure from his father's husky, barbarian sized frame. He exudes all the qualities one would expect from a prince, sharp features, neat dark hair, and arrogance in his voice.

The early morning breeze flows through the balcony, caressing large orchids spread across a wall. Timon stands at the banister looking out at the horizon. *How much longer must we endure the decadence of this world?* He ponders.

When he was thirteen, he was sent off to his cousins in Aryavan; he loathed the lot of them. 'Half-breed degenerates' is what he would refer to that royal family as.

Their predecessors had attempted to assassinate his father long before his birth, but fate turned the tables on them; that generation was annihilated from existence. Only one minor Aryan house remained to take up the mantle of sovereign.

As a pawn in his father's political game, Timon was to remain in Aryavan for five years, serving as a prisoner from his point of view. It was not all bad though, for he would learn their ways, but more importantly, their weaknesses. He secretly made plans for the future; ideas that would make the Aryans pay for his indenture-ship, along with everything else he didn't like about the world.

Something unexpected happened just after his sixteenth birthday, he fell in love.

Leena, an Illyrian noble girl, was sent off to Aryavan on her sixteenth birthday; the Illyrians practiced a similar form of 'Royal hostage' to the Atlanteans, but theirs lasted two years. Her presence made Timon's remaining time there bearable.

She was tall and elegant, raven-haired, with gentle features which made her appear kind; an attribute she naturally possessed. Leena always loved animals and helped the poor; there were so many poor souls in Aryavan. Both teenagers' stay in the kingdom ended around the same time. They were devoted to each other, so they made plans to get married in Atlantis.

It was a happy time for Timon, for the resentment he harbored since childhood was washed away by Leena's presence. Fate would intervene in their love affair; tragedy would strike the couple in Leena's hometown of Ganovce in Northern Illyria.

Ignoring every word of caution, Timon accompanied his intended wife to her home. They spent the winter there oblivious to the rest of the world, living a carefree life. One afternoon on their way to a transport bound for Atlantis, they were attacked.

Illyrian nomads descended upon the prince's party, killing everyone except Timon and Leena. The couple was whisked away deep into the unknown regions of the kingdom. Rape and torture were inflicted on both hostages until death would fall upon Leena. Timon was ultimately left to die in a swamp.

The memory still haunts the prince. Every day since he has sought a way to end the existence of the 'nomad scum.' Today, he is one step closer to see this happen, for secrets have been revealed to him. The priesthood has uncovered knowledge of a once mythical place called Lumeria. If the stories are correct about the power that exists there, then he can not only wipe the nomads out of existence, but he can also bring the world to yield. *For Leena,* he has convinced himself.

Timon stretches then makes his way back inside his large bedchamber. Fifty-feet away, two guards in red uniforms stand by the entrance; the Red-Guard, an elite royal order of mindless brutes, are always ready to serve their master. He walks over to his bed then looks at the lifeless naked girl lying there.

Her stomach is bloody from a half-inch wound; her neck is bruised from powerful hands that constricted around it. She was a mere servant who bore a small tattoo on the inside of her right forearm; the mark of a nomad tribe. The girl was an innocent refugee, serving the royal household faithfully for three years. Her innocence did not matter, for she was a nomad.

The prince walks towards the guards, "Get that out of my sight," he orders pointing at the body. "Burn the bed."

The guards open the chamber doors. Four male servants hastily enter. They collect the body with the prince's bloody clothing. As they hurry out, Timon's aide, Bana, enters the room.

Bana is a young, ambitious man in his early twenties. Son of a nobleman, he faithfully serves the prince and is privy to all his dealings. His neat, effeminate features fit well with his station. He has become arrogant with his high status.

Bana hurries in, "Your Highness, I have good news."

"It better be exceptional news Bana; it's too early to deal with you otherwise. What is it? Spit it out."

"The sacred texts have arrived. Lord Inias has it in his possession, and prince Varna will be escorting them here."

"Good," says the Prince. "Wine!" he shouts. An old bald servant hurries in; he stands motionless in front of the prince. "Well? Pour it you fucking twit." The frightened servant fills the cup, bows then leaves.

There is an awkward silence in the room as Timon gulps down his drink. Bana stands there, looking at him in his underwear. The aide has a particular inclination toward young boys, but this was a man, a prince no less. Silent lusting would be his only escape here; he gets lost in his thoughts.

"Bana!" the prince screams. "Where is Varna?"

"He left before sunrise," Bana responds, a bit flustered.

"And? Nothing? Get out." Timon is amused, knowing he has reminded Bana of his place in the scheme of things.

"Yes, your highness." Bana bows then makes his retreat.

The prince makes his way to a corner desk drawer; he drops a thin gold necklace with a blue opal gem attached. He took the piece from the dead servant, a trophy of sorts. It was turning out to be a good morning.

-CARRELL'S SHIP, ON THE BAY OF ATLAS-

The water approach into the capital goes through the 'Bay of Atlas.' It's a busy port, with dozens of sea vessels traveling daily. The waters leading up to the rocky cliffs are calm, crashing gently on to the high towers rising from beneath the ocean. A one-half mile apart, the towers reach 328 feet in the air, with large circular observation spaces at the top; glass windows wrap around the multi-level platform.

Inside the protected bay is the seaport itself. Giant circular port landings are scattered in the watery enclosure, with a variety of vessels parked alongside each other: military vessels, cargo ships, fishing boats, all litter the piers.

One mile out from the approach towers, a small passenger ship is inbound; the 'Rusty Anchor.' It's a crude vessel, probably older than any passenger on board; that is except the old Captain Carrell. It appears at first to be constructed out of wood, but it is a metal alloy with a painted illusion.

Hungry seagulls do nose-dives near the ship, scooping up their breakfast with enthusiasm. Some of the passengers run about the deck to look at the singing birds and the skyline of Atlas. The skyscrapers appear majestic behind the light mist in the foreground.

A ten-year-old girl runs along the deck holding her doll; her country dress flows in the wind. She smiles when she sees the ivory colored temples on the cliffs for the first time. The birds begin to intrigue her as they fly overhead, so she runs to the portside railing to watch them dive after their meal. A pair of large dolphins catches her attention. She is beside herself.

A man, huge by eight-year-old standards, steps behind her to block the early morning sun. Captain Carrell is a weathered old sailor, with a scruffy beard and skin of a leathery texture. A pleasant 'Grandpa-type,' with a pipe full of tobacco in his mouth, wearing a beat-up old captain's hat.

Carrell smiles at the girl, "Be careful missy, if ya fall in…they'll eat ya." The little girl is terrified. She scans the crowd back aft for her mother then runs off.

The captain smiles, knowing that he'd rather have to deal with a scared girl than a drowned one. *The brat was too close to the rails*, he tells himself. On his many journeys from Parthon to Atlas, someone always ends up in the water, but he has been lucky so far. He spots Alexius at the bow.

Carrell first met Alexius the day of his birth. The sailor saw a pregnant woman jump off the cliff in Parthon; luckily, he was able to dive in after her, successfully saving both lives. Since that day, Carrell has had the family of Lord Arias as his patron, bestowing wealth on him. For this old 'sea-dog,' the ocean is where he chooses to call home. He has been fortunate to join Arias on many adventures; oh, how he longs for those days.

"Quite a view isn't it?" he shouts out to Alexius after sucking on his pipe.

"This place has not changed. You still telling that stupid dolphin tale?"

The old man smiles, "Gives them a good fright each time. I'll bet she falls in before the towers."

They both look for the little girl. They see her hugging her mother safely in the center of the deck. Alexius pulls out one square piece of currency; the body is platinum with gold borders, with a golden emblem in the center; it is worth ten gold pieces. He slams it on a raised platform, encouraging Carrell to do the same.

"This place has not changed; garbage polished to look like pearls. Magnificent garbage all the same," Alexius points out.

"You should see Egypt then," Carrell says enthusiastically. "Not exactly the capital of Atlantis, but a different kind of magnificent."

"Any advice old man?"

Carrell looks over his right shoulder. He notices two beautiful prostitutes looking their way. The girls let the wind raise their sheer dresses, showing off the goods underneath. They blush with their seductive smiles.

"Sure," Carrell says in a serious tone, "I'll give you the same I always do, stay away from the 'Furry Chariot or you'll be a poor man by morning."

They both chuckle, and the old man slaps the younger one on his back. Suddenly, the boat engines stop, making the seagull's songs louder.

Blue beams shoot across the waters between the towers. A giant wall of light manifests itself, shimmers then disappears. One advantage the seaport has against any would-be ocean intruders is an invisible field barrier, able to withstand speeding crafts. The high towers scan incoming vessels, then decides whether to let them in or send them to a watery grave. Fortunately for this lot, it has been deactivated.

The boat engines hum to life, the craft pushes off. Passengers who haven't grabbed something substantial, rocks back suddenly. Everyone hears a scream then a splash. The little girl went over the side; not learning to hold on to the rails when looking for dolphins.

There is a look of disappointment on Alexius' face. The old sailor takes the cubit with a smile. They both look on at the skyline as the boat stops once more.

-EARLY MORNING AT THE FURRY CHARIOT-

At the edge of the busy commercial district and a residential one, exists the exclusive 'Furry Chariot Club.' The building is five levels high, sitting at the corner of 'Market Street' and 'Ocean Avenue.' It marks the very edge of the two districts.

The front of the building is adorned with expensive flowers, all spread out to give an appearance of elegance. The marble stairs are short, twelve in total, which leads up to dark, heavy doors. Urns are lit at the entrance, creating an ambiance of a temple; but this is no temple.

The interior décor of the receiving room teases the visitor with exotic paintings scattered amongst photos. There are also pictures of past events; a collection of erotic celebrations. The carpet is a rich burgundy color. There is always pleasant incense burning. The first person you will meet is a young, scantily clad, host or hostess.

Identification is required before proceeding further; those meeting you enforce this rule. A pair of inconspicuous guards, whom you shall never see, silently observes incoming patrons. Once your IDs are scanned, your credit established, you are free to follow your concierge.

The first area you will see is a long bar, stretching along the wall to the left. Behind the bar, at the center, there is an enclave with mirrors for walls; it seems quite out of place at first, but for the vain at heart, it's a welcoming spot. To the right is a moderately sized standing area, about 30 feet square; it ends at a stage for live entertainment.

Continuing past the end of the bar open booths appear; they can seat six in a semi-circle comfortably. These booths give way to a private area, with a more 'cozy' appeal. At first glance they appear open, but with the tap of a switch on the table, a barrier of light surrounds the booth, hiding whatever sordid activity is going on inside. At the end of the area is the manager's office.

The place is quiet now, with yesterday's crowd already disbursed; only a handful of people are moving about. The city's overnight workers usually visit at this time, either for a meal on the second level or a romp with one of the club prostitutes.

A single female sits at the bar holding a steaming cup of coffee; she's in her late twenties. Her long red hair is curly, falling comfortably on her petite frame. It matches her hazel eyes perfectly. Even though she stands at five-feet-seven inches, is 110 pounds soaking wet, her fiery temper manages to get her out of trouble, but mostly into it. Those she has inflicted her brand of mischief on refer to her as 'demon,' everyone else calls her Lyra.

Lyra sips her drink, nervously shaking her dangling feet like an overactive child. She occasionally checks the band on her left arm. She is interrupted by a well-dressed middle-aged man who came down a nearby stairway; his collar has the emblem of a city councilor.

The councilman stops at her side, "I think I am in love," he announces. He pulls a stool close. "You're new. How about an early morning ride?"

Lyra slams her cup on the counter, smiling at the man. The loud 'thud' alerts the manager, Rovina.

Rovina is a 'no-nonsense' woman, medium build, raven hair, and not only the manager but also somewhat of a sister to Lyra; her uncle Yanis is Lyra's guardian.

Lyra smiles seductively at the man, "You want to play do you? I'm not cheap. You look like you can afford to lose some coin."

The aroused Councilman moves closer to her, brimming with expectation. She spins on her stool, meeting his gaze.

He looks at her well-defined legs wrapped in expensive leather, then runs his hands up her thighs. She slaps his hand away then gives an innocent look.

"Three gold pieces," the councilman offers. "I've always wanted a redhead. Say, is it red down there too?"

"Seven and you can find out," she plays.

He dips in his pocket then holds out a handful of silver and gold cubits; he looks hesitant, "All I have are five-ers."

"I take those too." She gives him a naughty smile. He smiles back, beginning to rub his body on her.

His expression quickly changes to panic as Lyra now holds a thin blade to his testicles. He feels the point begin to pierce his trousers. Fear is quickly overcoming him. Lyra looks at him with a smile.

"Do I look like a working girl?" she grumbles. The Councilman nods, grunting his acknowledgment which aggravates her more.

Rovina quickly steps in, "Now now, the young lady here is a guest. How about I introduce you to some of our exclusive girls?"

As she begins to pull away from the relieved man, Lyra grabs three cubits from his hand while kissing him on the cheek. Rovina gives her a dirty look.

A beeping sound emanates from Lyra's armband. She reads the incoming message. She happily picks up her mug to slurp on the beverage. She stops then looks around; no one is near. She reaches over the bar, grabs a small bottle, then generously pours some of the liquor in her coffee. With as much haste she returns the container. Rovina approaches just in time to see the theft; all she does is shake her head.

Lyra pretends to be innocent, "Did master Yanis leave yet?"

"He just did. And would you stop attacking the customers," says Rovina as she makes her way behind the bar.

Lyra rattles her ill-gotten coin, "It has been a profitable morning." She gets serious. "The bitch just sent orders."

"Have some respect," Rovina chides. "What are they?"

"The books are at the 'Broken Temple,' in the old quarter."

"The abandoned one, by the river? No one goes there, not even in daylight. You'll need backup."

"No time. I need to get there, fast."

"Meet me by the waterside. Get Liviana her books, and maybe she will release you this time."

Lyra looks up at the ceiling, "It's not much to ask. To return to Egypt. To be a simple bar-wench?"

"You're never satisfied being simple at anything," Rovina points out. She makes her way to the glass wall in the center. A tap of a switch raises a section of glass, allowing her to disappear down a flight of stairs.

-BEHIND THE FURRY CHARIOT-

A rhythmic 'sloshing' sound can be heard from the water hitting the edge of the high retaining wall. Rich green moss covers the stone which spreads along a descending roadway to the left; a jetty jots out to the waters at the end. To the right are some stables belonging to a neighboring business.

Rovina is stroking the mane of an elegant horse, trying to calm the animal. About ten feet away from her, a hover-bike sits under a small shed. The vehicle is sleek; it looks like one of the newer models on the market. She sees a parking violation sticking out from under the seat.

Lyra strolls around the corner on the narrow cobblestone, oblivious to Rovina with the horse. A map on her band distracts her, up until she runs into the horse.

There is fear in her eyes, "You're not serious. I am not getting on that!" she exclaims with disgust.

Rovina shakes her head, "I just don't understand why you are afraid of horses."

"No," Lyra protests, "keep that thing away from me," she warns.

Rovina points to the hover-bike.

Lyra climbs on the bike. As she sits, she tosses the ticket on the street. She dons the

159

accompanying helmet as the engine ignites. The crisp sound brings joy to her face.

"Uncle Yanis will be back just after noon," Rovina yells. "Please return before he does. And oh, if you put a scratch on that, you'll have to pay for it."

Before pulling down the visor, Lyra looks at Rovina, "I am just a poor little bar-maid," she declares sarcastically.

The bike rises three feet in the air when the stands retract. Lyra engages the throttle, speeding off in an instant.

CHAPTER 14:
FROM MY
HANDS TO
YOURS

A light mist rolls over small hills just outside the
dusty Illyrian border-town of Harappa. There is a
slight layer of frost on the ground mixing with the
brown color of the land. Some trees are scattered in
the landscape, not the kind you will find in the lush
forests of Illyria or Atlantis. These were the kind
you would find in an arid place. Such was the
condition of this one-time oasis called Harappa.

Before the Great War, this was a lush land
teaming with wildlife. Harappa was a trading town
on the border of Aryavan; the truth is that it was
more Aryan land than Illyrian. The people were pure
Aryans who took advantage of the economic
prosperity of Illyria, while still adhering to their
Aryan culture; the same holds true three thousand
years later.

Devastation from nuclear-type weapons
overcame the area. Deserts formed, life was
decimated. It was not until a mysterious group of
refugees settled here that the town was resurrected.
Since then, Harappa was considered neutral territory
during the Illyrian conflict with Aryavan.

Today, the town is a sleepy one, with a
population of roughly fifteen thousand strong.
There are no armies here, nor are there any from the
ranks of the Priesthood. Only religious sorts who

follow some ancient cult, long dead to the rest of the world.

The town itself covers an area of 377 acres. Stone buildings inside Harappa's walls glisten with the ever-present sun. Foot traffic is frequent, although you will see many ox-drawn carts. There is a feeling of poverty in the place; this, of course, is what an outsider accustomed to the more delicate things would feel.

With their heads covered with cloaks, Liviana and Mica make their way down a dirt street, heading towards a remote corner. An ancient temple exists there. Today is a special day, a holy day. It's one where the religious gather to pay homage to the long-dead Mithra, a goddess from the 'time before.'

Mudbrick buildings litter the narrow street filled with open-air peddlers. Flowers, ceramic ornaments, fruits of all kind are displayed. These are offered to the 'holy-rollers,' as they make their way to the temple. *Why would one ever think these people are Illyrians when they are clearly Aryans?* Mica thinks to himself.

"What?" Liviana asks.

"I didn't say anything…except that I'm hungry."

"Oh don't start. We're almost there." Liviana stops at a baker's stall, grabs a loaf, drops a coin, then breaks the treat. "Here." She gives him the smaller piece.

"Some wine would be nice," Mica complains but silences himself after getting a sharp look from Liviana.

They walk briskly to a corner, eating the bread; it is baked with cheese and a generous serving of cilantro.

The thickening crowd can only mean one thing; the temple is near. A left turn merges into a slow-moving crowd of hundreds, flowing into a bottleneck at the temple entrance.

The structure is constructed of limestone with intricate carvings on the walls. Demons, strange animals, warriors drape every square inch of the temple's face. It is a haunting image to see the peculiar religion existing in this backward part of civilization. The many devotees chant names of long-forgotten deities, bearing no resemblance to anything the strangers have witnessed before.

"What makes you think the old crone will see you?" asks Mica.

"My father once told me that she is the keeper of secrets. I cannot trust that Lyra will retrieve the ancient texts, so we come to Old Mother to learn what we can."

"If anyone can get those books, it's Lyra."

Liviana looks at him curiously. She hands him her unfinished portion of the bread, which he takes gratefully.

"Even though she will cut your throat the first chance she gets; you still praise her?" Liviana asks.

"I deserve it, just don't tell her that," Mica admits.

They begin their push through the crowds, squeezing past all sorts of worshipers; old, young, smelly, clean. The task seems almost impossible at this point. Nevertheless, they carry on, hoping to gain an audience with the one called 'Old Mother.'

-THE STREETS OF ATLAS-

Vehicular traffic is as it always is at this time of the morning, unforgiving. The noise of the hustle and bustle is ever present in the commercial district. Tall buildings block out most of the sunlight.

High Priest Calis was gracious enough to pick up Alexius at the pier, a gesture welcomed by the young soldier.

They sit in the back of the comfortable car making their way to the local garrison. The journey from the port district to their destination, which is located on the opposite end of the city, would usually take thirty minutes without traffic; in this mess, it will be another hour before they arrive.

"The one thing I miss about the country is the free open roads. Not this infernal noise and commotion," Calis explains.

"The price to pay to live in this cesspool," Alexius admits.

"Yes, I suppose you are right. So, you are still determined to make your way to the Far Wes Continent?"

Alexius smiles, suspicious of Calis. "That's what's planned unless fate intervenes."

There was something about this priest, an unnerving feeling. Alexius could not put his finger on it just yet. The interest Calis had taken in him was uncomfortable, with an ever-present sense that it had something to do with Arias' journal. More importantly, the family heirloom he had inherited seemed to be mixed up in the theft of the ancient books.

"I can't wait to see Deidra," Alexius says. "She will be upset I did not ask her to meet."

Calis struggles to find the right title, "Is she your…"

"No…" Alexius answers smiling, "…just a friend. I've known her half my life now. She is a loyal confidant."

"It's good to have trustworthy friends these days. I hope you will consider me as such."

The driver is becoming frustrated, which is evident in his grumbling. He very aggressively swings the car into a nearby alley, then speeds down a clear path to another street.

"The day is young. Tell me, Lord Calis, what was my father and his secret circle up to?"

There is some hesitation from Calis. He begins to speak, but then has a look of fear as he glances at Alexius' window. A large truck slams into the side of the car, sending it crashing into a wall. Everything instantly goes black.

A five-foot-seven slim figure dressed in dark clothing and a cloak jumps out the truck and makes their way to the smoking vehicle. Shattered glass is everywhere. The wind blows over the figure's hood, revealing a female in her mid-twenties, with a blonde head of hair pulled back tightly into a ponytail. Subtle tattoos mark her face.

The traffic has stopped. People stare at the agile woman making her way to the crash. No one attempts to step out to help, they only observe.

The attacker yanks off the door between her and Alexius; he is unconscious. She drags the soldier's large frame with ease, not looking back at Calis' motionless body. She loads Alexius into her vehicle then gets into the cab. With some maneuvering she clears her truck from the area, quickly disappears through an alley.

It doesn't take long before the emergency services arrive. Pedestrians have now gathered around the crash site, looking on at the seemingly lifeless High Priest. An older lady begins to weep when she recognizes Calis.

A paramedic attending to the injured man raises his hand to another, giving him a 'thumbs up'; the weeping lady sighs with relief. As with any event in Atlas, the media arrives, setting up their broadcasts. Still, no one knows what just happened.

-SOMETIME LATER, IN THE OLD QUARTER SEWERS-

One marvelous innovation of the first builders of Atlas was the complex sewer system. They by no means invented it but improved upon older models from Hyperboria. It is as complex as the subway system, with tunnels leading to various parts of the city. Each area has a designated address which can be traversed by refugees and villains alike.

They all look the same; murky, damp, dark, filled with rodents. The dismal surroundings do not affect the woman currently observing her chained prisoner. She stands quietly against a wall. Six feet in front of her, Alexius is tied to a metal pipe.

A thick chain wraps around his wrists, traveling seven feet up to the ceiling. He hangs from his wrist, stretching his body to the ground. His knees are bent, his head is down, his body is limp. Slowly, he begins to regain consciousness.

Everything is blurry as his eyes open. The pressure on his wrists is now becoming apparent, he begins to straighten out his legs, standing slowly. There are only a few inches of relief as the chain eases tension. He looks at the female.

"Who are you?" Alexius demands aggressively. He shakes the chains, testing their strength.

"I am Ayala, a watcher of the old order," the woman responds.

"What the fuck do you want with me?"

Ayala moves closer, never smiling, never expressing emotion. She looks up at her prisoner, paying attention to her distance. She knows he could wrap his legs around her, or fire off a kick.

Ayala looks Alexius in the eye, "My master has sent me to collect you, and for the secrets you carry."

"Look, lady, I don't know your master, and I don't have secrets. Now let me down!"

The watcher dips into a concealed pocket in her jacket, producing a small cylindrical device about six inches long, one inch thick.

A small needlepoint at the tip worries Alexius; he begins to struggle. "What are you doing with that?"

"Blood contains secrets which can be hidden away," Ayala explains. "Only to be revealed by those who know how to find them." She lifts his shirt, exposing skin, then sticks the injector into the bare flesh. "Secrets are in your blood…or not. My master will decide."

Alexius' blood flows into the tube. *She couldn't do this when I was out?* He thinks to himself.

For a moment, Ayala's guard is down as she secures the cylinder. Alexius uses this opportunity to pull on the chains, lifting himself off the ground. As he rises, he raises his right knee, connecting it with the watcher's jaw. She stumbles back. He drops back to the floor then springs back up again, flipping his body with upward momentum.

His feet are flush with the stone ceiling for a split second. He springs off toward the ground, head first. The tension created on the chains as he yanks with his fall, causes the metal pipe to break. The chains fall free to the ground.

He uses it as a weapon, connecting the surprised watcher across her body. She falls to a corner, quickly moving to avoid another blow. Alexius removes the chains then springs at Ayala; he is surprised at his sudden agility. He glides down on her, channeling his power into his right fist, throwing it at the watcher's face. She moves like the wind. His fist crashes into the stone wall, creating rubble in its wake.

Ayala connects him with a powerful kick to the face, sending him reeling. Alexius blocks her path, causing panic to step in. *If I could get to the river,* she contemplates. She sees a nearby crevice with a channel. She charges, aiming at Alexius' stomach.

He blocks her quick hands. He picks her up, slams her on a wall while still holding on to her; he slams again, and again, like a dusty rug being beaten on stone. He feels her body go limp.

Alexius tosses Ayala's body towards a far wall. Her head hits hard on the stone. Her body rolls into a depression then splashes into the water.

It flows towards an outlet to another area leading out to the river.

~*WATCHERS*~

Since the time of the forefathers, there has existed the order of the watchers. They were numerous once, but through the ages, up until the time of Persephone, there were only dozens left. The order had seen a decline due to flaws in their engineering; intentional genetic manipulation. They were a hybrid race designed by the Anuk.

Initially, they were made to assist the great Anuk rulers in all things; military matters, religion, even government were areas they served. They were, in essence, the first Priesthood. As eons passed, there was little need for the sect of unique humans, for the multitude of man seemed to be a more docile workforce.

A watcher is primarily a hybrid of Anuk and man; not a mixed race as in the later interbred population, but rather the product of DNA encoding. Like a mass-produced vegetable, watchers were grown at specialized facilities. The early products made to live for thousands of years; companions to the long-lived Anuk of their age.

After the forefathers' time, when the Anuk only lived a fraction of their predecessor's lifespan, the watchers' genome was manipulated; they were subdued, life shortened. Some heretics described it as being 'domesticated.' Their worth was devalued to that of servants, serving the house to which they bore allegiance.

Watchers were now susceptible to an encoded 'death date,' which ensured they would expire after they were needed no more. Ironically, a secret band of watchers began to procreate, evolving past what Anuk scientists had programmed out of their genome. This miracle in part ensured the race would live on. The future generations were not numerous as hoped, and they did not possess the abilities of their ancestors.

Speed, stealth, enormous strength persisted; super intelligence did not. The 'loyalty' trait was still ingrained in them, but at the onset of the Great War, the order fractured into heretics and loyalists. One side served Thoth of house ENki, the other house ENlil.

Some survived the 'Black Death,' in part to their mixed heritage, but many died off. Soon they faded into myth. They exist in the shadows; a mystery lost to antiquity. They only now emerge at this time of the awakening, and their intentions are unknown.

-AT THE BROKEN TEMPLE, OLD QUARTER-

The old-quarter of Atlas is a dismal place. It is home to some of the less fortunate citizens and refugees from the borderlands. Ghettos are spread out in a three-mile radius, plagued by rampant crime.

A small town exists near a river that flows into the ocean. The residents there are mostly poor merchants, serving the area as best as they could. They even have a small bazaar by the water, peddling their merchandise to earn an honest, and sometimes dishonest living. The civil patrols do come by, but they allow the illegal activities to persist; here corruption runs deep in the police force.

Nearly twenty years ago a grand temple stood near the river; now it is just a dilapidated shell of what it once was. When cheap urban housing was being constructed, a street formed from the temple onwards. The structure in a way serves as a marker to the edge of the township.

The temple was never torn down, as it was looked upon as holy ground. That did not stop vandals from ransacking the insides, nor did it prevent drug dealers from setting up their stations within. Today, it serves as a meeting place for Prince

Varna of Aryavan, and Archon Inias. Two cars are parked in front of the broken building.

Varna steps out of his vehicle. He is a sharp looking man, about thirty-six. His features are rugged and muscular, his skin tanned from the eastern Aryan sun. He sports a neatly cut short beard, which accentuates his short hair and expensive dark clothing.

He steps on to the deteriorating stairway, then heads to a group of five men standing at the entrance. He sees Archon Inias smiling warmly at him. He also notices the four bodyguards who are carrying side arms. He laughs at the thought of betrayal; he welcomes it.

"Archon Inias," says Prince Varna.

"Your Highness," Inias responds with a smile. "I trust you were free from incident on your way here? Shall we go inside? These parts are not kind to royalty; less so to nobility."

Varna smiles at Inias' reference to himself as being 'nobility.' It is true, he was soon to be bestowed with the title of Archenias, 'The Grand High Priest of the Priesthood,' and High Priests were usually considered 'Lords' in their own right; but these mere men were not noble in Varna's eyes. The two men disappear into the structure, followed by a servant carrying a chest. The others remain outside.

Unseen by the group, a solitary figure is observing the activity behind a far wall. Lyra drops her binoculars to check her sidearm. She carefully retreats alongside the wall towards a far entrance to the place.

Inside the temple, broken statues, garbage, and graffiti are everywhere. The interior is dark; water dripping makes an echo in the filthy surroundings. Varna and Inias stand not too far from the entrance, taking advantage of the light outside. Inias' servant holds quietly with the chest in his hand. Varna looks at the servant, then back at Inias.

"Oh not to worry, he can't hear a thing," Inias explains. "Most of the personal servants in the priesthood are deaf. We see to it early on."

"Are these the books for Timon?" Varna asks pointing to the chest. The servant opens the box, displaying the sacred texts. Varna picks one up.

Inias smiles, "Nomad terrorists attempted to steal these in Illyria. A strange coincidence is it not? What do you suppose Prince…"

"Who knows what my cousin's intentions are," Varna quickly interjects. "I am not privy to his motivations."

Inias decides not to press the issue. He looks at Varna trying to read the Anuk symbols. He tried to translate a few passages himself, but the entire attempt was all too frustrating. There were many interpretations of each word. Each carried a different meaning based upon the pronunciation.

"I mean no disrespect," Inias interrupts, "can you read the text?"

Varna slams the book shut causing an echo, "Sadly, my family's lack of pure blood ancestry dismisses us to any…pure knowledge. No, I cannot read the text." He tosses the book back into the chest.

"This transaction will not be on record as agreed," Inias states.

Varna nods. He moves closer to Inias, "I am afraid I need more of your assistance."

There is a brief silence; Varna motions the servant away. He dips into his jacket to retrieve a small tube.

Curiosity overwhelms the Archon, "I am your servant of course. What is this?"

"From the expedition Timon has in our southern islands. You know the secret one to find Lumeria."

Inias' eyes widen with the accusation. He becomes noticeably uncomfortable; his lips tremble, "Did they find it?"

"I do not know. All communication has been lost. These are all the groups' transmissions for the past year. There is no trace of the expedition."

"The high priest assigned was a dear friend," Inias expresses solemnly.

"I sometimes wonder," Varna begins looking at Inias' head, "who is the more powerful, us the royal bloodline of the Anuk, or the priesthood." Inias takes the tube with shaking hands. "I will send you the encryption keys later on," Varna informs him.

"Have you seen the transmissions?" Inias asks.

"Yes," Varna responds. "Most of the data is corrupted. What survives are only images, archaic symbols, more of the ancient tongue."

"Then best let Prince Timon have it."

"No," Varna snaps, "not yet. He gets his books, I have this, for now. You know how impatient Timon is. Best give him a complete report." He grabs Inias' hand. "Just as you are powerful Archon Inias, so am I. I consider you a smart man. This particular item stays within the privy of you and me." Inias nods and then bows.

Suddenly, a loud 'boom' from a weapon echoes. The servant drops to the ground clutching his sides. Another shot echoes more intensely; this time a trail of smoke follows a projectile heading to the exit walls.

An explosion rocks the interior. Debris falls between Varna, Inias, and their exit. The Archon frantically ducks inside an enclave. Varna does not move. Instead, he looks around for the attacker.

Lyra is behind a broken wall, about thirty feet away from Varna. She sees him smiling. *What the fuck have you gotten yourself into?* She thinks. She decides that avoiding a fight will be in her best interest.

"All I want is the chest!" Lyra shouts.

Varna smiles, "Then you will have to come get it" he announces arrogantly. "Don't be shy…come on."

A shot flies towards Varna. As the hot projectile nears his head he shifts his body, it misses. Another bullet comes his way, with the same result.

"Are you fucking shitting me?" Lyra mumbles.

She looks out at the cowering Inias. The servant is crawling towards a hole in the rubble. Varna has his hands in the air, still smiling. She pulls her hood over her head, checks her pistol, then begins her charge.

While running Lyra fires her weapon. He once again successfully avoids the bullets. It doesn't take long for her to reach him.

Varna expertly deflects the small female's blows, disarming her in the process. She gets an unexpected kick through to his stomach, which sends him reeling back. He glances over at Inias who has grabbed the chest. He is almost at the exit hole.

Varna picks up an iron rod, then sends another to Lyra; she picks it up. They strike at each other, whirling and connecting the rods, engaged in a deathly dance. At one point Lyra is locked in close to Varna, but he does not deliver a devastating blow; he is enjoying himself.

"Did you think that it would simply go from my hand to yours?" Varna asks as he pushes her off, relishing in her frustration. "It's a shame if I were to kill you now."

"It's a shame that I would disappoint you," she responds.

173

The rods slam into each other. Varna knocks Lyra's weapon down. He grabs her then tosses her several feet across the room. He looks at the exit hole once more; Inias is gone.

"I'd love to stay and fight," he declares, "but I have to go. Come find me; show me what's under that hood."

He runs towards the makeshift exit. Inias' men begin firing their weapons at Lyra. She grabs her empty gun. She dives across some rubble.

It doesn't take long for Lyra to make it outside. She runs down the concrete alley, heading to her hover-bike. To her horror, she sees a large man attempting to start the vehicle. *It figures I'd get robbed. Rovina is going to kill me,* she complains. She pushes herself hard to reach the thief before he takes off.

Alexius is on Lyra's bike, struggling to start the thing. He finally engages the igniters, evident by that glorious hum. He taps some switches, the stands retract. He is about to engage the throttle when he feels someone grab on to him. A second later shots fire past his head.

"Go!" Lyra screams.

More shots ring past them as they speed off down the alley. After a minute of traveling at nearly 120 miles per hour, Alexius slows the bike. He brings it to a stop at the edge of the ghetto. He turns to see Lyra's furious expression.

She slams the butt of her pistol on his temple, sending him falling to the ground. She slides forward looking at Alexius rubbing his head.

"Serves you right for stealing my ride," Lyra says before speeding off.

Alexius shakes his head, admitting that a girl bested him. He did, after all, try to steal her bike. *This is just not my day. I'd better call Deidra,* he decides.

CHAPTER 15: IT'S IN THE BLOOD

In the sewers there are always some things that never go away; the dark, the dampness, the ever-present dripping of water. Everywhere there is always water dripping into something, creating that infernal 'drip' sound. If one were to live down here all their life, it would not be such a bother, but for Samiri, it drives him crazy.

The creature who sits in a dimly lit enclave was once a man; what exists now can barely be considered one. He appears to be in his fifties, with long dark, greasy hair. His clammy white skin has a texture of oatmeal in the candlelight, which goes well with his sinister face. His clothing is a 'mish-mash' of old filthy rags, filling his medium frame and short stature. There is an air about him, a stench you can say, of death and misery.

Samiri has lived in Atlantis for a long time. He was a companion to Alexius' father, Arias. Together with Darius, Calis, and on many occasions the King, these five adventurers would travel the world for whatever glory held their interests. Not much is known about him except that he is a foreigner; Illyrian most likely.

His attention is currently on his meal. He sits on a wooden chair held together by thin dark rope. His metal dinner plate is on a stone table, which he managed to shape out of a broken column. He regards his meal with delight; a swirl of potatoes, rat meat, with moss for garnish. Thin fingers with overgrown nails claw at the roasted rodent. He picks it up, bites into the flesh, relishing the flavor.

There is a tunnel across from the chamber he sits in. Approaching light with accompanying footsteps make their way through the stone passageway. He looks at the intrusion, protecting his plate as if he is about to be robbed. Calm overcomes him when he sees Prince Timon. That resolve disappears when two Red Guards appear behind the prince.

"How dare you summon me like a commoner!" the prince screams as he nears the wretch. Samiri springs off his seat.

"Forgive me, your highness. I meant no ill."

Timon puts his hand over his nose as he stands next to Samiri. He looks at the dinner plate and scowls, "Well, what is it?"

Samiri raises a bony finger, "Agents of our enemies have entered Harappa. They must not be allowed to converse with the one called, Old Mother."

"What the fuck are you talking about? Who is Old Mother, and why should I care?"

"She is the keeper of forbidden knowledge."

"That is just a myth; a legend cooked up by fanatics. An old tradition long lost with my ancestors. Besides, Harappa is Illyrian sovereignty; you want me to start a war before it's time?"

"Surely you have allies who can do your bidding?"

"Surely you have minions that can do yours! Take care of your problem. I have my own concerns." Timon backs off from Samiri, unable to bear the smell.

"We cannot let…" Samiri stops mid-sentence when the prince glares at him.

"We?" Timon asks. "Who is this, we?"

Samiri takes a step back, "Very well my prince; I shall do what I can."

Timon begins to leave. He stops at the center of the chamber before entering the tunnel. The dingy walls are annoying him.

"Why do you continue to refuse my offer for better accommodations?" Timon asks.

"My condition forbids sunlight as you know. The sewers are my only refuge," Samiri explains.

Timon grunts to himself. He steps in a puddle which aggravates him some more. "I've been fortunate to be without prying eyes for a few weeks. I think it's safe to indulge in your welfare a bit." He begins his retreat from the place but stops again. "Oh, I almost forgot; get your potion ready, we have a candidate." This time he leaves.

The footsteps disappear down the tunnels from which they came. Left alone at last, Samiri walks over to a portion of the stone wall. He touches what appear to be mere scratches on the stone; these are in reality hidden switches.

As the wall slowly swings open, the sound of stone dragging on stone causes a rumble. Samiri quickly enters a hidden tunnel. It is a short walk ending at another enclave. He sits on a stone block then stares down at a console; it doesn't look like any in Atlantis.

The tap of a few symbols causes a screen to materialize in the air close to the wall. The images are just static. Samiri patiently waits for something, maybe someone to appear. He looks down at the ground at his loathsome feet. Longing for the dinner plate overcomes him.

-DEIDRA'S APARTMENT-

One of the perks of being a captain in the Atlantean Foreign Legion is the ability to have one's own lodging. The Foreign Legion, after all, was

177

always on assignment; at times for years on end. But for the small contingent stationed in the capital, they can enjoy some little luxuries.

With the influx of troops returning from Illyria, Deidra was lucky to find her apartment at the rate she did. Rent was not cheap here. Finding decent housing on a soldier's pay, well, that was like finding a needle in a haystack. She earned one thousand ducats, or gold pieces, each month. Her rent was four hundred ducats.

Nevertheless, the apartment was on the second level of a busy restaurant on 'Food Alley' called, 'Number one Aryan food restaurant.' It was spacious for a single person, with a large sitting room, and a bedroom of comparable size; what else could she possibly need? Because of her unwanted house guest, additional space is desirable.

Running water from the bathroom can be heard in the sitting area. Deidra fumes as she checks the clock; Alexius has been in there for almost thirty minutes. She jumps off her comfortable couch to storm into the bedroom. She sits on the bed looking at the bathroom door.

"Chow is going to be mad with the amount of water you're wasting!" she yells. "You're not rubbing one out are you?" The water stops.

"Who is Chow?" Alexius yells back.

Alexius finally comes out of the bathroom. He looks at Deidra attempting to pout; she appears awkward trying to be a girl. He smiles at her feeble attempt.

"He's the landlord. He owns the restaurant downstairs," she explains.

"Enterprising fellow. Hey, thanks again for picking me up."

"No problem your majesty." She drops down below the bed to pull out a bag. "Today I was your taxi, your slave. Here, you left this at the crash."

She drops his leather bag on the bed; she did not know why she was angry with Alexius. It could be because she found out about the attack from the news reports or the fact that he refused to go to the hospital. It could also be that after all this time, she is still listed as his emergency point of contact. She folds her arms observing him rummage through the bag.

Alexius retrieves his father's journal. He knew this would put her in an even fouler mood.

"Is that it, your stolen book?" Deidra says pointing.

"It belonged to my father, see here." Alexius opens the page with his family crest, then to the part which mentions him by name. "By right its mine." He gives it to her.

Deidra looks at the inscriptions. She fans through the pages ending at the map of Cappadocia. A moment passes as she reads, then she returns the journal to him.

"Whatever is going on is beyond anything I'm prepared to get involved with," she declares.

"You don't have to get involved with anything. This burden is mine to bear."

"And what about today? What was that all about?" she asks.

"I don't know. I don't know much of anything anymore. What I do know is that I cannot go to FaW-C. I'll have to convince Andros to change my orders."

Alexius pulls out a small case from the bag. He opens it up, displaying two layers of trays containing money.

The hard currency system throughout the empire was simple. Since Atlantis was the most influential civilization, their system is honored by everyone. One ducat is worth ten silver pieces; one silver is worth ten bronze; one bronze is worth five coppers; one copper is well one copper.

For the snottier folks, there were the higher denominations called cubits; they were slightly larger than a coin, rectangular shaped, with a body of platinum. A pure platinum cubit is worth one thousand ducats; there are other denominations all the way down to a cubit that's worth ten ducats.

"No," Deidra protests.

"But I haven't asked anything," Alexius says while smiling.

"If Andros changes your orders, you can't stay here. I was lucky to find this place fully furnished. I'm sure you will find something too." She looks at the money, "You can stay at a snotty lodge. Whose money is that anyway, I thought you didn't have any."

"It's a loan from my brother. I don't trust anyone but you. Come on. It will be like old times."

"That's what I'm afraid of," Deidra grumbles under her breath. "You do know you're not sleeping on this bed."

"If I had a pair of tits you would let me," he jokes. Deidra hits him with a pillow.

He quickly gets dressed as Deidra picks up the journal again. He makes his way to the other side; she doesn't complain.

"That bitch today stuck me with something; took blood." He points to the needle marks near his abdomen; the area is turning blue.

"Should have gone to the hospital," Deidra says sarcastically.

She tosses the book into the bag. She turns to see Alexius falling asleep. *Sleep you little shit. I hope you get your orders changed,* she admits to herself. It was too early to go to sleep, but she was exhausted; it was only eight O'clock. She reaches over to the nightstand to touch a small switch. The lights go out.

-SACRED TEMPLE AT HARAPPA-

It is midnight at the pagan temple. It was a busy day with Old Mother seeing nearly two hundred supplicants; over one thousand remains. The holy day does not end with the sunset, but instead, it continues for seven days. The twelve hundred or so worshipers will have another chance to see the revered one. For now, they all sleep on the spacious five-acre grounds behind the temple.

Small tents are scattered around an open garden area. Green grass that spreads out like a carpet is almost an unnatural occurrence in such abundance. Water fountains flow into a long rectangular enclosure. Two figures lurk once more in the bushes, again on the holy ground.

"I don't know why we can't just wait for daylight. We only have one hundred fools ahead of us," Mica fusses softly.

"The truth is, they don't see the real Old Mother," Liviana explains.

There is some confusion on Mica's face, but he puts off asking his question to scale the nine-foot wall ahead of him. Liviana effortlessly jumps to the top. She lays flat on the surface then sticks her hand out towards him. Once the two are at the top, they scurry across to some thin overhead pipes.

They shimmy across a twenty-foot gap, over a deep gorge; the drop is 97 feet into a dried-up ravine. After a couple of feet away from the wall, they attach lines to the downward sloping pipes to begin a rapid descent.

The pipes end at a conical mountain's ledge; it looks like a giant ant hill. More of the dusty mountains litter the desert behind the temple grounds.

With some effort, they make it across. As the pair drop to the dusty ledge, they look out to their left at the open desert and the night's sky in the horizon. Stars fill the darkness, and a small moon provides some light.

"What is it, like just after eight in Atlantis? It's Happy hour at the Furry Chariot," Mica ponders loudly.

"Be quiet," Liviana reminds him.

They make their ascent along the ledge; it narrows as it goes up to the top. The journey is not a long one before reaching a small cave. The pair stops at the entrance, cautiously peering in.

Mica scans the space with his band; a hologram materializes above his arm, displaying an empty cave. They enter looking around the small area. The blue light illuminates the low ceiling and flat ground. A metal circle, about six feet in diameter, beckons ominously by just sitting there.

Liviana looks at Mica then at the floor, "Well, we've come this far." They both step onto the platform.

"How'd you know to come here anyway?" Mica inquires while holding on to Liviana.

"I didn't. It's just a memory from childhood."

The edges of the perfect circle light up as they begin to descend to the inside of the small mountain.

~*LIVIANA (Age 05), HARAPPA*~

The rumble of a large craft invades the serenity of the desert afternoon in Harappa. The Atlantean transport hovers next to small mountains behind the ancient temple. The craft positions itself next to a cave. A ramp extends to a dirt ledge, allowing a large man to stride across; he carries his little daughter in his arms.

-LATER THAT NIGHT-

A fire ceremony is underway on a cliff; the landing is sizeable, able to hold a comfortable gathering of seventy people. There is chanting, dancing in circles, with the required smoking of sacred herbs.

In the center near the fire, a bundle of blankets covers Liviana. She is sweating profusely; her body is desperately trying to release her from the clutches of a deadly fever. It is no ordinary fever, for this illness had taken her mother's life two days earlier.

Strange men had abducted her and her mother during their trip to Illyria. Her mother was infected with a deadly virus; Liviana was sentenced to be slaughtered. In a surprising turn of events, she killed the attackers, as young as she was, but not before she was infected. Her father found her after an exhaustive search; everyone knew he would destroy the world to protect her.

Now, they turn to the one known as 'Old Mother,' to bring forth her ancient medicines; this was not the figure who sat in the temple just beyond the mountains; that was a decoy. The 'Old Mother' who saved Liviana was never one to be seen by ordinary people.

~AT THE BOTTOM OF THE MOUNTAIN~

The platform completed its descent, leaving Liviana and Mica facing a deep grotto. At the center is a marvelously carved stone platform. Raised above it is a gentle waterfall. A tree sits in the middle, quite out of place in this desert. A pond holds water with an eerie electrical glow.

Off to the right, seated eighteen feet up into the rocks, a dwelling can be seen. A solitary candle burns in a cavity in the shape of a window. The air is fresh, giving a pleasing atmosphere of peace in the place.

Mica turns off the light from his armband. He looks at Liviana with disbelief in his eyes. He feels her hand taking his as they stroll to the stone platform.

183

"This is the real Harappa Temple," Liviana explains. "Old Mother lives there." She points to the stone dwelling. "We will wait here."

They drop to the ground, with Liviana leaning on the short inside wall, and Mica cuddling up on her. There is no smart comment or complaint from him, just a silent form of reverence for the place. They close their eyes to take whatever gift of sleep they can have.

-BACK AT THE TEMPLE-

The area with the tents is quiet, with no one moving about except three figures dressed in dark clothing. They walk about as if searching for someone. Like a pack of wolves, they step through the area, peeking into the tents.

One of the men points to an area at the far wall, pondering on their strategy. He raises his hand to wave the others over.

-PRINCE TIMON'S ROYAL OFFICES-

The skyscrapers of Atlas rise high into the sky; some reach over 100 levels while others stand a mere 30; Prince Timon's office spaces occupy the twenty-first floor of one of the many shorter capital buildings. It was not as high up as he would have preferred, but he rarely spent any time in this place.

Timon's audience room is spacious, with high glass walls bringing the life of the city inside. There is a corner for working, an area for eating, one for entertaining. Tonight, he hosts Prince Varna, Bana, and two high-end escorts.

The two princes sit in the entertaining area, reminiscing about stupid things. Bana fumes in the kitchenette, preparing refreshments with two almost naked girls.

"Get away from me you creature," Bana hisses as one of the girls caresses his arm. He looks over to the men, wishing he was in their midst.

The chest of sacred texts sits on a center table; the men stare at it.

Varna point to the chest, "Are you going to share Timon?"

"Are you sure you want to know what I am up to cousin?"

"I can make a good summation of what you're doing." He looks over at Bana. "Us Aryans are not as oblivious to the world as you may think."

Timon chuckles, "I would hope not. Go ahead then, enlighten me."

"Our alliance…" Varna pauses. Satisfied they can't be heard, he continues in a whisper "…to attack the Illyrians is not enough for you. So, you've been searching for Lumeria, for the power allegedly hidden there."

"That's good. I knew you would figure it out eventually."

"You could only keep your so-called research in the southern wastelands hidden for so long."

There is a smile on Timon's face. "It was honest research at first. That is until some artifacts were found. They presented clues, directions to the mythical Lumeria."

"You do realize that is all it is, a myth. Do you really think you will find power there? More importantly, if it is real, can you control it?"

Timon picks up one of the books. He fans through the pages, stopping at a random section. He displays it to Varna. "These books were part of the great library of Thoth, our ancestor. In it contains the ways and means to control that power."

"You're hedging your bets. You don't think Aryavan is ready?"

"I know you are not ready." Timon's accusation puts a scowl on Varna's face. "Don't be naïve Varna. If we went to war with all of Illyria today, your forces would be decimated, and mine would be crippled."

A brief silence passes; Timon begins flipping through the pages.

"Can you read it?" Varna asks.

"Barely; my sister can," Timon responds. He looks over to Bana, "Wine!"

As if on cue, Bana sashays over with a silver platter of expensive wine glasses. The two girls join the group, with each taking a pitcher to a prince. Timon returns his book to the chest then looks at Bana.

"Be a good boy now, secure those will you," Timon says to Bana.

Bana grabs the chest. He takes it to an open safe just above a fireplace. A roaring fire crackles beneath. He sticks the chest in the safe then taps a brick on the ledge. A large painting slides across the wall.

"I would have thought you would want those at the palace," Varna points out.

Timon looks at him intently, "Trust me. They are not safe at the palace. Too many sticky hands. No, they shall be safe here." There is a look on Varna's face, one which shows he is not convinced.

"Very well," Timon says. "They are merely baiting a lion."

"Bait? All this is a game?"

"It's a very, very big lion," Timon says while playing with his escort. "If you attack it head on, you may get eaten, but, feed it well; it will lead you to its den. When it's asleep, then you attack."

The girls giggle, not caring what schemes are being discussed. They only do their job, and they do it well. The princes continue to entertain themselves with the girls. That is Bana's cue to go outside to chat up one of the servant boys.

-LATER-

The audience chamber is dark; it is midnight. Timon and his guests have left, seeking entertainment elsewhere. They will not return tonight, for the social escapades of the princes are well known.

A slight rumbling comes from the ceiling; sounds like drilling. After a few seconds of the noise, a tile slides off revealing a gaping dark hole. A hood pops through with red hair falling out of the garment.

Like an insect dropping to the floor, Lyra attempts to be as quiet as she possibly can. She activates her armband, bringing up a 'V' shaped field of light. As she faces it to the walls, hidden areas are revealed. She doesn't see what she wants, so she makes her way to the fireplace.

"Now where would you be? Ah, obviously," she mutters as the image of a safe is displayed. She hurries to the front door.

She carefully drags a cabinet to the door, attempting to block the way in. Not satisfied, she piles a chair on top of it. She freezes as movement can be heard coming from outside. It is silent once more. Lyra runs back to the fireplace. Her armband begins to 'beep,' which startles her. She quickly touches her earpiece concealed beneath her hair. She is more annoyed that she did not silence the thing rather than the call coming in.

"What?" She snaps at Rovina on the other end.

"Where are you? You were supposed to stay here until I returned."

"I can't talk. Is there any change? Did something happen?"

"No...just get back as soon as you can." Rovina hangs up.

Lyra looks for a hidden switch through the 'V' field. She sees it; success, the large painting slides off to the side.

The safe's door has a series of buttons with a display. This would not be the first secured container Lyra has had to break into; included in her resume of mayhem is the occasional high-end theft. *This should be a quick in and out. Great name for a restaurant. Hmm, I'm hungry*, she muses.

With lock picking tools in hand, Lyra begins to work the mechanism. She attaches a tiny transmitter the size of a fingernail near the display, then continues to stick her 'picks' in the old-fashioned key-hole. She smiles with the ease at which her band's digital helper is cracking the combinations. Suddenly, alarms go off.

Instantly guards are at the door, pounding, pushing. Lyra tries to remain calm.

"Work the lock, work the lock, don't look," she tells herself.

The pushing on the door intensifies. A crack appears. Guards shout from outside; *How bad could it be...two, three?* Lyra wonders. She continues to work the lock, but then curiosity takes over; she looks at the door. *You Looked!* She complains.

A victorious 'click' brings relief to Lyra's panic. With haste, she tosses the books in her waiting satchel. *Time to leave,* she declares silently.

The doors burst open. Seven guards rush in desperate to catch the thief. One draws a pistol. Before he could get a shot off, a vase hits him squarely on the head.

The other guards surround Lyra, trying to push her in the center. The hole in the ceiling is too far away, and the goons are blocking the door. She looks behind her at the wall of glass. *No bitch, don't do it!* She warns herself.

They are 21 floors up. The structure is sloped slightly; this gives Lyra an insane idea. There would be no time to contemplate success or failure; two guards begin shooting at her. She dives for cover behind a couch.

She quickly taps a switch on her armband, bringing up a display of her hover-bike. She points her pistol at the glass wall. She empties her gun. Shattering windows let the howling wind blast in. Trying her best to avoid the bullets, Lyra dives out.

Fear overcomes her for a moment; that wash of uncertainty that blasts through your soul. Her body hits the downwards slope of the building, dropping rapidly. She desperately tries to steady herself. There is a straight drop coming up, somewhere around the tenth floor; she has to hurry.

She stares at her knees, fearful to look beyond that. Her stomach clenches up; even more than it did at the first fall. Gravity is pulling her down, the wind is blasting across her face, and her backside is numb from the ride down. She anticipates the drop off the side then leans her body forward, pushing off the edge.

There will be no time to think, with only one chance to get it right; she unhooks a small box from her belt. The casing falls apart revealing a thin coiled line with a hook tip at an end.

She sees the hover-bike rising rapidly on the third floor, then the sixth, now level with her body. She misses it by a foot. Quickly, she launches the line at the bike's frame. The cord wraps around a protrusion to secure itself.

The line quickly tenses up as it absorbs Lyra's falling weight. She holds on for dear life, trying not to scream with the pain of the constricting cord around her arm. Her fall is slowing as the bike begins to descend; hover-bikes could fly at altitudes of 120 feet.

Shots fly past her head from the guards high above. The bike fires thrusters as it nears the third level, then the second, now the first. Lyra is on the ground, ready to throw up whatever junk she ate earlier on. She frees herself of the cord, jumps on the bike, then speeds off.

That was a close one, she admits to herself. Now the problem was her cargo; it was too 'hot' to take back to the Furry Chariot. She speeds through her pre-planned escape route; narrow alleys seem never ending on her way to safety. There was one place Lyra could think of that would work as a hideout. She smiles with determination then realizes *Damn it. I've got to pee.*

-AT THE SACRED TREE IN HARAPPA-

The soothing darkness accentuated with the glowing blue light from the pond water has put the two visitors to sleep. They lay like children, bundled up together in the corner of the raised platform. Not much would be able to wake the exhausted travelers, not even the approaching intruders.

Three men come upon them behind the short wall. They look at each other signaling their intentions, trying not to make a sound. This would be an easy kill, a quick bounty.

Two men make their way behind the sleepers, positioning themselves close to their victims' throats; they draw daggers. The third intruder stands over them with his rifle pointed, ready to shoot. The rifleman nods to the other two. Their blades move in to make their cuts.

A subtle noise alerts the third man. He looks up quickly. The other two pause, expecting trouble.

An old woman, no taller than five feet, holds a staff three feet off the ground. She slams it on the stone floor creating an intense wave of light.

There is a sound which starts as a low drone, then turns into a high pitch, matching the light quickly flowing towards the intruders.

The men scream as the beams pierce through their bodies, dissolving flesh. They appear to be burning where they stand, like paper embers flying off in a light breeze. It takes but seven seconds for their screams to end; their bodies now turned to ash.

Liviana and Mica are awake, frozen in place, looking on in fear. They both snap their heads back to see the one called Old Mother standing there with a smile on her face.

"Old Mother," Liviana declares in awe.

Their savior stands there looking at them with love on her face. Her grey hair, weathered clothing, and delicate appearance makes her look like a grandmother, but more importantly, safe. They just lay there, not sure what to do next. Old Mother looks at them with a smile.

-SAMIRI'S LAIR-

It is the early morning above the sewers of Atlas; of course, down in these parts, it is always perpetual night. The creatures of the dark always move about not caring what time it is. This holds true in the lair of Samiri.

The wretch sits on the ground close to an urn with a roaring fire. He has a small pouch in front of him; he regards it as if praying to the contents. A sound in one of the tunnels alerts him. He grabs the pouch, quickly hiding it in his tattered rags. Ayala appears limping.

She is bloody; a sight Samiri cannot recall ever seeing. She makes her way over to the urn, stopping three feet away from her master. She holds her broken arm then looks down to the ground.

Samiri is irate. "You have failed me yet again. One simple task and you could not even do that," he snarls.

"The soldier surprised me; he is strong. I will not fail again."

"You let the son of Arias beat you. You should have prepared yourself."

The watcher's eyes widen at the mention of 'Arias'; it is as if she is surprised. She puts her hand in her inside jacket pocket, holding on to the cylinder of Alexius' blood.

191

"Well, did you at least draw his blood?" Samiri asks.

"No, master. I failed at that too," Ayala says while regarding the floor.

Samiri's anger begins to show on his face. He wants to spring up to her throat, to rip out her spine. As he starts to move his sacred pouch falls out of his rags, making a rattling sound as it hits the ground.

"Get out of my sight!" he screams.

Ayala turns away from Samiri. She limps off to a side tunnel, still trying to process the revelation of Arias' name. She looks at her master. He has resumed the worship of his pouch. She continues her departure, happy to be away from that creature.

Samiri empties the pouch's contents. Three small broken parts of a golden disc scatter on the stone. He arranges them into the circle they once were, but there is a piece missing. All the parts are metal, with gold plating over them.

Out of Samiri's sight now, Ayala creeps next to a small drain; dirty water flows from places all over, emptying into the underground pipes. She retrieves the cylinder of blood, and cracks open the seal. She pours the contents into the flowing water then lets the vial fall.

CHAPTER 16:
NO.1 ARYAN
FOOD
RESTAURANT

The sun is up in Harappa. The events of the past hours were unexpected; disturbances were things Old Mother was not used these days. She has lived here for a long time, unscathed by the conflicts of the world. She now stands in her stone carved home, stirring a large steaming pot of porridge. Her guests sit at a wooden table, anxiously waiting for breakfast.

A crisp autumn air flows through the always opened windows; the magnificent tree is visible from here. Small potted plants sit on the window sill with small insects buzzing around them. Laughter echoes from outside. Liviana jumps off her wooden chair to observe. Old Mother walks by Mica and rubs his head.

"Are those children from the temple?" Liviana inquires.

"Oh no, they live here in the canyon. My caretakers, you can say; their family roots go back deep." She chuckles like a happy granny.

She places a small bowl in front of Liviana, then a large one for Mica. She smiles as she walks to the pot. She stirs some more while inhaling the aroma.

Old Mother waves at Mica, "Come on children, help yourselves."

The pair dart to the stove like hungry children. They heap the porridge into their assigned bowls, eager to start the meal. When they return to their seats, they find Old Mother sitting there, ready to watch them eat; it's as if she just materialized at the table.

"Thank you. You are too kind," says Liviana.

"You and I have seen our share of hardships," Old Mother says to Liviana as she hobbles over to Mica. She caresses his head once more; he is just 'soaking it up.' "But these children, they are about to face horrors."

Liviana looks at Mica, happy to see him content. "What do you know about the sacred 'Texts of the Amon-I'?' she asks Old Mother.

"Be careful of that word…Amon-I," the old woman cautions with a smile. She hobbles back to the table.

How did she make it down below so quickly? Mica silently wonders about the events earlier in the night. He continues to eat his meal. Old Mother looks at him as if she heard his thoughts.

Her face is stern now, "It is a name lost to time; one which an ancient evil has been pursuing."

"I am afraid they already have the sacred texts; we are attempting to retrieve them at this very moment," Liviana interrupts.

"The time of the awakening is at hand," Old Mother warns. "Even if you find the resting place of the forefathers, then, only the Amon-I will return their essence."

Liviana is confused, "I do not understand, what is the Amon-I?"

"It is power, lost for countless eons." She makes her way to Liviana. "Be warned. The texts contain the ways to return the forefathers to the world; this return needs their essence, or else they will rise with the untampered might of their race."

The words sink in for a moment. Amon-I was translated in the old tongue to mean 'A history.' Old Mother is now telling them that the Amon-I was an object of power.

Liviana runs her hand over her head, frustrated with the new complications, "We need the Amon-I to resurrect the forefathers properly, is what you're saying; the sacred texts list the procedures?"

"That is one way to put it, yes. Less poetry, but yes," Old Mother responds. She looks at Mica. "Did you know that some of the great poetry today was first composed by the Watchers?" Mica shakes his head.

"Where do we find it?" Liviana asks.

"The texts will guide you, but first, ask yourself, why do you seek Lumeria?"

The question gives Liviana some pause. "I know of the power hidden there, but I do not seek it. I am trying to prevent war; to save humanity from annihilation."

Old Mother smiles; she sees the frustration on Liviana's face. "War is a part of the great cycles; a tool by which life cleanses itself from age to age. When the great civilizations are gone, who do you think will inherit the world?"

"I don't know," Liviana admits.

Mica looks to Old Mother, "What about the artifact we are seeking?"

"The 'Key to Lumeria,' fashioned by the great Thoth himself." Old Mother stares past the window as if remembering a time long forgotten. "He was the keeper of forbidden knowledge, the master of a high order. The only Anuk availed of the secrets of the forefathers.

He foresaw the coming events of his time, so he constructed the key in secret. From any of the ancient structures, the key can access the magic of the gods. More importantly, it will allow its keeper to traverse the many dangers of Lumeria."

"So, the key is only secondary to the Amon-I?" Liviana asks.

"It is, but do not underestimate its importance. It was entrusted to a special line. If the line survives, then they are the ones to use it."

"Who is the line?" Liviana inquires.

"A mystery to be solved," Old Mother chuckles.

"And the Gem of Persephone?" Mica asks.

"A curiosity," Old Mother says. "The name surfaced sometime after the Great War. It is possible it is a simple Anuk trinket."

Liviana wants to ask more questions, but fears that she will end up asking the wrong ones. She ponders on what she has so far, which was not much more than she already knew. She suspects that Old Mother will not tell her all that she came here to find out. *The answers are in the texts* she convinces herself.

"You said 'an ancient evil' pursues the Amon-I. You meant Timon?" Liviana asks.

Old Mother smiles at her. She moves in close to hold Liviana's hand, then looks at Mica examining the broken disc on his chain. Liviana helps her to the window plants. They pick up small tin cans then begin to water the little pots.

"Does he know he's playing with a Watcher's key?" Old Mother smiles while watering.

"It's broken; what harm could it do?" Liviana jokes.

"Timon is but an instrument whether he knows it or not," Old Mother explains. "War is coming, and if the agents of evil find Lumeria, they may raise the forefathers, or attempt to destroy them."

"Essence or not, I'm afraid war will bring their wrath," says Liviana

"Then pray we get those books," says Mica. Liviana is startled; Mica has never been able to sneak up on her. "Those are odd plants," he points out.

He caresses the royal blue colored leaves on a burgundy vine. His touch causes the release of golden-like pollen into the air, which shines brightly for a few seconds. Old Mother caresses his face.

"That's the Orchid of Sana; it means 'to you. It's part of the sacred Lotai flower." Old Mother explains. "It can heal many ailments with just a sip, program the mind if needed, and," she looks at Liviana and caresses her face as she bends down to look at the leaves, "kill."

Mica looks at Old Mother and kisses her on her silver head of hair.

-EARLY MORNING ON FOOD ALLEY-

The sun is not up yet in Atlas, but the city is already alive with activity. There is always something going on, with lots of hungry people roaming about. In this part of the commercial district so close to the city center, the famous 'Food Alley' is always open for business.

There is a multitude of cuisine available here, catering for every discerning taste. From fancy restaurants to 'fast food' ones, offering Illyrian, Aryan, and Atlantean dishes. The area is always busy at day or night, with a recent business model taking hold of the entrepreneurs; they call it 'Take-out.'

A moderate-sized food delivery truck is parked on a sidewalk just in front of a small green and white striped awning. Neon signs glow stating 'No. 1 Aryan Food Restaurant." An apartment window is just above it, displaying a large sign announcing, 'Vacancy.'

The restaurant opens well before sunrise. The eating space is small, holding two rows of seating which can seat six comfortably; they number eight per row, ending at a counter before the kitchen.

A wall separates one side of the booths from another more spacious room.

The owner, Chow, is from the far eastern shores of Aryavan. He is a proud immigrant to Atlantis. He is short, a bit round, gray with a bald spot, and has a lazy eye. It is hard to determine his age; at first glance, you would think he is in his sixties.

His thick Aryan accent makes his speech hard to understand. He has a habit of switching from the common tongue to his native one instantly; mostly to scream at the cooks behind the kitchen wall. There is always a symphony of knocking pans on steaming pots, mixing with his Aryan curses.

Chow makes his way from the kitchen to a pair of hungry customers; soldiers, dressed and ready for breakfast. He regards his new tenant, Deidra, and her friend Alexius with respect. A bell at the top of the front door 'dings,' using Chow to turn to welcome the incoming customer. His smile quickly turns to a frown at the sight of the red-headed mess rushing toward him.

Lyra stops at his side with a look of desperation, "Chow, I have to pee!"

"Crazy bitch, of all places on food alley, you come here?" Chow responds.

Lyra pushes past chow. Alexius begins to raise a finger to point but decides to leave it alone. He notices her satchel and wonders, *It can't be her.*

"You in trouble or something?" Chow asks as he hurries after Lyra, who is now in the kitchen area.

"Or something," Lyra responds. She enters a small section at the side then rushes into the bathroom.

She quickly sits on a stall, anxious to let her agony disappear. The resounding relief brings joy to her face. Finally, peace and quiet after a few hours of avoiding the authorities. She looks at her precious bag. She did not care about the contents or what Liviana wanted with it. All she cared about was that this was her opportunity to get out from under the 'Witch's clutches.'

~LYRA~

When she was a child of just six, Lyra lived on the Dalmatian coast in Illyria. Her family was not part of the aristocratic class, but they were comparably successful. Life seemed simple as a child. Her days were spent in school, accompanied by the more fun, mischievous affairs she found herself in.

Her father was always absent, *Dead somewhere,* is what she told people. Her mother got involved with some unsavory types, and eventually had to be incarcerated; Lyra was left with relatives she loathed. That was her excuse to further her criminal career.

She befriended one of the temple slaves, Mica. Together they escaped their gloomy lives through made up adventures. One day, she learned of the real possibility of her father's death. With Mica's help, she snuck into the Grand Temple to pray for her father's soul. She was caught, flogged, and sent away. She lost her only real friend that day.

Ten years would pass before she would run into Mica, and they would pick up right where they left off. One obstacle was between them, however, Liviana. She was a sophisticated woman, and Lyra regarded her as a threat.

Once she realized that Liviana treated Mica as a brother, her entire outlook changed. The adventures she dreamed about were now becoming real. As the years passed, there was no task too small for her. She gained a reputation for excelling at criminal endeavors: theft, pirating, smuggling, large-scale destruction, public indecency, were only some of the charges against her in Northern Illyria.

As any resourceful criminal finds out at one point or another, their past will catch up to them. On a routine smuggling job, Lyra was caught and charged for all her crimes; death was imminent. Liviana would be her only savior. Instead of the hangman's noose, she was sentenced to be a slave for five years in Egypt. She served her time then became a ward to her former master, but she is still indebted to Liviana. Now she has a chance to pay her debt and retire peacefully as a 'happy bar wench' in Egypt.

Lyra looks at the satchel, wondering where she could hide it. She looks around, unable to see any break in the ceiling; but then again, that would be too obvious. Suddenly, she remembers something.

Chow smuggled illegal mammoth tusks in his restaurant back in Egypt, and always kept his product in the walls. *There has to be something,* Lyra insists and begins looking around the floor.

Frustration overcomes her with the absence of any hidden vaults to be found. She embraces the fact that she will have to convince Chow to help her hide the stolen items.

Lyra breathes deeply before walking out. As she steps into the adjacent room, she runs into Chow.

"You wash hands? This restaurant," the little man protests. "What you have there?"

There is commotion outside; raised voices sounding official. Lyra rushes out with Chow to the kitchen; they peek through a hole in the wall. Three policemen are questioning the customers. The civil patrols were known to be 'Hot-Heads,' always looking to exert their idea of authority on the populace.

A cook's coat and hat on a rack catch Lyra's eye. She quickly puts the items on; Chow helps her tuck in her hair.

Three police officers enter and begin looking around. "A criminal may have fled here," one officer barks.

Chow points to a door at the end of the kitchen, "Woman run through, went out back," he says. "Stink like garlic." Lyra discreetly punches him.

The three men hurry out the back way, pushing the kitchen workers as they run through with their guns drawn. The iron door shuts with a 'bang,' ending the commotion. The cooks return to their steaming pots. Lyra runs into the bathroom.

She strips out of her clothing, pondering on whether or not she should tell Chow about the books. She shouts for the little man.

Chow enters the private area, offering Lyra a small package of clothing. He looks at her in her underwear, blushes a bit before giving Lyra his package.

"You pay later," he informs her.

Lyra takes the package. She struggles with the knitted shirt, which is at least one size smaller than she needs; the trousers fit, but they are shorter than expected, with the ends of the legs stopping at her knees. She looks ridiculous.

"What the fuck Chow!" Lyra complains as she turns to a mirror.

"Crazy bitch this not department store," Chow says throwing up his arm. "These grandson clothes. What they want?"

"Better you didn't know. Say, can you hold something for me?"

Chow thinks for a moment, "You rent upstairs apartment, and you keep your ill-gotten product here."

"No!" Lyra says sternly.

"Then take your merchandise somewhere else. I have respectable tenants upstairs now; don't need likes of you. They soldiers, with rank and money. I make them take you away!"

A thought popped into Lyra's head. If Chow's new tenants were as he claimed, then the likelihood of the premises being searched just dropped. But why pay for an apartment when she had free lodgings at the Furry Chariot?

"Fine you lizard; I'll take it. How much?"

"Eight-hundred ducats."

Lyra's mouth opens. She shakes her head, "Forget it. Find someone else to screw with. I'm not in the mood."

"Okay, Okay. Five-hundred, and you get me discount for strip show at Furry Chariot."

"Four-hundred and it's a deal, but I pay by the week," she says while shaking Chow's hand. He retrieves a key then passes it to her.

Lyra drops to her knees and then kisses Chow on the cheek. "You will always be my Chow-Chow." He blushes as she caresses her hands on his face. "And no, I didn't wash my hands."

Chow fumes as Lyra hurries up the back stairs. He mutters some curses in Aryan and then picks up a waiting platter. He makes his way outside grumbling.

Alexius and Deidra look at the incoming platter with steaming egg soup and bread. They take the bowls gratefully.

"What was that all about?" Alexius asks Chow.

"That just police being a menace to society. Oh, you have new neighbor, she move in today."

"You mean the girl who was running from the patrol?" Deidra points out.

"Oh no, redhead demon my friend from Egypt. She works for me from time to time." He leans in close, "Her family owns the Furry Chariot."

Alexius' face lights up; so too does Deidra's. Chow retreats into the kitchen area.

"Do you think Andros will help you out?" Deidra asks Alexius.

"I doubt it," he answers. "If anything he wants me gone from here. FaW-C will be the perfect place to let me roam out of sight."

"That's what you wanted isn't it?"

"I thought I did."

"Go to Stavos," Deidra suggests. "I am sure he will help." She remembers some news and gets excited, "The rumors are true. He is starting a campaign in the wastelands. It's quite 'hush-hush.' Prince Timon himself ordered it."

"Stavos will send me right back to Andros. Where in the borderlands?"

"Anatolia, then across to Cappadocia."

Suddenly, Alexius remembers a passage in the journal; a part that tells him 'The key to power begins in Cappadocia.' This campaign is one he must be a part of, and groveling to Andros may be the only way to achieve this. He continues to slurp his soup, as he hatches a plan.

CHAPTER 17:
THE LOYALTY
OF FRIENDS

Situated at the western edge of Atlas, the armed forces of Atlantis headquarters occupy an impressive sixteen hundred and twenty-eight acres of military property. It has over eight hundred buildings, an airport, and fifty-two miles of private roadways. This facility is no garrison, but tradition has kept the reference alive; the first military established here considered themselves a remote outpost of the once glorious Hyperboria, and it has always been referred to as 'Garrison' ever since.

Unlike Atlantean bases in far-off territories, this one is magnificent. It is a blending of old with new architecture, where the wide-open columns of marbled buildings give way to structures of steel. There are some training fields on the perimeter, which the foreign garrisons have mimicked.

In the center, there is a quarter mile long reflecting pool, with 108 flags standing on each side; they represent all the units of the Foreign Legion. If a flag is at half-mast, a unit is back in Atlantis; they may be in the capital or one of the other regions of the continent. At full mast, the flag signifies that a unit is still deployed. If it is lowered almost to the concrete ground, this means it has expired.

Along the side of the reflecting waters, administrative buildings rise to fifteen levels. At the head of the pool, a large 'old-style' structure reminds the residents that this was the first camp of the brave men and women, who first arrived on these shores.

The receiving area of all the administrative buildings is the same, spacious, bright with light streaming in from outside. Large panes of glass form outer walls, showing off the flag poles. As one enters, there are several greeting counters spread along the space, with soldiers at the desks screening visitors headed to various departments.

A young slim baby-faced male soldier, posted to the desk for 'Administrative Services,' quietly reads a trashy book behind his counter. He ignores the glares from Alexius, who sits on a row of visitors' chairs across from him. Occasionally, he glances over at the annoyed captain, hoping he would not come over again; frustration fills his face as his fears are realized. Alexius lumbers over to his desk.

"I've been waiting here for one hour! Is Commander Andros in or not?" Alexius growls.

"He is captain. It should not be long now," the young man responds with a hint of arrogance.

What is this military becoming? Alexius asks himself. He reaches over the counter to swat the book from the soldier's hand.

Alexius points a finger, "The next words out of your mouth better be 'Sorry for making you wait, Sir. You can go up now, Sir'. Say it, or I'll smash that pretty face of yours."

"Sorry for making you wait, Sir" he repeats in a trembling voice. "You can go up now, Sir."

"Thank you, corporal, don't mind if I do. And stand at attention; don't move until someone dismisses you," the captain orders. The soldier acknowledges and springs up.

Alexius makes his way to a lift, smiling at his triumph. As the doors close, he looks at the soldier, whom he suspects will notify Andros of the event.

It doesn't take long for the lift to reach the 13th floor. The doors open in a busy office space, with staff members moving about in haste. It is a mix of civilian and military personnel, each with their assigned duties, carrying about their routines. *A bunch of bureaucratic monkeys*, Alexius thinks.

He doesn't care for the lot, mostly because none of the soldiers in the administrative corps ever had to be out in the field. They lived lavishly and were always clean. Andros is one of them, responsible for the entire department. He was a brute who tried to 'flex his muscles' every chance he got, like in Illyria. The truth of it all is that he is an aristocrat playing soldier.

The path to Andros' office is clear, with no aides rushing to stop Alexius, just questioning glares from some of the older soldiers. He sees the private area, with an attractive civilian female sitting behind a counter. As he approaches closed doors, he is expecting some protest from the receptionist; there is none, which raises some suspicion. He pushes the doors and marches in without apology.

Andros sits behind his desk calmly reading the morning reports. He does not acknowledge Alexius, which he knows will annoy his brother-in-law. His passive aggressive way of dealing with *this screw-up* always pleases him.

"Andros, I need your help with something," Alexius announces as he strolls in.

"Commander," Andros says in an authoritative tone. "You will address me as

206

Commander within these walls, and everywhere else in Atlas, do I make myself clear, captain?"

Well, it eventually had to bite me in the ass, Alexius admits to himself. He thinks back to his outburst at Andros, in his father's private room.

"Commander," Alexius says calmly, "I respectfully request your help with an urgent matter." Andros drops his papers to look at Alexius. He smiles.

"What is it this time?" the Commander inquires, "Trouble with the authorities? Gambling debts? You were not a mere hour in the capital, and you were abducted; probably by one of your criminal associates."

The accusation does not bother Alexius. *There will be no pleasing this villain; besides, he was the one that blocked a rescue attempt. No, be calm, and don't smash his head on the desk.*

Without hesitation, Alexius makes his request, "I want a reassignment to Commander Stavos' campaign."

There is a brief silence. Andros did not expect this from Alexius. Running away to the Far West Continent was the perfect solution for the menace; after all these years, he would be rid of this embarrassment of a soldier. Now, there was a chance he would share in Stavos' glory, ultimately returning to Atlantis with more pride and arrogance; but then there was the chance he would be killed.

"Done," Andros declares, still smiling. "I will arrange it."

"Thank you, Commander," Alexius says, trying to hide his surprise. *This was easier than I thought,* he admits to himself.

He stands calmly, waiting for dismissal. Andros waves him away, so he quickly makes his exit. He closes the doors and then looks at the pleasant female receptionist. He ignores any inclination to suspect something sinister, *maybe*

Andros is warming up to me. He shakes his head with the comfort that things will never change.

-OFFICE OF COMMANDER STAVOS-

This office occupies spaces in the old main building at the head of the reflecting pool. Those that traverse the wide halls are of a higher rank than the personnel in the other buildings. Generals, Admirals, and the Commander of the Foreign Legion, Stavos, all pride themselves on being the elite amongst the armed forces.

Although ranked as a Commander, Stavos' unique responsibility to all units of the Foreign Legion does put him above his peers. He is an average sized man, standing five-feet-eight inches, medium build, and some would say, of merry character. His short hair is neat, and his features sharp; evidence of him being a 'chubby child' is on his cheeks, a fact which is frequently referred to by his friends. He is popular with the troops, beloved some would say.

Stavos' office is laid out as a soldier's would be, sparse with little decoration. Some pennants hang on the wall, showing off his previous commands' achievements, and many trophies are displayed on a high ledge. The layout is reminiscent of any Archon's office in the field, with the only thing lacking being the extravagance. He sits quietly at a desk waiting for his visitor to arrive.

The dark blue office doors open. An aide motions Alexius inside. Stavos does not stop staring at his morning reports, reminding the Captain of his previous encounter with Andros.

Not wanting to offend the Commander, Alexius decides to show off his crisp military bearing by offering the proper respect to his mentor.

"Glorious morning to you Commander Stavos, Sir!" Alexius shouts with an Atlantean salute.

A brief moment passes, then Stavos' morning reports rise to his face, barring Alexius from witnessing the increasing laughter. Stavos cannot contain himself any longer, so he drops his hand.

Stavos is red in the face, "What in all that is wretched are you doing?" he laughs.

Still standing in his rigid pose, Alexius explains, "I just came from that twat's office. Just making sure you didn't turn into a twat while I was gone."

The Commander rushes over to Alexius to embraces him, slapping his back as long-lost friends do. He releases him and then goes over to a wine pitcher. He pours for the both of them and picks up two cigars.

"So, afraid to see what FaW-C has to offer I hear," Stavos says while he lights Alexius' cigar.

Alexius begins to choke, "What the fuck is this?" he complains, but still puffs away. "Tastes like rancid feet."

"It's from Faw-C you pussy. I thought you should at least have something from there since you won't go."

"I'll get to FaW-C one day. Not today I'm afraid," Alexius says.

"No, because tomorrow you leave for Anatolia. I am so happy you just don't know it. The thought of depending on a bunch of stinking recruits to pacify the resistance is just, sacrilege. It's your fault you know."

"Me? Oh no, I didn't ask to be assigned to Illyria. It was Andros' petty attempt to get me out of Atlantis. You could have stopped him you know."

"I tried," Stavos explains. "The moron has a way of manipulating those above his rank; not me though you little shit, don't even think it. You and Deidra weren't the only ones displaced you know. I lost most of the loyal officers of the '13th.'"

"That's what you get when you make a noble a soldier," says Alexius.

"You're one to talk," Stavos teases. "If I did not know you, I'd swear you shat gold and talked like those cunts in the Senate."

"That will never be me. I am a low born commoner who somehow ended up with forced nobility, or at least that's what my mother said." Alexius pauses and has slight regret for his last quip.

Stavos looks at Alexius sip the wine and pretend not to care that he mentioned his mother. "My condolences for the loss. I can't very well say your loss, but a loss all the same. Come, drink with cheer, for tomorrow you rejoin the path to glory." They toast to the upcoming campaign. "So, which pair of tits brought you to your senses?"

"Nothing like that I swear. I'm just reevaluating some things, that's all."

"Good, because after this campaign, I'm requesting you be assigned as my assistant, receive a higher rank and all that good horse shit."

Alexius' face brightens, "It would have been a better campaign if you were coming along old man."

"These pussies think I should fight from a desk. Smell the blood from reports, and plunge my pen in cabinet briefs. I would give anything to be back on the battlefield."

Alexius raises his cup, "It would be a glorious campaign then wouldn't it?"

The doors burst open with an aide rushing in. He is out of breath, trying to announce someone. Before he could get a word out, he bows as Prince Timon enters with Bana close behind him. Stavos and Alexius quickly jump to their feet and bow in unison.

"Commander Stavos," Timon says in his commanding tone while striding over.

"Your Highness, this is a surprise," Stavos says reverently. "This is one of my Captains, Alexius of house Badur."

Timon looks Alexius up and down; a moment of envy overcomes the Prince as he regards the taller man's stature. Timon is not built like a warrior, but his Anuk heritage did allow him to be as powerful as ten men Alexius' size.

"Yes, your brother is the Lord of that House, isn't he?" Timon notes.

"He is your highness," Alexius responds.

The Prince casually walks over to Stavos' desk, observing the wine cups, cigars on an ashtray, and papers littered about.

"I knew your father," Timon says to Alexius. "I admired him deeply. His passing was a great loss to the royal family," He calmly steps in front of Stavos. "Stavos, I want you to join me this afternoon; there are some things I wish to discuss."

Stavos' face turns red once more, "It will be my honor." He tries to contain his excitement.

"Good. Come to the palace at say, four."

Timon turns and makes his retreat. Bana opens the door, and they both disappear.

"You'd better change clothes," Alexius jokes.

"Why, what's wrong with these?" Stavos asks seriously.

"You've got stains all over your trousers."

"Shut up you twat."

"I'd better leave you to get your good panties on. I have somewhere to be." Alexius grabs Stavos' arm tightly. "Good to see you old friend." He slaps his shoulder then makes his exit.

"Stay out of trouble," Stavos yells. "You'd better make that transport tomorrow."

Alexius grunts at him as he leaves the office.

-HOSPITAL AT CITY CENTER-

The medical centers in the commercial district of Atlas are well equipped for any urgent care. They have the latest cutting-edge equipment available anywhere in the empire and are free for all its citizens. There has always been a long-standing tradition since the time of Hyperboria, that the spiritual, and health care of all people will be free, available forever; today, at least health care is free.

The priesthood controls a large hospital near the city center. Elite clientele goes there, such as the royals, nobles, and the clergy. The occasional senator may be cared for at the facility, but only if their patron is of the top tier class.

Alexius and Carrel stand over Calis' bed. They are in a large private room, which may be as big as Deidra's apartment. They look at the unconscious man hooked into medical equipment.

"He is a good man you know, despite being a High Priest," Carrell says softly.

"I only just made his acquaintance, but he does seem different than the whole stinking lot. How do you know him anyway?"

"This man saved my skin a few times, and I saved his. It was a long time ago when I would on occasion, accompany Calis and your father on their adventures."

Alexius looks at the old man, curiosity overcoming him, "You've never talked about your, adventures. What were you all up to?"

Carrell smiles, "Well, there's not much to tell really." There is an obvious hesitance in his voice. "We were all young, and got into lots of things; they more than me. There was this one time I had to save young Calis here, and your father from being served up as dinner to an African tribe of little men. I found them in the wilderness, ready to be boiled in large pots." He pauses to light a cigarette.

"Well?" Alexius asks anxiously.

"I offered the chief a heard of donkeys and a barrel of rum in exchange for their lives. The chief agreed."

There is a miserable look on Alexius' face, "That's the stupidest made up story I've ever heard."

He shakes his head at the old man, who smiles at him. "I'm going to find something to eat. You want anything?"

"I don't suppose they serve ale?" He watches Alexius walk off, ignoring his request. He turns his attention to Calis, "You better wake up you hear. I am too old to watch over him."

-HOSPITAL CAFETERIA-

Patrons to the hospital cafeteria do not have to wait in lines or endure the sub-standard food as in other places. They type in their order at a table or booth, and a server would arrive shortly with their meal; quite the convenience in this elite institution.

It has been a long time since Alexius had to visit a hospital; he rarely got sick. He sits quietly at his table, waiting for his meal. Looking around at the people seemed to be the only thing to do. His casual glances end on a patch of red hair sitting two booths away from him. *It can't be,* he gasps. His server arrives with his tray.

Lyra is quietly enjoying a sandwich, taking her time to chew her food. She is uncharacteristically dressed in a stylish shirt and skirt. Her hair is brushed. She is instantly startled as Alexius slides into her booth.

"Excuse me!" Lyra exclaims loudly with annoyance.

Alexius grins while pointing, "It is you. You hit me over the head, remember?"

"What are you talking about you baboon, I don't know you." Lyra looks at him carefully, then notices his soldier's uniform.

"Alright then, answer me this; you just moved into Chow's right?"

"Oh, soldier boy. Are you arresting me?" she asks sarcastically.

"What? No. I am Alexius, and you are?"

213

"Trying to enjoy my meal." She realizes he is not going away. "Lyra. Alexius huh, that's a girl's name. What, your mother didn't like you?"

"No, she hated me," he responds. "What are you doing here? You are not staff, not with that hint of criminal mischief about you."

"Shouldn't you be out killing something? No wait, you're killing my patience."

"Killing my patience...that's rich. Are you always this rude to your neighbors?"

Lyra was not in the mood for small talk; she wants him to leave. It would be smart she decides, to make nice with the new neighbor, just in case the authorities find themselves at Chows.

"Alright," she says politely, "first of all, you were trying to steal my bike, which makes you a criminal, and..."

"You were shot at," he interrupts, "which means you were up to no good. Then you were hiding from the civil patrol."

"You have quite the imagination."

"Look, I get it. Don't let the uniform fool you, for I'm always up to no good. Stealing your ride though was not intentional."

"Sure looked intentional to me."

"I was in a car with High Priest Calis," he explains, "this bitch crashed into us and then abducted me. She held me in the sewers under the old quarter, so when I escaped, I wanted to get out of there as fast as I could. There was a bike, so I tried to borrow it."

"So after you escaped your crazy girlfriend, were you going to return it?" She lets the sarcasm sink in. "How do you know High Priest Calis?"

The question throws Alexius off, "What? Oh, he knew me as a child. He is acquainted with my family and all that. He seems like a good man." Lyra is silent, chewing on her sandwich.

"Is he in danger or something?" she asks.

"No. The doctors say he will regain consciousness soon, and his body is healing." He bites into his sandwich. "What are you doing here?"

"Stealing stuff." Lyra slips out of the booth. "By the way, I'm only renting the space at Chows. I'm not staying there. So don't come looking for me."

Alexius picks up his sandwich and follows Lyra. He sees her head to a lift and wants to follow; *that's not why I'm here,* he chides himself. He continues in the opposite direction.

Carrell is sitting on a chair facing the window, falling asleep. He quickly wakes when Alexius enters the room. He gratefully accepts the half-eaten sandwich.

"If you don't mind, I'll be heading back to the pier," says Carrell.

"Go on old man. Take care of yourself out there." Carrel smiles at him then leaves.

Alexius stands over the priest once more, looking at him with curiosity. Suddenly, Calis grabs his hand. His eyes slowly open while he attempts to say something. Alexius puts his ear close, trying to make out the whisper.

"Find Liv…" Calis begins. He is too weak to speak loud enough for Alexius to make sense of what he is saying. "Livi…" His eyes close once more.

The sun is dipping behind the buildings on the horizon. The room's lights brighten to a comfortable level. This reminds Alexius that he has to meet Deidra at the apartment.

-MARKET SQUARE AT THE OLD QUARTER-

The sun has set, signaling the nighttime activities in the Old Quarter market square to begin. It exists just beyond the river and hosts a variety of entrepreneurs. Leather merchants, slave merchants, and exotic animals all occupy their place in the bazaar. Even though this place is in the more dangerous part of the city, there are always affluent visitors walking around browsing the wares; with their security detail of course.

An unmarked transport recently landed just at the outskirts of the ghetto; it discreetly brought Prince Timon and Commander Stavos to the area, along with six of the Red-Guard soldiers. They all wear regular 'street-clothes,' allowing them to blend in with the crowds. Their walk and demeanor, however, does distinguish them from the rest of pedestrians.

"Your Highness, are we drinking with the common folk this evening?" Stavos asks cheerfully.

"Don't call me that," Timon snaps. "We are just simple wanderers, heading to questionable destinations."

"Very well. May I ask where it is we are going then?"

"Somewhere private, without curious ears to catch our whispers."

Both men duck into an alley entrance behind a blacksmith's shop; not long after, the six guards follow. No one is paying attention to them, for this is business as usual in these parts.

They pass by two men fighting with a crowd of four just looking on. Closer to a corner, a figure lurking in the shadows offers the group drugs. They casually enter a small tea shop.

The lights are dim. The place is empty. An old woman sits behind a counter, not paying the visitors any mind at first. She slowly gets off her seat, hobbles to a door close by her table, then points to a darkened room.

The eight men enter; Stavos is relieved to see three tables spread out in the small space. Oil lamps are lit and hang near two ledges, giving the room an ominous feel. Timon sits, which prompts the rest to follow. The old woman brings a tray with a pot of tea. With trembling hands, she puts it on the table. As she turns to leave, Timon grabs her hand and places a gold coin in it. She smiles and walks off.

"I lived in Illyria for a few years, did you know this?" Timon asks. Stavos shakes his head. "It was common practice to send the royal children to live with our cousins in Aryavan. There I met an Illyrian girl. I fell in love with Leena, and I was at peace with the world."

He pauses for a moment to remember the time spent with his beloved. Stavos sips his tea.

"She was the dearest thing to me," the Prince continues. "Treachery snatched her away. Since then I vowed to purge the world of the evil and decadence that plague our civilizations. Corruption, poverty, but most of all, defiance, all of which you can see in this ghetto."

"A noble task, but an impossible one I dare say," Stavos says.

Timon gets closer, "I now have the chance to accomplish this. Your campaign in the borderlands, there is something I need for you to do."

"Command it, and it shall be done."

"I seek an artifact, one lost through the ages. It belonged to my ancestors, and is of great worth to me."

"Tell me where to look and I shall," Stavos says proudly.

"Not looking, rather taking; one of the nomad tribes possesses it."

"Are you certain?" Stavos asks with some surprise in his voice.

"I am. My source is infallible. The leader is an outlaw named Darius. An Atlantean wanted by the Senate for treason."

"I know who Darius is, I remember," Stavos states. "He murdered Lord Arias of house Badur."

"I want you to lead the campaign yourself. Start in Cappadocia," Timon orders.

This is what Stavos has been yearning for; a chance to get out on the battlefield once more. And now, charged with this great responsibility, he regards his prince with respect and love.

"The Senate will never allow a move on Cappadocia. It is protected," Stavos reminds the Prince.

"Who is the more powerful, the Senate or me?"

"Apologies," Stavos says humbly.

"You will meet resistance, be certain of it. Stavos, no survivors, do you understand?"

"It shall be done," Stavos promises.

"Do this for me without question, and you will be rewarded with the highest honor; you shall be raised to posts nearest my person."

Stavos stands, and then humbly bows. Timon stands, and within seconds the Red-Guard rise; the chairs 'screech' on the floor, but this does not break Stavos' reverence. Timon puts his hand out to Stavos, who then reverently kisses it.

"I am your humble servant," Stavos declares.

The prince retracts his hand, and motions that it is time for their departure. He heads for a back door in the room, which leads out to an area behind the tea shop.

They walk several paces down the moderately lit alley, then Timon points to a broken, moldy wall. A couple of stray cats run out from in front of it, making their descent on a short stairway. The group makes their way to the stairs and follows the cats.

They come upon a heavy wooden door with a small closed window cut into the top portion. Timon retrieves a small purse of coin then beats his fist on the door. The window opens. A ghastly man appears peeking through it.

"Moira," Timon announces as he passes the purse to the doorman. A short while later, the door creaks open.

"What does that mean?" Stavos asks.

"Fate," Timon explains, "or what has been dealt to you. An expression to honor an ancestor. These fools believe she is the goddess that dispenses fate."

The group enters through the door; the path ahead is a damp tunnel. The door closes behind them, bringing on the total darkness. Fire torches can be seen hanging on the walls forward; crackling and glowing brightly as they descend into the sewers.

After a short walk, they come upon an entrance to what appears to be a vast chamber filled with a rowdy crowd. The noise and clamor echo as everyone tries to get a glimpse over a wooden banister. Beyond the rails is a drop some fifteen feet into a circular area, where two men are engaged in bloody combat.

Timon and Stavos rush to the edge, pushing through the crowd, eager to see the current match. It is an even pairing, with two bulky men doing battle with their fists. Stavos is intrigued.

"Your father outlawed these games," he shouts to the Prince. "I remember when I was a young recruit; we purged the city of such sordid establishments."

"The great king is gone," Timon responds. "It is only natural that things return to how they once were. That is after all, what he sought; a return to the old ways."

Stavos smiles, eager to start the entertainment, "Are we betting then?"

"You may," Timon answers. "We have to see someone first, come."

They make their way to the edge of the banister at the beginning of narrow stairs. Stavos catches a glimpse of two figures he knows. He stops to look carefully.

"What is it?" Timon asks.

"Alexius and Deidra," Stavos answers with a smile. "I should have known."

He raises his hand in an attempt to get their attention. They spot him. He can see Deidra smiling from ear to ear. He looks at Timon, who is pointing down the stairs. They make their way below quickly, leaving the rowdy crowd behind.

CHAPTER 18: THE STINK BENEATH THE STAIRS

The roar of the crowd is fierce at the lower levels of the sewers. Timon has led Stavos into a room just below the arena. They sit in a dank, smelly space, which appears to be an office. An old crone is rummaging through a broken ceramic urn.

She is hideous, short, hunched, in desperate need of sunlight, and has a head of wiry silver hair. Some bones of unknown origin adorn her head. The crone's smile reveals several missing teeth. Her bony fingers are long with dirty fingernails. She retrieves a small bowl with what seems to be blue fire. Settled within the strange flame is a vial with an unknown substance.

Stavos sits uncomfortably close to Timon on a moldy couch. He is panicking inside, worried that there is something sinister about to happen. He fakes a calm demeanor as the crone approaches, but his anxiety is beginning to show. Timon looks at him, smiling, patiently waiting for the old woman to finish her moving about.

The hag smiles at Stavos, raising her dirty index finger, "Is he the fighter tonight?" she asks in a raspy voice. The Prince shakes his head.

"It is I who shall be fighting," Timon informs her. He throws a coin purse on a nearby silver platter, bringing some relief to Stavos.

221

"What shall it be my prince?" she asks while placing her bowl of blue flame next to the Commander.

Stavos looks at Timon then back at the woman; they were supposed to be incognito. A whirlwind of possibilities enters his head, hoping that the Red-Guard were right outside. He quickly calms down when he realizes Timon chuckles at him.

"Relax," the Prince says. "She knows who I am. She runs the games. I am grateful for her discretion. I am in the mood for something, big."

The crone gets close to Stavos, "His Highness is a loyal benefactor," she explains.

She grabs Timon's right hand, alarming Stavos; before he could spring up in protest, the prince pushes him down.

The crone closes her eyes then spits into Timon's palm while she chants something in an unknown tongue. "It is difficult to tell. There is high energy in the ether. The ancestors do send their favors tonight." She hobbles away to her chair.

Stavos stands, anxious to leave. Timon pulls him back down. He notices a metal door in a corner opening. The creaking is loud but quickly dissipates. Samiri slithers into the room.

Timon smiles as he looks at the villain, "Commander Stavos, meet Samiri. He is a…" He struggles to find the right word, "holy man."

"Begging your forgiveness your highness, but I am not religious," Stavos explains; his heart is racing.

"Neither am I," admits Timon, "but no matter, he is. On your mission for me, I require that you indulge us in a small ritual." He nods to Samiri, who quickly makes his way to the now frightened and squirming Commander.

The old crone hobbles over to plant a dirty hand on the soldier's shoulder. They open his shirt. He is about to push them off, but Timon's mighty hand secures him to the chair. The disgusting couple smile as Samiri exposes Stavos' bare flesh.

Samiri's wrinkled face gets close to Stavos, "Not to worry Commander, this won't hurt, much."

Samiri picks up the vial from the flames; his hands appear to be unburnt. He grins as he brings the flask close to Stavos' chest, pouring slowly. The bright blue liquid is thick and penetrates the flesh instantly. Stavos' screams bring delight to the old crone as she chants once more. With the last drop dissolving into flesh, Samiri closes his eyes as he joins the crone's chanting. Stavos passes out from the ordeal.

-AT THE BANISTER OVER THE ARENA-

The crowd has settled down as the last match ends. There will be a brief intermission. It's the perfect time to indulge oneself at the bar, which is serving a more potent beverage than what's offered in the surface establishments. For those who can't make their way to the bar, a squad of boys and girls run about taking drink orders and making deliveries.

The dirt arena below is being prepared for the next match. Alexius and Deidra drink their drinks while complaining about their betting strategies. Deidra's girlfriend Cleo comes stumbling towards them; she is drunk. She hangs on to Deidra before planting a passionate kiss.

Cleo smiles at Deidra, "All this makes my blood boil, I feel, alive." She grabs Deidra's crotch.

"And horny," Deidra responds. "Come on, one more match. Then we're leaving."

There is a sour look on Alexius' face, "I'm not betting with you two anymore," he complains.

"Don't be a sourpuss," Deidra teases as she hits him in the stomach. "I'll give you double or nothing on the next match. Which color, blue or green?"

The trio had worked out their own 'side-betting' amongst themselves. Crude displays would show the names of the upcoming contenders, allowing patrons to place their bets on a fighter. These three took it a step further; before the names are announced, they betted on the fighters' side of the arena. One corner is blue, and the other is green. They did not have a clue as to who the contenders were. Their only hope was that fate would bless their color.

Alexius shakes his head, "Alright, blue."

The girls laugh, impatient for the next match. Alexius finishes his drink. He does not realize that Stavos is standing behind him.

"Seems I'm missing out on the party," the Commander says with a smile.

The girls instantly sharpen up. They relax after Stavos puts a finger to his lips. They move closer to give Stavos a tight hug.

"Well don't look at me, I'm not hugging you," Alexius says sarcastically.

A bell rings as the names of the contenders are displayed. The crowds retrieve small devices from their pockets to begin their betting. Heated discussions drown out friendlier ones, while scantily clad barmaids push through the rabble.

Stavos pulls out his device, "A little illegal affair is within our rights I think. It is the night before a deployment after all."

"I didn't know you partook in these games, Sir."

"Please Deidra, in here I am not your superior officer, you are not a Captain. We are just old friends who are enjoying a bit of blood and betting," Stavos explains.

"Wait a moment," Alexius says, "you said 'within our rights,' does that mean what I think it does?"

Stavos nods with a smile, bringing much joy to the group. They are interrupted by a loud bell signaling the start of the next match. They look down at the dirt, anxious to see the fighters. There are at least several cubits at stake between the three gamblers.

In the green corner, a seven-foot beast of a man appears. The crowd goes wild. 'Digger!' they yell; 'Digger,' being short for Grave-Digger. He wields a large broadsword, wearing nothing more than a pair of brown shorts and a black helmet. Alexius shakes his head as the girls laugh, expecting an impending victory.

In the blue corner Timon appears, wearing a helmet and the leather pants he came in with. He swings his sword in controlled patterns, getting himself ready to do battle. His size is immensely dwarfed by the giant he is about to face. The crowd does not acknowledge his handle of 'The Undertaker.' They keep on shouting 'Digger!'

Stavos' eyes are on the Prince, "So what are the odds?"

"Double on blue," Cleo answers.

"I'll take it," says Stavos.

"What, you don't like money?" Deidra asks.

Stavos winks at Alexius who shakes his head, expecting to be paying the wenches shortly. A petite barmaid brings them a new serving of drinks and cigarettes, which they take gratefully.

The bell rings. The fighters rush each other. Swords smash together, echoing that metallic 'cling' with each contact. The larger man is strong, easily overpowering the prince. Timon miscalculates a lunge; the giant connects him with the heel of his boot.

He slides across the dirt crashing into the stone wall. The giant is on him with the broadsword in the air. The steel comes down hard, barely missing its target. It appears that Timon moves with superhuman speed, dazzling the crowd. He gets behind his opponent.

The giant roars in anger but then is furious as he gets the back of his thigh sliced. Timon flips in the air, lands in front of his now kneeling opponent. He begins to slice into flesh, occasionally smashing the hilt of his sword on the man's face. There is no more fight in the giant.

Timon raises his hands in the air, feeding off the crowd's chant for blood. He looks at his kneeling opponent; there is defeat in the man's eyes. He pierces his sword at the top of the man's shoulder, then down to his chest. The body falls lifeless to the ground. The crowd goes wild with the spectacle.

A bell rings ending the match. Four attendants run out to remove the defeated giant. Another two quickly begins evening out the dirt with their brooms. Timon hurries to a small tunnel on the blue side, striding triumphantly like a conquering warrior.

As he exits through the arena door, he is greeted by Stavos and his officers. He removes his helmet, causing the juniors to drop on one knee immediately; Stavos remains standing, bowing.

"Please, get up," Timon says calmly. "This is not a place one needs to be recognized."

"Excellent match your highness," Alexius says. "Next time you need a bigger opponent."

The words bring a smile to Timon's face. His jealousy of Alexius was creeping up again. Somewhere in his mind, he asks himself, *why I should feel this way about a mere soldier.*

"Maybe not bigger," Timon responds as he looks at Stavos. His gaze shifts to Alexius, "More affluent maybe. How about it my lord, shall we?"

Stavos' smile disappears, "Surely you jest. We deploy tomorrow," he protests.

"I promise; it will not be a death-match," Timon reassures Stavos. He puts his hand on Alexius' shoulder, "Your ancestor Badur fought the house of ENlil on their first arrival to Atlantis. That was ages ago, but it is still in our nature to fight, won't you say?"

"If his highness wishes it," Alexius says to Stavos while he strips off his shirt.

"I wish it," Timon proclaims in a harsher tone. He walks back to the arena.

"Deidra, blue or green?" Alexius asks while he hands her his shirt. He removes his necklace. "Protect that with your life," he whispers to her, looking at his heirloom.

The prince walks through the tunnel, stopping at a small armory. Alexius starts towards the tunnel while looking back to the group; they look at him as if he is a condemned man.

Deidra makes sure Alexius sees her, "Green!" she shouts.

The short pause between matches is almost over. The new contenders are announced; Timon in the blue corner, Alexius in the green. They each wear a protective helmet and wield swords. The artificial lights brighten, causing the sweat on their shirtless backs to shimmer. The crowd is shouting 'Undertaker!' pumping up the prince's ego. There are no cheers for Alexius' handle 'The Immortal.' The bell rings, they charge.

Both fighters rush each other swinging swords high then connecting the blades. The clashing of steel is quick, fierce, with both men moving with calculated rhythm. Dust kicks up within the wake of their footwork. For a moment it seems as if they are evenly matched.

Timon uses his smaller size to outmaneuver Alexius. He blocks an incoming sword to his right side with an upward stroke, plants his right foot into the dirt, then forces his left fist through the opening he created. Within a split second, his fist connects with Alexius' jaw, sending him reeling back several feet in the air.

Undertaker sprints to his downed opponent, slicing his sword downward but misses his target as Alexius rolls away. Distracted by how fast he moved, Timon is surprised by a sturdy heel connecting his face. He spirals to the ground.

What have I done? Alexius screams in his head; he did after all just 'floor' the prince of Atlantis. The rage in him quickly takes over, however. Timon is back on his feet, he is angry. This fight will now be with fists.

Alexius catches Timon's mighty right fist as it plunges toward his neck; the left fist fires off. The Prince is strong. He can't hold back the force much longer. He slams his head into Timon's temple, disorienting him. He smashes his fist into Timon's jaw sending him flying off in the air. The prince crashes on the ground, unable to get up.

The bell immediately rings, which is unusual, for a defeated fighter has to yield, or lose his life; this is the only way a match will end. Stavos rushes out to the arena with the Red Guard. They pick up the unconscious prince. Alexius raises his hands. The crowd screams 'Immortal!'

-HOSPITAL AT CITY CENTER-

The private wing of the hospital is quiet; far removed from the ever-present activities of the lower levels. At night time it feels deserted, with only a small dedicated staff ready to serve their elite patients.

Calis regained consciousness hours ago. He has had many visitors since the accident, but now he thankfully has only one, Carrell.

"It was not easy getting this; that's three you owe me," Carrell says to Calis. He empties a vial of dark blue liquid into a cup of water; the contents instantly transform into a thick substance with tiny shimmering specs of gold.

"Thank you, my friend," Calis expresses gratefully. "I need to get to Rovina. She may be in danger."

"Not to worry; Lyra has the books," Carrell explains.

"That miserable child," Calis complains as he gets off the bed. "She's more than likely keeping it for her selfish ends. Don't be surprised if the little criminal sells them, or worse, sells them to Inias."

"All the same, she's hidden the books. Won't even tell Rovina where they are."

"Where is she?"

Carrell smiles, "At Chow's; she's taken an apartment there. As fate would have it, so has Alexius."

The weakened High Priest grabs the sea Captain as he tries to walk, "Let's hope fate allows us the courtesy of not letting them collide."

"I take it you want to see Rovina?"

"Yes, and I'll be giving Lyra a piece of my mind; she will bring those books to us, one way or the other."

Carrell helps his friend get his things together. With some luck, the staff will release Calis. With more success, they won't ask any questions about the quick recovery.

-CHOW'S APARTMENTS-

One prerequisite to living in Chow's apartments is the understanding that the landlord is very, very cheap. He has strict rules about wasting utilities; for this reason, the water pressure drops considerably at night. Also, the lights outside the apartments are shut off one hour after sunset; only the lighting for the restaurant remains.

Deidra struggles with Cleo to carry Alexius up the dark stairway to their apartment door. Thankfully, light from outside shines through a window on the second floor. Alexius is bloody and limps up the stairs. They reach the top to face the door; the girls struggle to keep the behemoth upright, for, in addition to the pain, he is intoxicated.

Aggravated with Alexius' state, Deidra lets go, "Drag his ass in," she tells Cleo.

"No," Alexius mumbles, "Since the bed is not big enough for the three of us, I'll just go over there." He points to Lyra's apartment.

"Are you stupid?" Deidra asks.

"You're really asking that?" Cleo jokes.

"Yup," Alexius confirms. "She doesn't live here, she told me so."

"Oh let him Deidra, do you want him making a mess in your living room?"

"You know what? I don't care," Deidra says.

Cleo lets go of Alexius' arm, leaving him to lean on the wall. She goes over to Lyra's locked door. She quickly retrieves an all-purpose tool from her bag to pick the mechanism.

"My friends are criminals," Alexius jokes. Cleo smiles as the door opens. Both girls toss him in Lyra's apartment.

The place is dark and shows all signs of not being lived in. Alexius locks the door behind him before making his way to the bedroom. He falls on to the neatly made up bed, ready to welcome the sleep that is descending on him.

Fifteen minutes of quiet allows Alexius to drift off, but suddenly, he hears the door open. Panic overcomes him; *She said she was not staying here. It could just be Deidra or Cleo.* The sound of Lyra grumbling confirms his fears; *she lied.* He rolls off the bed then dives beneath it.

He sees expensive boots entering the bedroom. They make their way to a corner, then Lyra's butt drops in his view; she squats in front of a wall to open a hidden panel. Moments later she pulls out a leather satchel, the same bag he saw her with last night.

Lyra drops the bag at the foot of the bed before pulling off her boots. Her skirt, shirt, and underwear fall to the ground, then the legs disappear into the bathroom.

What's in the bag? Alexius wonders while he slides as best as he could to it. He manages to reach a strap and pulls it closer. The bag tumbles over, exposing an edge of one of the books.

There is something familiar about the color of the binding. He decides to investigate some more. Before Alexius could pull one out, the legs return. He retracts his hand quickly then holds his breath. The legs stand there, four feet away from his face.

Lyra picks up the bag then returns to the bathroom. Alexius exhales, not sure of what to do next. He wants to leave, but his curiosity is getting the better of him.

He hears running water from the bathroom. *What's the worst that can happen? She screams? I get thrown out?* He ponders. With determination on his face, he marches into the bathroom. As he steps in, Lyra cracks him over the head with a solid marble statue. The ornament falls to the ground with Alexius.

With a triumphant look Lyra point to Alexius' unconscious body, "That's what you get for trying to rob me; wait." She squats down to look at his face. She fans away from the alcohol fumes, "Soldier Boy."

-THE NEXT MORNING IN LYRA'S APARTMENT-

Sunlight streams into the bedroom from a window, hitting Alexius's face. He slowly opens his eyes, feeling the pounding in his head, the soreness in his body, the restraints around his wrists; iron restraints attached to the wall.

He looks at the shackles, slowing realizing
that he is lying on Lyra's bed, naked, with only a thin
white sheet across his waist. Panic creeps in. The
bindings are tight, but somewhere in the back of his
pounding head, he feels, no he knows, that he can
easily break through them. He begins to pull on the
restraints but stops when the door opens.

Lyra casually struts in with a mischievous
smile on her face. She stares at Alexius and
wonders; *does he really think he could break those chains?
Idiot*

"It's awake. Good, I'm about to leave,"
Lyra says.

"Look here wench, release me this instant!"
Alexius grumbles.

Lyra sits on the bed then lifts the thin sheet;
she giggles. "I guess you're not very happy this
morning." She frowns, "Or is it always like that?"

Alexius is furious. He begins to tug at his
restraints once more. The wall starts to crack.

Lyra panics when she sees a crack forming,
more worried about Chow than Alexius, "Hold there
soldier. I'm just having a bit of fun. Calm down. I'll
let you go."

"Let me go now, or I'll…"

"You'll what?" she interrupts. "Break into
my room, and rob me?"

Lyra puts her hand over her mouth and
gasps. She knows the fake damsel act is annoying.
She giggles then jumps on the bed to straddle him.
She slowly gyrates her hips, playfully teasing him.

"Get off me, where are my clothes?"
Alexius screams.

"You saw my naughty bits, so I see yours."
She taps his chest with her index finger. "I had
Brutus help me tie you up. He has your clothes."
She pinches his nipples. "He is very fond of big
tough girls like you." She taps his nose then rolls
off.

232

"Who the fuck is Brutus?" Alexius asks, a bit calmer now.

Lyra smiles mischievously, "He is your soon to be rapist husband. Oh, I'm robbing you. Call it compensation for my troubles." She blows him a kiss as she walks out.

As soon as she disappears, a seven-foot giant lumbers in the room, smiling; it's Brutus from the Furry Chariot. His head is big and matches his oversized body. He is dressed in brown trousers which could be heavy drapes, a white shirt the size of a ship's sail, and a black sleeveless jacket. It doesn't matter to Alexius that Brutus appears to be a simpleton; the thought of the impending rape is sending him into a panic.

Brutus offers a friendly smile, "Little man no be fraid. Brutus bring friend."

The gentle stare of the creature calms Alexius a little. He looks at the big face smiling at him as if they were playmates.

"Friend? What friend?" Alexius asks.

Calis calmly walks in then nods to Brutus, who leaves. He notes Alexius' look of horror has given way to disbelief. He places some clothing on the bed, along with the heirloom.

"Do you have any idea just how embarrassing this is?" Calis points out.

"You're embarrassed?" Alexius asks in an annoyed tone. "I had a run-in with a demon from the underworld." He looks at Calis with some curiosity, "How did you…I left you in a state of…"

"It's not important right now," Calis cuts him off. He frees Alexius from the restraints. He notices Deidra looking in.

Alexius quickly gets dressed. His necklace drops on the bed; Calis picks it up. He looks at the ancient symbols and smiles.

"Your father's part of the key," Calis reminisces.

"I should have expected you would know about this," says Alexius.

"Keep it hidden," Calis cautions. "There will be time enough to explain. I am sure you have some understanding that this is important?"

Alexius nods as he straightens himself out. He could hear Deidra giggling with Cleo in the other room. "Lyra's parents should be flogged, and her father's cock chopped off for bringing that into the world."

"Maybe that's a bit harsh," says Calis. "It might be that she had a criminal for a mother. Let's go. I am sure Chow will be having a fit right about now."

They leave the room, headed downstairs to calm the angry landlord. Calis knew that he would have to appease the Aryan somehow, even if it meant paying for a year's worth of rent for both apartments. He suddenly realizes the brilliance of Lyra's idea to keep the books away from the Furry Chariot. *Maybe this could be another safe house*, he muses.

CHAPTER 19: THE GAP OF CORA

In each of the civilizations there exist multiple swaths of territory aptly named, 'The Wastelands.' In Illyria, it's the tundra coming down from the once glorious Hyperboria. In Aryavan, there are barren deserts that were once rich with life. In Atlantis, on the landmass across the small sea just east of Egypt, there is the scorching desert of Rekem.

This was once a land full of lush woodlands, rivers, streams. Now, it is covered with red and orange sands rising high like mountains. The ground is beaten by the wind and heat, creating flowing sand tracts which appear like giant serpents from afar. For thousands of miles the desert stretches, a blinding reminder of what weapons of mass destruction can accomplish.

The expanse is named after a prosperous trading kingdom that once thrived here. It was an outpost really, founded by an Anuk prince belonging to a minor house of ENki. They were artists, carving unusual structures out of the igneous rock. Far removed from the major conflict of the great houses, they thought they would be safe in their oasis.

Red structures were hewn into small hills covering 102 square miles. Many were decorated with marble and rose granite edifices, along roadways paved with asphalt. A reservoir supplied water from a nearby lake, serving a population of twenty thousand. The pride of all the residents was a magnificent palace which also served as an assembly hall, constructed in the city center.

Today, this gem called Rekem lays hidden in the desert. It is also the secret dwellings to the King of Atlantis. The population is made up of nomads, runaway slaves, and fugitives from all three civilizations; they number nearly ten thousand.

Life here is not bad. Despite this rock city being in a desolate place, it is also a citadel for one of the hidden nomad civilizations. Underground streams provide water. Smugglers frequently bring in goods and agents of 'The Master' supply an abundance of weaponry.

~BARISH~

Barish was the firstborn of King RU, who was the son of King Tiberius, begotten by King Rigel, the heir of King Atlas. Rounded off to the nearest century, Atlas lived for 900 years, Rigel for 700, Tiberius for 900, RU for 800, and Barish for a mere 400 years. These were all pureblood Anuk, direct descendants of the forefathers of house ENlil.

The last, pure direct descendant of this line will be Liviana when the King dies; Timon is only a half-brother to her, born to an Aryan princess of human and Anuk heritage. This fact is only known by the immediate family but was revealed to the prince shortly before he was sent off to Aryavan.

In his youth, Barish was carefree, devoid of any interest to rule. He often found himself immersed in literature and history. Archeology was his passion, but war would change that. His siblings were all killed in the first Egyptian uprising. Those who survived ultimately died off at the onset of a mysterious plague.

Barish's own family was killed in the conflict between Aryavan and Illyria; treachery almost put an end to his house along with the line to the forefathers.

Barish is still an Anuk worth beholding, for even though he is 372 years, he is exceptionally young when measured against the lifespan of his ancestors. He stands six-feet-four-inches, is a muscular 220 pounds, and wears his head of long and flowing red hair; it matches his short, well-groomed beard. At first meeting, one may think he is a warrior lord of old.

Now, in self-imposed exile, he is the secret symbol of hope for the nomadic peoples of the civilizations. Together with the mysterious Nebpkara, he rallies the disenfranchised, the rejected, the weak, to a cause still hidden to the masses. All they are aware of is that this great man helps them live in a world controlled by the corrupt.

Sleep often escapes the King, more so when Liviana visits. It has been three days since she arrived from Harappa, bringing revelations from Old Mother, and the gem of Persephone. That mysterious stone no one knows anything about, but the King knows. He remembers quite well where he hid it.

Barish strolls across the well-polished marble floors of the stone palace. It is far from being one of the magnificent dwellings his ancestors would call a royal home. For him, it is comfortable. Plants adorn stone walls, accentuating paintings of grand landscapes of Illyria. Columns spread across the massive hall, rising to the forty-foot ceiling. It is almost midnight; Barish silently ponders the information from Old Mother.

He is startled by a sound coming from behind a column. "Papa," Liviana announces as she rolls into view holding a large goblet of wine.

"At this hour?" Barish asks, pointing to the goblet. "Between you and Mica the wine stores will be dry before the next moonrise."

Liviana gives him a questioning stare, "You've got that much?" she jokes.

"Daughter, if there is one thing I've learned over the years, it's to keep you away from good wine." Barish takes Liviana's hand, "When are you going to tell that boy about his true heritage?"

"One day I suppose; when I know I won't lose him for it."

"Why aren't you asleep?" asks Barish.

"Why aren't you?" Liviana responds. "I went to your chambers, but you were gone." She pouts as her father takes the goblet. "It will be three months before I can get away from the capital. Is it wrong to want to spend my last hours with my loving papa?"

Barish takes a drink as they make their way to a stairway leading to the ground floor. Lights embedded into the wall brighten as they pass, providing a soothing dull glow to the area. They head to a large opening leading outside. It is dark out. The wind howls across the canyon.

"Why do you insist on keeping up this, walkabout of yours? Come home!" Liviana complains.

"It has been the tradition of our people since the beginning of time. I will return when my term is up," the King insists.

"It has been twenty years now; the prescribed period is ten. You do know the tradition only suggests wandering in insolation; it doesn't say it has to be in a wretched desert." Liviana grabs the goblet. "Why didn't you name an heir before you left?"

The King smiles. The wind is cold, causing him to drape his arm around his daughter. They stroll across to what is referred to as 'The Monastery'; a grand structure carved into the canyon walls.

"How can there be an heir to Atlantis, when there is an heir to the world?" Barish mutters to himself. He has heard this question from her and countless others before.

"I didn't quite catch that," Liviana complains as the wind howls, but quickly forgets her inquiry as they climb some short stairs. "Why are we here?"

The lights automatically turn on in the stone building. Burnt umber on dark sienna colored ceilings shows off their splendor up high. There is an altar with a small flame in a clear urn directly in front of them; an eternal fire which is always lit.

The flame has been burning for the better part of 300 years. There is a peculiar flicker tonight; not the usual red with yellow, but an intense blue.

There are rows of seating before the altar with a pathway down the middle. They make their way to the fire, stopping just in front of it. Father and daughter stare reverently into the flames, embracing the slight warmth which it brings.

"Why did you seek out the gem of Persephone?" Barish asks in a serious tone. His uncharacteristic tone causes some concern for the Princess.

"I don't know," she responds. "I saw the reference in Arias' journal, then again in Rihzon. It was a mere coincidence that I found it." Very rarely has Liviana had to explain herself to her father.

"Yes, I suppose it was," Barish mumbles.

"You're acting weird. Should I not have brought it here?" Liviana asks.

"It's perfectly fine that you found it. It's just everything seems very real now."

"All that we have done, all that we are doing, to what end are we racing towards? Why is our house so determined to resurrect the memory of a heretic queen?"

Barish gives her an angry look, "Watch your tongue child," he snaps.

It was all confusing to Liviana. She resigns herself to sip her wine. Her eyes widen when her father produces the Persephone gem. He holds it up to the fire.

The ruby-like stone sparkles, creating purple streaks of light that bounce off the walls. Very casually, the King drops the gem into the eternal flame; Liviana protests. At first, nothing happens, but then the fire rushes into the ruby as if it got pulled in. Darkness envelopes the area. Then a soft burgundy glow emanates from the gem.

"What is it?" Liviana asks looking on in awe.

"A relic from the time of the forefathers," the King explains. He puts his hand into the urn, much to Liviana's horror; she calms down when it is obvious that the object is quite cool. "Do you know what this is for?" Barish asks. Liviana shakes her head. "It is but a mere container," he explains.

"For essence?" she asks as she waits for the gem to fall in her palms. Barish nods. "Who's?"

"A tale for another time," Barish says with a smile.

"Father!" the Princess grumbles.

"Daughter," the King responds. He leans over and kisses her forehead.

"Very well," Liviana concedes. "I should know better than to try to get answers before it's time." Barish smiles as he grabs her arm. They begin walking back to his palace.

"Timon has sent the Foreign Legion to Cappadocia. Even now they make camp at the 'Gap of Cora'; I suspect they will attack Darius soon," explains Barish.

This news causes alarm with Liviana, "We have to help him!"

"There are one thousand warriors ready to face them. I have dispatched more from the Illyrian highlands. Our spies could not get information out from the capital quick enough; Darius is trapped."

"You know what will happen if Timon gets his hands on the artifact," Liviana says in a panicked voice. "Why won't you just let me kill him?"

"For all that he is, what he is becoming, he is your brother."

"I have to go. If I leave now I can get Darius out."

"No!" Barish exclaims. He stops to look at Liviana intensely. "You must return to Atlas to recall the Foreign Legion. Convince the Senate to end the campaign."

"And Darius?" Liviana asks.

"Calis is on his way to get him out."

"You could stop this you know," Liviana says a bit calmer.

"Even if I returned today, recalled the Legion, put Timon in chains, it will not stop the machinery of war that has been brewing for centuries. You know what will come when the forefathers return?" the King asks. Liviana nods then rest her head on her father's chest.

"Send me to Nebpkara instead," Liviana says. "Together we can increase efforts to bring down the priesthood."

"That road, unfortunately, has been closed. The Master's focus now will shift to consolidating the nomads."

"When will I meet him?" Liviana asks.

Barish kisses her head instead of providing an answer. They look at the star-filled sky, wondering if their friends will be safe.

-CAPPADOCIAN MOUNTAINS-

Long before the Great-War, this part of the Anatolian plains has been a haven for wandering tribes. The volcanic rock rises from the valley floor, creating small conical mountain stacks which over time, became assorted dwellings for the settling inhabitants. It is now a small city of nomads, which have always been ignored by the Atlantean governors.

The people who live here today are peaceful; they casually mix with the Illyrian traders who cross the borders, and from time to time, visit the Atlantean city, about one hundred miles away. They are led by a man they affectionately call 'Chief.'

He has lived here for nearly twenty-six years, with a small family, and a royal order of protection for the city from King Barish himself. This area is off limits to any form of invasion or settlement from any force of Atlantis.

Chief is in his late fifties, five foot nine, of medium build. Most of his grey hair has dropped off, with only a thin layer left to tease his age. His tanned skin is similar to the rest of the population, but his square jaw exaggerates distinct facial features common to Atlanteans. While the nomads say 'Chief,' those from the continent of Atlantis call him, 'Darius.'

Five miles outside the conical stacks of Cappadocia, is a tranquil green valley. Darius with a party of twelve armed nomads stands behind a line of trees. Just past the tree-line is an empty flat swath of land. They patiently stare out there, minding their horses.

The engines of a small transport craft roar by as it glides into the valley, settling softly on the flat area. The nomads can see Illyrian markings with those of the priesthood. It was not uncommon for pilots to park their crafts this far outside the city; they did so mostly because of the anti-aircraft batteries posted around the mountains.

Before the craft's engines whine down a ramp opens. High Priest Calis jumps to the ground. He stops as if in pain but collects himself quickly to make his way to the tree-line.

Darius smiles as his longtime friend limps towards him. He embraces Calis tightly, for he has not been in his company for several years. They head for a small field-table with two chairs. As they sit one of the nomads brings tea; it is a welcoming drink to fight the cold wind.

"It's a shame we meet under these circumstances," Darius says to Calis in his thick, loud voice.

"Then we'd better get going," Calis responds. "Stavos' camp is only five miles away. The only way out is through Illyria. I'm afraid it will be just a matter of time before they close the borders. Today, time is our enemy."

"They still have to get past the Gap of Cora. As far as I'm told, the Senate holds the Legion in contempt for marching on us."

Calis leans closer to Darius, "Do you really think complaints from senators will stop Timon's forces from invading? No, my friend. As delicious as this tea is, we don't have time for it. Let's go." He stands and is startled by the sound of moving riffles. "Come on Chief," he protests.

"I will not leave my people. If death is what awaits them, then my fate will be no different," Darius explains.

"The warriors should be waiting for the soldiers at the gap. You can still get your people to safety. Have the Illyrians arrived yet?" Calis asks.

"What do you think?" Darius asks with some annoyance. "The wild men from the highlands are late for their funerals. No, we will seek shelter in the Forbidden City; many have already made their way down there. Besides, no outsider has dared enter those tunnels in three thousand years."

"There is more at stake here than your death wish. Give me the artifact then." Calis puts his hand out to Darius, waiting for his part of the key to Lumeria.

There is a smile on Darius' face, "Well I don't have it with me," he explains. "What if you didn't come? I was not going to have it rattling about in my pockets."

"Fine you old goat. Let's get it. You'll have to tell your people not to shoot my transport down."

"You're not going in there with that thing. I don't control the perimeter defenses." Darius gestures to one of the nomads, who bring a pair of horses.

"You are the Chief aren't you?" Calis notices the incoming horse. "What are you doing? I'm not getting on that filthy beast. Keep it away I warn you." He steps back from the horse, apparently afraid of it.

"Tell me something," Darius demands as he climbs on his horse, "how do you suppose Timon knows I have my part of the key? Only you, Barish, and Liviana knows its location."

"Treachery exists somewhere within our ranks."

"Then why am I giving it to you? What if you take it back to Atlantis, straight into the Lion's den?"

"Don't you dare," Calis warns. "I will give it to Arias' son. He is here you know, with the regiment."

"Alexius?" Darius pauses for a moment as if hatching a plan. "Then I will give it to him."

"How are you going to get it to him, by buzzard?" Calis asks sarcastically. "No, I have befriended him, and when he returns from this awful campaign, I shall place it in his care." Darius points to Calis' transport.

"Get in your ship. Wait for me at the far side of the river Halys. It's beyond the perimeter guns so you will be safe. If I see the son of Arias first, then…"

"Hide," Calis interrupts. "He thinks you killed his father."

"And you couldn't tell him otherwise?" Darius complains.

"I took an oath never to reveal certain things…that was one of them." He notices the frustrating glare from Darius, so he shrugs. "Fine, it was a gamble on my part; I encouraged the belief that you killed Arias so he would seek you out."

"You're a bastard Calis. That's very conniving." Darius rides away.

"I learned that from your sister!" Calis shouts.

-THE GAP OF CORA-

This narrow stretch of canyon runs for nearly one mile from the main travel lanes down to the outskirts of Cappadocia. The narrow path is the only way into the nomad city by roadway; air traffic is closely monitored by heavy batteries that keep vigil on all the approaches.

The gap was aptly named after the sixteen-year-old princess Persephone of Hyperboria; 'Kore' was the name she used to hide out amongst the locals; over time the name changed to 'Cora.' As the story goes, Persephone was captured by Illyrian wild men from the north and was being transported through Anatolia in secret via a large caravan of 2000 migrants.

She escaped somewhere in the wilderness, then found herself in the Cappadocian mountains. There she befriended the locals who hid her from the Northerners; her captors eventually considered her lost or dead, so they moved on.

Fortune would favor Persephone once more, for entirely by accident she discovered a long-abandoned sub-terrain city. It was a carefully designed network of tunnels with rooms plunging nearly four hundred feet into the ground, spread over a five-mile radius. The conical mountain stacks above the surface were mere dots when compared to the size of the underground dwelling spaces.

This city was built by her ancestors, during a period in history lost to all but the Creator himself. She did also discover a small cache of weapons amongst riches left behind by the previous occupants. Being the petulant child that she was, she orchestrated the return of her captors to the canyon. Eventually, the wild-men were massacred.

A river of blood flowed through the canyon. Since that time Persephone was never regarded as a child again. Her father's enemies knew she was a force to be reckoned with, so they no longer threatened either her or her concerns.

Her uncles who ruled Illyria granted the Princess a massive portion of the land, which she, in turn, sold off, except Cappadocia. She then freed all the slaves in the domain. Persephone never revealed the secret city to anyone except a chosen few.

Even though the Great-War devastated the region, and the forces of Atlantis claimed the land for the empire, the people who come to Cappadocia know that Persephone is still the sole owner of all the properties contained therein.

This fact does not concern the current forces of Atlantis who inhabit the 'Gap of Cora.' The heavily armed regiment has finished doing battle with the nomad terrorists. Hundreds of bodies lay prostrate on the canyon floor; blood flows from the Atlantean and nomad dead. Several attack aircraft from both sides smolder from their crashes. The 'Gap of Cora' once more flows red.

Commander Stavos' camp is just beyond the gap's entrance. Red tents of Atlantis are spread out on a small area of flat land. Heavy troop transports and attack crafts are parked on a designated airfield. Support vehicles hastily re-arm the ships. Soldiers run feverishly to and from their stations.

The troops wear their fatigue well. Most have never seen battle, for they were recent recruits at a training base in southern Illyria. Now they were soldiers, blindly following the orders of their Commander.

Stavos' tent is the largest in the camp; the fabric is a rich red color, with a gold standard standing proudly at the front. The entrance's flap is closed, which means there is a gathering of officers inside.

A female soldier walks briskly to the flap then boldly enters. Inside, Alexius, Deidra, along with two other officers observe the soldier as she greets Stavos. She hands Alexius an encrypted message tube, salutes Stavos then promptly leaves.

"It has a royal seal," Alexius observes. He hands it off to Stavos, who then tosses it on top of his small desk.

The Commander is not his cheerful self, "Good work today. It appears we have stopped their resistance."

"Are we making camp then?" Deidra asks.

Stavos shakes his head then walks towards the exit, "Get the troops mobilized; we are moving into Cappadocia."

Deidra looks at Alexius, then back to Stavos, "Sir, they are wary…"

"Do as ordered Captain!" Stavos snaps.

"Yes Sir," Deidra responds.

"Now all of you get out!" the Commander orders. The group leaves through the flap. As Alexius begins to leave Stavos grabs his shoulder, "Not you Captain."

He returns to his desk with Alexius following. He picks up the tube. Alexius opens a portable receiver on the desk. Stavos promptly inserts the tube. The screen flickers to life. Prince Timon's image appears.

"Stavos, I want you to clean out Cappadocia," the recording begins. "Remember, wipe out every living nomad. Find Darius, and bring me my artifact!" The image flickers away.

Surprise fills Alexius' face, "Darius? He is here?"

"Wine!" Stavos orders. Alexius brings a pitcher with two cups. "I take it you know the story of Darius and your father?"

"I only recently learned of what happened," Alexius answers as he touches his shirt, feeling for his necklace. "What artifact is the prince searching for?"

"A family heirloom." Answers Stavos. He shuffles some papers on the desk. "But he wants Darius' head. Help me accomplish this. Rise with me to the halls of glory."

Stavos produces a picture of Darius when he was younger, along with a rendition of what he may look like now. Just below is a picture of a small octagonal artifact with engravings in the old tongue. Alexius is relieved as the heirloom is not his. He notices infrared scans on the desk.

"These look like dwellings; families not warrior camps," Alexius point out on the scans.

Stavos finishes his wine, fills his cup, then quickly downs the drink. He is sweating profusely, even though the temperatures outside are a few degrees above freezing. Alexius looks at him with concern but decides not to inquire about his friend's strange behavior of late.

It was just four days ago when he ran into Stavos with prince Timon at the underground fight club. There was nothing out of character with the Commander then, but the next day, there was an anxious way about him. They made their way to Cappadocia with haste, barely set up camp, battled the nomad warriors. Now without rest, they were about to storm what looked like dwellings.

Then there were the physical signs of anguish in Stavos. His eyes were bloodshot with bags forming under his eyelids. He was always sweating as if his body was trying to burn out an infection. He was quick to get angry, and rarely made any sarcastic comments about, anything. *There is something wrong with him*, Alexius acknowledges silently.

"Do you know what a nomad child turns into?" Stavos asks, "A warrior! This is our chance to stamp out the disease, here, now!"

Horror overcomes Alexius, "You're talking about genocide; mothers, children, families."

"You're a fucking soldier!" Stavos points out. "Those little shits will turn into the dead out there. Before that, they will wait to slit your noble throat the first chance they get. Don't go soft on me now. Tell you what, you and Deidra can plunder when we are finished." Alexius looks at him as if he got caught with his hands in the coffers. "I know about your exploits."

"Deidra is innocent; any wrongdoing should fall on me," Alexius says quickly.

"Yes, she is. A fine soldier, whom I foresee will command the Foreign Legion one day." He grabs Alexius' shoulder, "You and me my friend will be amongst the living gods, like the heroes of long ago."

There was a time when the thought of glory would entice Alexius to whatever means necessary to achieve it. Now, there is a bitter taste to what Stavos is feeding him. The small ache in his stomach is quickly turning into nausea. He notices that he has been spinning Chloe's 'magic bracelet' for the entire conversation. Suddenly, his mind escapes to thoughts of his niece and nephew, the priest Mathias with his dead grandson, and the faceless civilians who they are about to massacre.

There would be no escaping the events to come.

CHAPTER 20:
THE LIES WE
ARE TOLD

The river Halys is a quarter mile wide, stretching for 734 miles through the land. The rough waters beat on rocks near the banks, creating foam in its wake. It separates Cappadocia from the nearby Illyrian border some two miles away.

The Illyrian transport craft Calis arrived in sits on a grassy area near the banks, with the engines 'spun up,' ready to depart at a moment's notice. Some twenty yards away near the riverbank, its passenger paces impatiently.

"Hurry you fool" Calis grunts to himself.

Why doesn't anyone listen to me? He did not want to be out here in the open. He should have been within Illyrian airspace with Darius by now. Then there is the risk of his sudden trip to Illyria being found out by the new Acheniaes, Inias; that would ensure some uncomfortable questioning from the intelligence arm of the priesthood.

His contemplation is interrupted by the pilot shouting from the ramp. He looks at the man. *This cannot be good.*

"Your holiness, we have incoming!" the pilot screams.

As if on cue, three Atlantean fighter craft dart overhead; they are a quarter mile away, 800 feet up. One breaks off from the formation then banks steeply to the right, pulling a sharp turn while descending toward the river. The remaining two fire missiles into the Cappadocian landscape, causing anti-aircraft batteries to engage.

Calis begins to run towards his craft but freezes when he notices the single fighter angling towards his position. He shouts to his pilot, "Get out," but the man is already engaging his engines, attempting to lift the craft off the ground. A missile from the fighter shoots off to the escaping vehicle; within moments it hits, exploding into a massive fireball.

The force of the explosion knocks Calis off his feet, sending him plunging into the roaring waters. The fighter speeds by then pull up sharply, beginning its ascent into the clouds. Debris from the Illyrian craft drops into the river, missing the unconscious priest by inches. If he doesn't drown for the next mile of his travel, then Calis will be stranded in the wilderness that waits.

-AT THE FOOT OF THE MOUNTAIN STACKS-

Atlantean soldiers are formed up just outside the mountain dwellings; rows of armed troops waiting for the air assault to end. Faint explosions are echoing in the valley; signs that the bombing of the perimeter batteries is successful.

The command vehicle is a crude tough-looking small truck, parked at the front of the ground troops. Stavos sits calmly in the front, carefully examining a thin screen on his lap. A display of live infrared images is being broadcast from field equipment planted at the mouth of the caves. He scrolls through the information, searching for any signs of the inhabitants.

He turns to his Corporal sitting in the driver's seat. The young soldier known as Fat-Boy is uncomfortable, as this is his first engagement as a soldier, and the bloodshed of the previous hours weighs heavy on his soul. The Commander decides that he needs a more seasoned eye to look at the screens. He turns to his right to look out the window.

"The caves are empty," Stavos declares to Alexius, who stands impatiently outside his door. "They must be underground; what do you think Captain?"

"It is possible," Alexius answers as he grabs the display. "Or they have abandoned it."

"Not likely. They are still there. Captain Deidra!" Stavos shouts, looking past Alexius. She runs up to the door. "Ready your infiltration force. Empty the stronghold if needed. I want Darius; kill everyone else."

The order brings a moment of hesitation from Deidra. She looks at Alexius and notices he is giving her a disapproving look. She has never been one to disobey direct orders, for she took her oaths seriously. No matter how cruel or inhumane the command was, she never questioned them. Unlike Alexius, she is properly programmed to follow orders, for the glory of the Empire.

"By your command," she acknowledges. She gives Alexius a steely look then runs off towards the back of the formation.

"Commander, these mountain caves are dwellings, civilians. It is possible all their warriors were killed," Alexius protests.

"You have your orders Captain."

"There has to be…" Alexius begins as he gets closer to Stavos, then whispers, "another way. There is no need to massacre an entire people. How can we stand in the halls of glory knowing what we have done?"

He notices the heavy bead of sweat on Stavos' face rolling down his clammy skin. His friend appears to be struggling inside, fighting an impulse. *One problem at a time*, Alexius cautions himself.

"Very well," Stavos announces. "If we find Darius the rest will be spared."

The concession is all Alexius could hope for right now. With any luck, Deidra will not meet any resistance, and Darius will surrender. More importantly, he wanted to confront the man accused of killing his father. He runs off to find Deidra.

-IN THE UNDERGROUND CAVES-

The inhabitants of the mountains have made their way into the tunnels beneath the surface. They carry on through the narrow passageways in droves, trying not to trample each other. Men, women, and children of varying ages; some carry light sticks, others have bags of provisions strapped to their backs. The ceiling is low, about six feet. Carved rock passageways are only ten feet wide.

Large circular stones stand motionless at junctions, ready to be rolled into place to block off the path to the surface. Muffled explosions rock the walls, causing dust and tiny pebbles to fall. Panic sets in with the mob as they attempt to all push forward at the same time.

Some armed warriors stand in crevices in the rock wall, observing the crowd and trying to assist when needed. An old woman falls to the ground, bruising her knees; she decides not to cry out in pain, but the mob is on top of her and her granddaughter. Darius jumps off his crevice to push the incoming waves off of her. He helps her up then grabs a passing man to entrust the woman and the girl to his care.

"Chief, they won't all make it to the lower levels in time! What do they want?" a warrior asks.

"Me," Darius answers. "Get the word out, start filling the chambers. It will ease the crowds for now."

"But the soldiers may find the people in the upper chambers," the warrior points out.

"With any luck, the entrance will remain hidden. If it's found, then my friend, their sacrifice will not be forgotten." Darius points to the passing wave.

The warrior activates a small communications device in his hand. He barks the orders to the rest of fighters. There are chambers littered on the levels, each capable of holding 100 souls. A rolling stone can secure the space at the entrance. Once put into place the rock will appear to be a small wall.

"You should get below; we can handle this from here," the warrior urges Darius.

"No. There is something I have to do; someone I have to find," Darius explains.

He pats the warrior on his shoulder then continues to help the crowd. His worse fear is coming to pass; the impending annihilation of his adopted people. He has lost all communication with Calis, which means he cannot get his artifact out of Cappadocia. He resigns himself to seek out Alexius, hoping that he can convince the soldier to abandon his orders and take up the responsibility Arias hoped he would.

-DEIDRA'S PLATOON-

Twenty-five seasoned Foreign Legion soldiers in black stand patiently in front of a small entrance to one of the mountain stacks. Deidra checks her sidearm; satisfied, she returns it to her holster then checks her daggers. The noise of running boots on gravel does not shift her focus; she knows its Alexius.

"Deidra, wait!" Alexius calls out.

"Your whining is boring me, no, it's aggravating me. We're here to do what we've always done, or have you forgotten?" Deidra asks in a rough tone.

"Stavos changed his mind; no killing, just find Darius."

"Just like that huh?" she asks suspiciously.

"Just like that," Alexius replies.

"You're lying to me again," Deidra says while continuing to check her daggers.

"You know I don't lie to you." Alexius grabs her arm then pulls her close.

"You lie to me every day. Let go of me!" Deidra shouts.

"That may be true," he admits, "but I don't lie about the important things. Look, I have a bad feeling about this; did we come here to kill warriors or civilians?"

"We exchanged our conscience for uniforms," Deidra points out. "Don't get your loyalties twisted. We serve the Empire, our Commander, and our Prince. Now move!"

She storms off to join her platoon. There would be no reasoning with her at the onset of battle, Alexius knew this. *There may only be one way*, he decides; find Darius then bring him to Stavos. He runs away from the platoon, headed for another cave opening.

-AT THE SECOND UNDERGROUND LEVEL-

The waves of retreating civilians have thinned out; many are concealed within the hidden chambers spread out along the tunnels, allowing ease to the congestion. Darius stands at a stone column rising from the ground to the ceiling; there are more of these here. Multiple tunnels are scattered at junctions that lead to unknown destinations; only his trusted warriors know where to point the people.

One of the warriors pushes her way to Darius. She clutches her communicator tightly. She looks at Chief helping the people.

"Chief, the soldiers have found the entrance!" the warrior exclaims.

"Then it is time to do what I must. Tell the others to find whatever hiding place they can.

Spread out and go deeper. Follow the markings as you have been taught; Hurry!"

The warrior runs off leaving Darius to wave over two more. The three men make their way to the upper level with haste.

-OUTSIDE A CAVE ENTRANCE-

Swarms of troops rush into the caves ready for resistance. Their orders are clear, round up the enemies, find Darius; kill everyone else. All of the grunts already had their taste of blood earlier at the Gap of Cora. They were fighting for their lives then, but now they will be participating in genocide.

Their Commander watches them disappear into the mountain; there is an anxious air about him. He sees Deidra and quickly strides over. She is looking around wildly as if trying to find someone.

"Are you sure you found the entrance?" Stavos asks Deidra.

"I am certain," she answers. "It leads deeper. The scans show at least eight more levels. Commander, it will take days to search the tunnels. The troops are tired, starving…"

"I don't care about who is tired or starving!" Stavos cuts her off. "I want Darius found and this place purged!" he screams. He walks off into the tunnel with Fat-Boy.

-AT THE FIRST UNDERGROUND LEVEL-

The tunnels are dim with the only light emanating from Alexius' light stick. The thin crude tube is three feet in length, with the top twelve inches glowing with luminous white light. There is evidence on the ground that there was a massive exodus here; torn clothing, fruits, vegetables, blood.

He stops his advance to look around the empty space; the brown rock walls seem to go on endlessly. Dark foreboding tunnels beckon him to enter the unknown, but he decides to refer to a more detailed direction. He retrieves his father's journal.

The drawings give some indication as to which direction will send him to possible gathering points. He studies the map intensely, dropping to the ground as he reads. He is startled by his communicator crackling on his belt. He looks at the screen; it's Deidra.

"What?" he snaps.

"Where are you?" Deidra demands.

"Never mind where I am." He pauses, realizing that he owes his closest friend more than a brush off. "I'm going to find Darius, then bring him to Stavos. Maybe I can stop this massacre."

"You ass!" she screams. "Stavos will have your head for this."

"Look, we have to find Darius right? Just trust me. Try not to get yourself killed." He switches off the device before Deidra can respond.

-AT UNDERGROUND LEVEL THREE-

Soldiers have halted their advance to set up a heavy gun in front of a circular stone. One soldier holds up a display for Stavos, showing blurry images of red outlines moving about inside a hidden chamber.

"Bring it down," the Commander orders.

The gun fires a wave of projectiles accompanied by circles of blue light. It is a combination of explosive pellets and sonic energy which maximizes the destructive force. Within seconds the rock barrier comes crumbling down, revealing frightened people.

Men, women, and children, huddle together in the stone room. They look at the soldiers as they enter, in particular, they observe Commander Stavos; he appears to be searching for someone. A senior man stands up, much to the protest of his companion.

"Please, we are unarmed, we have done nothing wrong," the old man states.

"Where is Darius?" Stavos asks.

258

"We do not know who that is," the man explains.

"I'll make this simple." Stavos grabs his pistol then shoots the old man in his temple. He continues to scan the crowd. "Shall we begin again? Where is Darius? Your leader!"

No one answers, but it didn't matter at this point. The Commander nods to soldiers. He steps out of the room.

The soldiers fire their weapons at the people. Screams being drowned out by gunfire fill the chamber. When the killing stopped, the soldiers resume their search.

-LATER AT UNDERGROUND LEVEL THREE-

Several wrong turns, and a drop down a shaft later has led Alexius to the third level. Frustration overcomes him as everywhere he turns looks the same.

He begins to run; several yards ahead he stumbles and falls near a column. As he starts to pick himself up, he notices the base of the column has an odd patch of what looks like dirty marble. A faded golden symbol is partially covered with dirt. He brushes it off.

The symbol is not familiar, so ignore it; no need to look for it in the journal for time was not on his side. Suddenly, he feels a rumble on the ground as if a rock from below was exploding. He remains still, listening for any sound emanating from the dark tunnels ahead; there is none. *The tube closest to the vibration,* he decides then runs into the dark cavity.

-AT UNDERGROUND LEVEL FOUR-

Once more another chamber has been discovered; the scene waits for the same result, just as with the previous four. Stavos is becoming impatient with the search; his troops are now beyond exhausted. He points to a mother and her six-year-old daughter. He pulls out his dagger while looking at Fat-Boy.

"Bring the child!" Stavos orders. Fat-Boy complies.

The woman screams as Fat-Boy reluctantly pulls the child from her arms. The little girl struggles, but the soldier's grip is tight. Stavos grabs the girl by her hair as he puts the blade to her throat. He looks at the mother with merciless eyes. He is tired of her screaming.

"Where is your leader?" Stavos barks.

The little girl's struggling causes the blade to scratch the surface of her skin. A bead of blood appears on the broken flesh, and then she suddenly goes limp. Stavos looks at her disappointed. He lets her body drop to the ground; the mother jumps up to charge Stavos. He plunges his blade into her neck.

"Poisoned blade," he explains to Fat-Boy with a smile. The soldier looks on, trying desperately not to let his Commander see his abhorrence. "Very well, purge them."

Gunfire erupts in the area. Within moments all is dead in the room. The soldiers step out and are ready to move on to the next area. As the echo fades, a runner can be heard coming their way. The soldiers point their guns in the direction, ready to fire. They drop their weapons when they see Alexius rushing towards them.

He stops at the edge of the group, breathing hard from the desperate run; Stavos passes by him, expressionless. Alexius notices smoke coming out of the chamber ahead; he pushes his way to it, expecting the horror he knew awaited him.

Blood is spewed on the walls; the dead are piled upon one another; the smell of Sulphur is stifling the senses. The dead girl's body twitches on the ground near Alexius' feet. A small stuffed rabbit falls out of her dress, rolling into a pool of blood.

Unbridled rage overcomes Alexius, like that of a caged lion ready to pounce on its jailer. He charges towards Stavos with hate in his eyes. Soldiers attempt to hold him back, but they are swatted away like flies. Seven men grab him; they struggle to keep him down. He tries to fight them off, knocking one on the ground, then slamming another to a rock column. More jump him, making a total of thirteen now.

One soldier slams his rifle butt on Alexius temple. Then another quickly discharges a stun device behind his neck. An unknown amount of voltage flows through the black box, which sparks as the energy hits the Captain's flesh.

Finally, Alexius drops, disoriented from the blow to the temple and the electric shock. He sits calmly on the ground while one soldier places restraints on his wrists. Two others lift his hulking body, trying to make him stand on his wobbly legs.

"Corporal!" Stavos calls out. "Escort the Captain back to the surface!" he screams.

Fat-Boy with the two soldiers drag Alexius away, leaving Stavos to push further into the abyss of tunnels. It will be a long journey back up, but the soldiers were grateful to be leaving the main group.

They struggle with the massive Captain up an incline to the third level. They carry on their task silently, with no one wanting to talk about what is happening.

"They are just people," Alexius says in a weakened voice.

"We are just following orders, Sir," Fat-Boy says.

Suddenly, a muffled explosion is heard. It is an unmistakable echo of the soldiers' heavy gun blasting through another rock door. The vibrations shake nearby columns, dropping pebbles to the ground at first. At this junction, the columns break, causing the ceiling to come crashing down on the group.

Heavy blocks smash the soldiers, instantly killing the two that were carrying Alexius, and crushing Fat-Boy's sternum. His head is above the rubble, with blood oozing out of his mouth. He turns his head slowly to the right.

Alexius' head sticks out from under the rubble. He is barely conscious. He sees Fat-Boy stretching his hand out, reaching for him. Flashes of Bain fill his mind, then of the nomad boy he killed in Illyria. The image of the little girl with her toy dominates his thoughts. He begins to weep. His tears absorb the dust on his face. He can feel his strength failing. His vision is blurry; his head is beginning to throb. A rock dislodges from the ceiling, quickly hitting him on his temple.

CHAPTER 21: THE PATH TO PROPHECY

The sun shines in the sky over a calm lake; the water is clear. The air smells of lilies, and everything is peaceful. The water rolling on to the sandy shore hits Alexius' tiny feet, pushing further up the sand, soaking his three-year-old body.

Delicate, but strong arms pull him onto a thin dress covering a very comfortable lap. He opens his sleepy eyes to see the sun burning brightly overhead. The silhouette of a young woman who feels like his mother looks down at him. Her long blonde hair falls on his face with a scent of lavender.

She hums a tune he knows but has never heard. The melody is putting him to sleep once more. He begins to drift off into peaceful bliss. He can feel her arms grip him tightly. Her loving embrace is overpowering his senses. He wants to stay here forever.

Alexius' eyes open; they burn from the dust particles lodged therein. His body aches and his head is about to explode from a headache. His vision is clearing, and his sense of hearing is normalizing; three men are talking nearby. He expects to be covered with rubble, but to his surprise, he is not. He tries to stand.

The men are startled as he stands upright. His adrenalin quickly pumps through his veins as he recognizes Darius. Instinctively, he reaches for his sidearm, but it is gone. He feels for his daggers, but as expected, they too are missing.

"Don't be afraid, son of Arias," says Darius.

"Darius," Alexius confirms and begins to wobble to the men. He quickly drops to his knees.

"We mean you no harm son," Darius says calmly.

"You killed my father. Let me return the favor."

"I don't think so," Darius says with a smirk on his face. His companions reveal their side arms. "Now that that's out of the way; we can leave you here to die or, you can put away your misguided anger, and trust me."

"Why should I trust you?"

"Because you have fallen into a much bigger game, one your father meant for you to enter," Darius explains. "I loved your father, and I did not kill him. You were left with this lie to protect a bigger one. Come, there is much to learn, and we don't have time."

The nomads help Alexius on his feet. Darius stands in front of a stone wall; he touches a small corner. The ground rumbles as the stone swings aside revealing a passageway. Electric lights slowly turn on in a small room, revealing a console at one end. There is another passageway opening up at the opposite wall.

-OUTSIDE THE MOUNTAIN-

Swarms of Atlantean troops exit the side of the mountain. They are all disoriented by the sudden sunlight attacking their senses. It will be an exhausting two-mile march back to the troop transports.

There is no compassion for them from the Commander. His mission is still incomplete. He cannot rest until he finds Darius, and Prince Timon's heirloom; but even Stavos has his limits. Against his better judgment, he has taken Captain Deidra's advice to regroup at their camp.

Deidra is at the mountain's entrance; she sees Stavos' vehicle drive off. She presses a button on her communicator and waits for any indication that Alexius' radio is still turned on. Her impatience is getting the better of her, so she checks her sidearm as she runs into the mountain.

-HIDDEN UNDERGROUND ROOM-

The surroundings in the dark chamber are eerie, cold. There is a hiss from air vents which travel all the way from the surface. The lighting is dim, and there is a soft blue glow from an old console. Darius is attempting to do something with the switches; Alexius is crouched in a corner looking at the activity.

He glares at the men from time to time, not trusting their motives. The console catches his interest when a screen materializes in the air. Images of hundreds of people huddled together move about in a three-dimensional show. He has never seen anything like this before.

"What is that?" Alexius asks with some bewilderment in his voice.

"These are our people, hiding from this atrocity." Darius selects a switch, causing the images to change to a map of the entire area. "We will be able to see where your soldiers are with this."

"They are not my soldiers," Alexius explains. "You can stop this if you surrender. What is your part in all of this?"

"I am just a humble advisor to the King, just like your father," says Darius. "It was Arias who taught me how to use this," he explains pointing to the console.

"Can you tell me what is going on?" Alexius asks with some frustration.

265

Darius nods to his men, "Make sure the path to the second level is clear," he orders. "Are you ready to listen, Alexius of Badur?"

"I don't have a choice do I?" Alexius asks with some distrust in his voice. "I don't know you, and I have to assume things are not always as they appear, so yes, I am listening."

"First, as I said, I did not kill Arias. Our enemies spread this lie. If you read his journal, you will find this truth." Darius retrieves the journal from his pocket and hands it to a grateful Alexius.

"I've not found anything to vindicate you, old man."

"There is a good portion written in the old Illyrian script; have it translated. You will realize that Arias describes the treachery of a man called Samiri. He suspected this villain was not whom he claimed to be. For many, many years, he was our trusted companion.

He sought something called the 'Amon-I,' an ancient relic. King Barish and the rest of us were seeking the lost land of Lumeria; the mythical resting place of his ancestors. It is during our quest that we discovered the awful truth of the past."

~DARIUS' RENDITION OF EVENTS~
"The forefathers came to this world from the heavens, ages ago. We do not know why, but they brought with them the means to bring mankind out from the mud, starting a 'Golden-age.' They set up civilizations and government, religion and education. They most of all never claimed to be gods amongst men. Two great houses ruled; house ENlil the primary, and house ENki, the secondary.
After thousands of years passed, when humanity was at peace with itself, the seven

forefathers retreated to Lumeria, to take the long sleep until the time they would rise again, at the end of Virgo, to judge humanity; humanity, a term given to all Anuk and man.

If peace weighs heavy on their scales, then a new 'Golden-age' will dawn. If war, pestilence, and chaos are rampant, then the cleansing will be imminent; the complete and utter annihilation of humanity.

During the age of the mighty Anuk King Shuru of ENlil, the seeds of conflict were sewn. The mighty watchers of old, an ancient sect, were stripped of their power and made to serve second to man. It was at this time that the first of many engineered plagues swept through the world, killing off millions of the Anuk, the watchers, and man.

A child was born to Shuru during these years of darkness, a daughter named Persephone. She was immune to the plague. Contained within her blood were the antigens to cure the deadly disease. She was hailed as the savior of humanity, and highly regarded after that; some secretly worshiped her, while others wanted to covet her.

Her love for Osiris of house ENki was frowned upon, as those houses within ENlil knew that any union between the two would pass on the royal bloodline. The firstborn daughter of Shuru was to inherit the world, and as such so would her offspring.

The Great-War engulfed the world with conflict and chaos. King Shuru and Osiris were murdered. The usurper from house ENlil sought an end to Persephone and her unborn child. They almost succeeded at the temple of the lion in pTah, Egypt. With the help of Thoth, Persephone escaped to Lumeria with a key that allowed her access to hidden Anuk technology.

From there she launched devastating weapons which destroyed the world as it existed. A plague was also unleashed, killing off most humans with Anuk blood. Nothing is known about her after this.

Before she escaped, Thoth transferred the essence of her unborn child to a sacred Anuk relic, a part of the Amon-I. He hid this 'Gem of Persephone' in the world, only to be revealed through clues before the end of Virgo.

Thoth passed on secrets to your ancestor, Badur, who in turn entrusted them to his descendants. Before the end of Virgo, house Badur would bring forth Persephone's heir, and bestow on him or her, the key to Lumeria.

The heir will raise the forefathers to judge the world, as the awakening can only be performed by such; a union between the direct lines of ENlil and ENki. Persephone and her child were the ones foretold in the ancient Anuk scripture; whether engineered or by divine providence."

There is a confused look on Alexius' face, "So as I am the last of house Badur, I have to seek out Persephone's heir to help raise the forefathers?" Darius nods. "There are a lot of holes in your story old man, and nothing to explain how my father died."

"Samiri," says Darius. He lets the name fester for a moment. "With knowledge of old, he seeks to kill Persephone's heir. He wants the Amon-I, the vessel which contains the essence of the forefathers. The Amon-I is more than a vessel, and this knowledge I do not have."

"Where is it then?" Alexius asks.

"Only your father knew," Darius explains. "Samiri thought by befriending us he would be able to find its location. This failing, he tortured Arias to his end and manipulated events which placed the blame on me. I fled Atlantis to lay in wait for you. Your father did write 'The path to the key of power starts in Cappadocia,' did he not?"

Some semblance of comfort overcomes Alexius; since learning about his father's murder, he had wondered about the cause for it. There is an air of trust about Darius, so he dips into his shirt to produces his heirloom. Darius smiles and does the same for his.

"This is for you," Darius says, "and this is when I must entrust it to your care." He pulls the octagonal shape off the chain and hands it to Alexius. "These two pieces must never fall into the hands of Prince Timon; none of the pieces must. He too seeks the power in Lumeria, but only for the conquest of the world. Do everything possible to prevent this."

"They fit together," Alexius says while examining the grooves of both. He returns his piece inside his clothing and puts the new piece in his pocket. "Now that the history lesson is over, we have more important concerns."

"Yes, I say that we do. You have to leave this place. Find Liviana," says Darius.

"The princess?" Alexius asked surprised.

"She is Barish's daughter after all and a trusted member of our circle. She will know what to do. I am afraid our mutual friend Calis was supposed to meet you, but he has seemed to have disappeared."

Darius touches some switches, showing the topography of the land outside Cappadocia. A red dot illuminates next to the river Halyr, with some ancient symbols next to it. Darius' scowls with worry. He presses another switch, dissolving the display.

Darius begins to shut down the console, "Calis' transport has been destroyed. We can only assume he perished along with it. We must go." He points to the tunnel and begins hurrying through; Alexius follows.

-SECOND UNDERGROUND LEVEL-

Running boots down a shaft accompanies the glow of a light stick. Deidra is following the path taken by the troops, trying to make her way to the last spot she was told Alexius was seen. She has a feeling he is down here; probably getting himself into a situation. Ignoring her soldier's instincts, she is determined to assist him in whatever stupid endeavor he is undertaking.

She stops her advance near a junction; voices are echoing down one of the tunnels. She draws her weapon while moving cautiously to the sounds. Faint light can be seen bouncing off a wall. She hears a reference to the notorious villain, 'The Master.' *This can't be good* she decides. She enters the area and stops when she sees the figures standing by a wall; Alexius is with Darius.

"Alexius move away!" Deidra screams as she points her weapon at Darius.

"Deidra, no!" Alexius yells. "It's alright. Put your weapon down. It's alright."

Alexius moves cautiously towards Deidra, getting in front of her aim and Darius. He knows she is exhausted, and will not be thinking clearly. Her only thoughts would be on completing the mission, which meant taking Darius back to Stavos;

he could not allow this. Darius quickly steps in front of Alexius.

"Please, there is no need for violence here." Darius pauses when two warriors run up behind Deidra. "We don't want any trouble."

"You're with them?" Deidra says to Alexius, "Really? Get your head out of your ass!"

"I can't let you take him to Stavos. You know I'm right."

"I will go with you if it means you leave this place," Darius says. He looks at Alexius, "And you, leave here quickly. Find the one whom you must." Darius motions his men to lower their weapons.

"I'm sorry Deidra," Alexius says while stepping closer.

"For what?" she asks.

Before Deidra could blink, Alexius punches her face. Her weapon discharges into the air as she steps back disoriented. Within seconds she crumples to the ground on her wobbly legs.

"For that," says Alexius

"We can get her to the surface," Darius offers. "You must make your way to the river Halys. Come, we don't have much time."

"I am going back to camp with Deidra," Alexius insists. "Look, Darius, I will protect this secret with my life, but I will not abandon my friend. I am going back to camp."

"Just like your father; very well. You should be aware then that a well-armed tribe of Illyrian nomads is on their way to your camp, about a day away. You'd best be gone by the time they arrive."

"I'll find a way, I promise." Alexius picks up Deidra and drapes her over his shoulder. He looks at Darius, nods, then runs off towards the surface.

-AT THE MOUNTAIN ENTRANCE-

A small transport craft settles on the ground then a ramp descends. Alexius had called for it on his way to the surface. One medic jumps out to wave him over.

With haste, Alexius gets into the craft with Deidra on his shoulder. He drops her on a cot before securing her restraints. *Oh shit, she can't wake up just yet,* he panics.

"Sargent," Alexius yells over the whining engines, "You have to sedate her. She is infected. I'm afraid she may harm herself." The medic acknowledges.

It will be a short fight to the camp, and he has to figure out how to get himself and Deidra away from the impending attack. The best thing to do will be to inform Stavos about the approaching warriors, then slip away during the fighting. It is a risky gamble, and he knows Deidra will never forgive him for dragging her along.

-LATER AT THE ATLANTEAN CAMP-

Sunlight is fading fast in the valley; the cold wind is beginning to sting. Many of the soldiers are outside, happy to be done with their task for today. They know it will be a matter of hours before they have to go out there again; to perform horrors in the name of the Empire. Nevertheless, they walk about the camp getting food, medical aid, and for most, forgiveness from the resident priests.

The Captains' tent is not far from the medical one. Since there are only two Captains on this campaign, Alexius is confident he will not be disturbed.

He makes haste with the packing, emptying a larger bag into his leather one. He grabs some of Deidra's things and throws it in with his. He is startled when the tent's flap opens.

"Deidra," he exclaims with surprise. She rushes towards him and slams her fist on his nose.

The attack caught him off guard; he drops to the ground.

"You are a fucking asshole!" Deidra screams. "That's for my nose." She clutches her fist in pain and then kicks Alexius in the gut.

The tent flap opens once more, this time Commander Stavos enters. He is a lot calmer than he was before. He observes the scene curiously. He looks at Deidra, gesturing her to leave, which she does promptly. Alexius is still on the ground, making no effort to stand.

"Did you get it?" Stavos asks.

"Get what?" Alexius asks harshly.

"Don't play games with me, Captain. You know very well what I am talking about. Deidra told me what you did; protected Darius from her. So, you either know where Darius is, or he gave you the artifact; which is it?"

Before Alexius can stand Stavos drops a knee on his gut. He quickly sticks the pointy end of his dagger into his friend's neck. He applies a bit of pressure, attempting to pierce the flesh.

"This is a poisoned blade. The scratches I'm making right now may not kill you, but it will cause some fatigue to your nervous system. If you want the antidote, you will answer."

"What happened to you?" Alexius asks as he begins to feel the effects of the poison.

He surprises Stavos with a swift punch to the chest, which sends him flying to the other end of the tent. He quickly gets up and lunges at his commander. There will be no way out of this one. No need to wait for the Illyrians to attack, for now, he is certain an escape has to happen; without Deidra.

Stavos counters his punches and delivers some of his own. He feels the power flowing through his blood as if his strength has increased ten-fold. He lashes out at Alexius, connecting him with a mighty blow. He dives to where his dagger fell, quickly picking it up, and ready to plunge it into Alexius' heart. He notices the octagonal artifact has fallen out of Alexius' pocket.

The rumble inside the tent has attracted several soldiers from outside. At first, they are hesitant to peer in. One of the soldiers sees Deidra pacing two tents over.

Blow after blow connects Alexius as his weakening body is beginning to fail from the poison. He is still stronger than Stavos and manages to pick up a metal box to launch it. Stavos falls. Alexius jumps on him. He delivers his blows now, hoping to subdue his attacker.

Stavos waits for Alexius to raise his fist then pushes his own through the opening, connecting his jaw. He can now get out from under Alexius. He pulls another dagger from his waist and plunges it into Alexius' chest. He rolls on top of the Captain.

The pain is unbearable, but Alexius tries to remain conscious. He sees Deidra and the soldiers enter the tent, looking horrified at the scene. Stavos is distracted. This gives Alexius a split-second opportunity to attack.

It is as if his hand was the wind, with everything moving in slow-motion but him. Power courses through his veins, he could feel it. His dying body is re-energizing itself. His mind is gaining a sharp focus unlike anything he had experienced before; *It could be adrenalin,* he thinks at that moment.

Alexius pushes Stavos up with both hands, sending him five feet in the air. He launches himself up to meet the motionless man, grabs his shoulders, and then twists his body in mid-air.

They begin their descent with Stavos' back facing the floor. Alexius yanks the dagger out of his chest and plunges it into Stavos sternum. All this happens within the blink of an eye. They crash on the ground.

Alexius drops on Stavos ready to pass out. He can hear the breath leaving his friend; dying breaths. Blood oozes from both their wounds. Everything seems to be going black, and then his body goes limp.

Deidra immediately pulls Alexius off Stavos, not sure of what else to do. The soldiers stare at the scene waiting for a command. Deidra checks Stavos' neck for a pulse but doesn't find any. She does the same for Alexius and sighs with relief. She puts her hand to her face, silently crying. Panic sets in.

"You're in command now Captain Deidra. What shall we do?" one of the young soldiers asks.

Deidra sees the private looking at her with anticipation. She did not know what to do. She considers what options lay before her. She could not cover this up, and Alexius surely would have to be sent back to Atlantis to answer for his actions. Atlantis sounds like the best option. It would take him far away from Darius, and hopefully, his brother would be able to help him.

"Take him to the medics," Deidra orders. "He goes on a transport to Libya, tonight. Get help, put the Commander's body in his tent. Let the priests perform their rituals."

The soldiers acknowledge and begin to drag Alexius' heavy body out of the tent. Deidra looks at Stavos' corpse. She adored him, and now she felt overwhelming anger for what transpired. She knows Alexius could be tried and put to death, but there was nothing she could do. Duty and honor demanded she stayed true to her office before any family or friend. She finds resolve in this thought.

Deidra notices Alexius' bag. She goes over to it to pack some of his things. To her surprise, she finds some of her articles in the bag. She silently sheds her tears, trying not to be overcome with emotion.

The octagonal artifact on the ground catches her eye. She picks it up. She knows it's Alexius' and tosses it into his bag. She throws it over her shoulder and leaves the tent, heading to the medics to check on her friend. It will be a long night.

-MIDNIGHT AT REKAM-

The palace is quiet since Liviana left. Once more Barish lives in anguish at the thought of being apart from his family, both his children. He strolls over to a communications device in his private chamber. He activates a screen and waits for the receiver to answer the call.

A figure with a brown cloak appears on the other end, with candles burning in the background. The image flickers for a moment as some encryption symbols flash on the screen. Satisfied that their communications were secure, Barish proceeds to greet Nebpkara, 'The Master.'

"Time has caught up to us old friend. Events are spinning out of control in the borderlands as Timon steps up his efforts to secure the key."

"*Are the texts safe?*" Nebpkara inquires.

"They are secure with Liviana's agents. I'm afraid that they may not be safe in Atlantis for long. I have told her to send them here with much haste."

"*That was the intent after all. Are there any news from Calis?*"

"He has gone silent. His last mission was to bring Darius here; both are missing."

"*Samiri you think? We can only assume the worst.*"

"No. He is still hidden from us. If he is to make a move, it will be soon."

"*What of the other concern?*"

"Calis was working on bringing him into the fold. Liviana does not know yet, but now I may have to inform her about everything."

"That may be something we cannot avoid. How do you think she will react?"

"She has always been a petulant child; it runs in her blood. I don't know old friend."

"Barish, my King, my friend, my brother; you know I cannot do what I must beg of you. I can only try to influence events to cleanse the world of religious heresy and hope there is enough time to hide from the forefathers, that which will anger them the most. In the meantime, please protect my son."

"You have my word. I will let you know of our progress. Goodbye Arias, my brother."

The King turns off his device and takes a moment to contemplate his next move. He reaches over to a small ledge and grabs a picture of Liviana when she was but a child. He puts it close to his heart and closes his eyes.

The time of the awakening is but months away, and this age had all but forgotten about the forefathers' return. Events are brewing which will ensure the annihilation of humankind, with only a handful of souls trying to prevent it. Atlantis is setting up Illyria for war with Aryavan, and the Aryans are oblivious to the attack that will be delivered on them afterward. Prince Timon is adamant that he will change the world and does not believe in what is to come. Therefore, his only concern is to find the power in Lumeria, to use it to conquer all.

Meanwhile, prophesy that was engineered ages ago is beginning to take form. The players have emerged, and the evil which orchestrated the events of the Great-War rises again. Persephone will have her vengeance on the house that destroyed hers, if not then all shall pay. Only her heir can raise the seven great Anuk. Only her heir can prevent it.

This is a time of prophecy, silently flowing from one age to another. Find the past to fight the future; understand the real foundations on which we build upon, and take heed of the day known throughout the universe as, Judgement Day.

ABOUT THE AUTHOR

Abdur has been fortunate to have traveled the world and has gathered an abundant collection of cultural and oral traditions, which adds to his fascination with ancient history. He is a US Navy veteran, whose forte is Naval Aviation & Intelligence, and education in Psychology.

Since leaving active duty, he has completed the television pilot for "Chronicles of Atlantis," along with seven episodes of the first season; "The age of Prophecy" books are a novelization of this endeavor. He currently lives in Virginia Beach, VA, USA.

31766362R00170

Made in the USA
Middletown, DE
07 January 2019